THE
CLEMENTINE
COMPLEX

THE CLEMENTINE COMPLEX

BOB MORTIMER

SCOUT PRESS

NEW YORK LONDON TORONTO SYDNEY NEW DELHI

Scout Press
An Imprint of Simon & Schuster, Inc.
1230 Avenue of the Americas
New York, NY 10020

First Scout Press trade paperback edition September 2023

SCOUT PRESS and colophon are registered trademarks of Simon & Schuster, Inc.

For information about special discounts for bulk purchases, please contact Simon & Schuster Special Sales at 1-866-506-1949 or business@simonandschuster.com.

The Simon & Schuster Speakers Bureau can bring authors to your live event. For more information or to book an event, contact the Simon & Schuster Speakers Bureau at 1-866-248-3049 or visit our website at www.simonspeakers.com.

Interior design by Hope Herr-Cardillo

Manufactured in the United States of America

10 9 8 7 6 5 4 3 2 1

Library of Congress Cataloging-in-Publication Data is available.

ISBN 978-1-6680-2416-4
ISBN 978-1-6680-2418-8 (ebook)

For Mavis

"Sorry to say, Pops, but you should have thought around this a bit more before you started."

PART
ONE

MY NAME IS GARY. I'm a thirty-year-old legal assistant with a firm of solicitors in London. I live by myself in a one-bedroom flat on a sprawling 1960s local authority housing estate in Peckham. My flat is just a five-minute walk from work, a state of affairs that pleases me, on those occasions that I wish it to. I'm on the short side of average height and come equipped with a large nose that borders on the comical if I wear sunglasses.

If you happen to clock me in the street, I will invariably be wearing my cheap gray suit with a white shirt and tie (workdays) or my brown corduroy jacket with jeans and a T-shirt (empty days). There's a good chance you might see my nose before you spot my clothing. My hair is neat and tidy with a short back and sides and a side parting engineered to resemble a semi-quiff. My brown eyes are almond shaped and have been described as both sad and welcoming within the same twenty-four hours. To describe me as anonymous would be unfair, but to notice me other than in passing would be a rarity.

My only real friend in London is one of my neighbors on the estate. I did make a good connection with a girl this past week or so, but earlier today that blew up in my face and smacked my arse with a fish slice. I thought she liked me, but it turned out I was very wrong. I think I was in love with her; in fact I'm sure I was, and being honest, I still am. I'm properly heartbroken, for the first time in my life.

My mum used to tell me that I was blessed with a good imagination and should use it to my advantage—to relieve any boredom and inject perspective and joy into my life. She would say, if you can imagine something that has never happened to you, then when you encounter it you will be better prepared to both appreciate and cope with it. Sadly, my imagination is not really working to my benefit at the moment, though to be fair to Mum it usually does.

Some people bury their faces in their smartphones all day. Not me. I've had the same old Nokia phone for years and years and have never bothered with social media and the like. I don't see the point of it; I've got enough strangers in my life as it is. So if I'm out and about I keep my head up and my mind stimulated by the sights and sounds around me: neighbors arguing (I might imagine it's over the need to replace a washing machine filter); a broken window (I imagine it was smashed by a child maneuvering an adult ladder); rust penetrating the wheel arches of a long-abandoned car (I imagine the car has been dumped by a wine merchant who went nuts); dogs sharing an interest in a spillage (I imagine the dogs are called Zak Briefcase and Lengthy Parsnips).

If these sights and thoughts aren't stimulating enough, I let my imagination kick into a higher setting.

For example, when I'm walking to work, I have to wind through the various access roads that meander between the blocks of low- and high-rise flats on my estate. Just before the exit from the estate is a grassed play area about the size of half a football pitch. (There used to be a seesaw, but I heard it was removed because some kid smashed up her face really badly on it. You don't often see any small kids using the area, probably on account of the cumulative dog dirting. Come to think of it, you don't see many young kids anywhere on the estate. They must be there, but you just don't see them.)

Often as I pass by this grassy patch a squirrel will stop in its tracks and stand on its back legs to have a good nose at me.

"All right, mate," I whisper to myself. "Your tail is looking well plump and very high, have you got something special on today?"

"Thanks, Gary," I reply on his behalf. "Nothing special, I've met this lady that I like and I'm trying to look my best. You should give it a try. You're looking a right mess, if you don't mind me talking around that fact."

"I'm just going to buy a pie. No need to dress up for that."

"What if you meet a beautiful lady at the pie shop? You'll wish you'd thought a bit more around what you look like . . . You'd think about me and say to yourself, *That lad was well prepared. He'd covered a lot of bases that I haven't even started to address.*"

"Yeah, maybe that could happen," I reply. "Thanks for the tip. So, where did you meet this new lady of yours?"

"You know what, it was exactly where you're standing. She was stood stock-still, just like you, singing a song about the Royal Mail or a cruise ship—something like that. It was hard to tell because her singing was so shit. But when I thought around how pretty she was I was very impressed."

"Well, you seem happy and I have to say you're looking the business."

"Yeah, things are looking up, and I've got a good feeling about your prospects, too. You should buy some cologne or at least think around doing something like that. I can smell romance in the air."

"I might just do that. See you around."

I walk on with a spring in my step and a good connection in my account. The idea of a romance is often a good source of hope for me.

I'm sure a lot of people have these little daydreams and flights of fancy to fill the passing of time, but I don't know if they realize how important they can be to inject a bit of balance and optimism into your life. I need a lot of that just now, especially given that, on the face of it, my life is bordering on the shit.

I'm in my car, driving to a meeting with a bloke called John McCoy. The prospect fills me with panic and dread. It's a make-or-break meeting for me and I just want it to be over and done with. At the moment I'm being held up by a bloke who's spilled a huge bag of onions on the zebra crossing and is unwilling to give up on them. I parp my horn in frustration, then silently apologize to the man and each and every one of the stray onions.

Let me rewind and explain.

2

ABOUT TEN DAYS AGO I went for a drink after work with a bloke called Brendan. He'd been asking to meet up for ages, and I'd run out of excuses. He works for a private investigators company, Cityside Investigations, who are clients of the firm of solicitors where I've been employed for the past two years. I don't know him that well, but we always have a little chat when he's in the office to pick up documents and flirt with the secretaries. He's about ten years older than me, skinny and short with wavy side-parted hair that gives him a slightly Tudor edge. He usually wears a blue or gray sports jacket with a beige turtleneck and deep blue, A-line denim jeans that sit slightly high above his pointy brown leather shoes. A hint of novelty sock is always deliberately on offer. His face is plain-looking, his nose a bit thin and sharp, the overall effect being that of a rolled oat. Yes—a very oat-y look that I often associate with Yorkshire squaddies.

Brendan thinks of himself as a "fun" character, and he probably is if you like the company of loud blokes. He talks nonstop and uses laughter as a form of punctuation. It doesn't matter that he hasn't said or attempted to say anything amusing; he still lets out a snigger or a tommy titter every third sentence or so. He seems to have little interest in what others say to him. I often think it must be nice to believe that your company entrances people. Must be a great confidence builder. I'm always willing to play along with his witterings, and in return he thinks I like him. I don't *dis*like him, but that's about as far as I would go.

I texted him as I finished work and told him I would be at my local pub, the Grove Tavern in Camberwell, around 7 p.m. When I arrived I noticed a colorful red-and-white striped bicycle leant up against the wall by the entrance. It crossed my mind that there might be a pissed juggler inside the building throwing his skittles willy-nilly at the light fittings. I would enjoy watching the repercussions of that sort of incident.

When I walked inside there was no juggler, but I immediately spotted Brendan, sat at the bar scrolling through his phone. He didn't see me. There were a few other people seated around but generally it was quiet and welcoming. The bar takes up one side of the room and on the opposite side are a series of curved booths with bench seats and backs upholstered in a burgundy velveteen material. A quick thought passed through my mind: what a good name for a pudding "velveteen" would be.

"*Would you be interested in a pudding, sir?*"

"*Yeah, maybe, what have you got?*"

"*We have a chocolate and orange velveteen served with clotted cream.*"

"*I'm not saying no to that, mate, it sounds very influential. I'll take one.*"

Then I remembered that I have little interest in puddings, let alone their manufacture, so dropped the thought onto the floor like a used bus ticket.

I sat down next to Brendan, and he started to talk.

"All right, Gary, what can I get ya? The bar is your oyster—ha ha ha!"

"I'll have a pint of IPA, thanks."

"Ha ha ha! Barman! A pint of IPA for my soppy mate here."

"Sorry I'm a bit late, Brendan, I was taking a statement from this bloke at work and he suddenly got a terrible sweat on."

"Whoa, a perspirer. They can be very egregious—ha ha ha!"

"Yeah, I agree. He seemed to get itchy first—you know, before the sweat kicked in. I wanted to ask if he was okay, but when someone is itching it feels like a bit of a personal thing to bring it up, so anyway . . ."

I could tell from his gaze over my shoulder that he had no interest in my tale. He interrupted without the usual unspoken consent.

"Look, it's fine, Gary, I hadn't even noticed you weren't here to be honest—ha ha ha! Here, listen, I've got a legal question for you."

"Well, I know I work at a solicitors but . . ."

"That's good enough for me. I'm not looking for advice, it's just I came up with what I think is an interesting legal conundrum—ha ha ha—so listen up. What do you reckon to this: This morning, right, I was having a coffee, on me own, at a table outside a café on the high street. Now, on the table next to me was this couple, and they seemed a bit fidgety—a bit unresolved, if you like. I've sniffed them out as a pair of illicits—you know, having an affair or whatever—ha ha ha! So, just to pass the time, I turned my phone towards them and started a video recording—you know, just for the thrill of it.

I recorded about twenty seconds and played it back to myself using my wireless ear buddies—ha ha ha! You could hear what they were saying absolutely clear as a bell—something about going to Dubai for a posh burger—but in the background you could hear the music playing in the café. I think it was Coldplay, maybe Oasis—who gives a fuck . . ."

My mind drifted away for a moment, and I looked over Brendan's shoulder towards the end of the bar. A pretty, dark-haired woman, probably a few years younger than me, was sat alone staring at her phone and sipping on a gassy drink. I acknowledged withinward that I fancied her, then refocused my attention on Brendan.

"So, the question I'm contemplating is this: If I had to play that video in court as part of my evidence, would the court have to pay royalties to Coldplay or Oasis? And, what's more, could either of those bands refuse to have the tape played without their permission? What do you think, Gary?"

"Err, it's a solid query, but not one I can help you with, Brendan. I know fuck all about copyright law. I just help with conveyances, drafting up wills, taking statements—that sort of shit."

As I was speaking, I glanced along the bar again and noticed that the dark-haired lass was staring directly at us, all the while continuing to fiddle with her phone. *Bit of a sullen expression*, I thought to myself, *but she might be interested in me, or what I attempt to represent.*

"So, Brendan, what's going on with you at the moment? You got a lovely big pile of investigations keeping you afloat?"

"Nah, not so much—ha ha ha!—I got taken off a big job by the boss a couple of weeks ago. Back to the grind serving the documents, the domestic injunctions, and the witness sum-monses. Selling stuff to the newspapers what we get off the local coppers. Started doing some debt collecting, too. I'm pretty good at it. I reckon it's because I'm small and unthreatening—ha ha ha!"

"I reckon it's because of your nose."

"How do you mean?"

"Well, it's so thin that a bloke could cut himself if he lamped you in the face."

"Is that a remark?"

"Yes."

"Well, it's untrue. You having that pint or not, big nose—ha ha ha!"

I picked up my pint and treated myself to a large gulp. I hated my first taste of beer all those years ago, but these days I can't live without its prospect. I was the same with corned beef and coffee.

"So, what was this big job you were working on?"

"I can't tell you that, mate, it's highly sensitive."

"Fuck off is it! Come on, give us a sniff. Let's have a think . . . Was it to do with staff fraud at a chemist's or a chain of coffee shops?"

"No, you're not even in the right playpen—ha ha ha!"

"Was it a celebrity divorce and you had to hang around the gym where the wife was having her noodles?"

"Nah, listen, I can't tell you, and to be honest you don't want to know. It's already got me into a palaver. The people involved are right nasty bastards. Let's just leave it."

His expression told me that it was indeed the end of this particular conversation, and I noticed that he hadn't laughed once during this exchange. He seemed a bit flustered, a bit flighty. The bluster was gone. I hadn't meant to put him on the spot, and in truth I felt a bit of an arse.

I changed the subject to the football. He changed it to the personal lives of the secretaries in my office. I changed it to electric vehicles and he changed it back to the secretaries. I went to the toilet.

As I stood at my favorite urinal I felt a sudden rush of the sadness feeling. I had been in London for nearly two years and still hadn't really made any worthwhile connections. I kept myself to myself at work, hiding away in my office and never socializing with any of my colleagues. We had nothing in common apart from our caseloads and work-related gossip about clients and court staff. This pub, I realized, was the beginning and end of my social life.

I could hear the chatter and sound of the fruit machine coming from the other bar in the pub, where I usually sit. I'm something of a regular in there. I go most nights when they're showing the football on their big-screen TV. I always sit next to a bloke called Nick and his mate Andy. They never invited me to sit with them; it happened naturally as the best view of the TV was from the three stools at the end of the bar. Our chats revolve around football and our jobs. At the end of the games they usually sup up quickly and make their way home. I don't even know exactly where either of them lives. I reached into my pocket to check on my phone whether a match was being broadcast that evening, only to discover I had left my phone in the office.

The face of the dark-haired lady entered my mind. She's very pretty. I haven't had a relationship since moving to London. I did take one of the secretaries from work out for a curry, but in the taxi on the way home we both got a terrible sweat on, and I abandoned the project right there and then. We've been very cautious with each other ever since. The only other date I've had was a year or so ago, at a local pub restaurant, where I'd arranged to meet a girl from an internet dating site. She had looked very viable in her profile, and the messages we exchanged were quite appealing. When she turned up, however, she had the largest, most powerful arms I had ever seen on a woman. She was short and petite in the general sense, but her arms would have sat well on a heavyweight boxer. She was obsessed with the concept of grip and torque and boasted endlessly about her power-to-weight ratio. After about half an hour of this I went to the toilet and made my escape via a side door. Unfortunately, she had predicted this move and was waiting for me as I stepped onto the pavement. She called me a wanker and then lifted me up onto the roof of a parked Range Rover before walking off, shadowboxing, into the night. I have never been tempted to use an online dating site since that evening.

I clambered back onto the bar stool next to Brendan. The dark-haired lady was no longer at the bar, and I briefly panicked until I saw that she had seated herself in one of the velveteen booths. I watched as she removed a book from her tan leather messenger bag and began to read. She seemed instantly engrossed by its content. Unlike some people, I'm not immediately intrigued by a lass sat on her own reading a book—it always seems a bit arch, even corny, to me. I mean, what's the big deal about books anyway? It's probably about futuristic military ducks or some such nonsense. Her drink was getting low. Maybe she'd have to come up to the bar soon. As

I was sitting there, Brendan had placed his cheap faux-leather briefcase on the bar counter. He was fiddling around with the brass-sprayed catches, trying to close the case.

"Nice bit of briefcase, that, Brendan. Are you pleased with what it achieves for you?"

"Eh? Yeah, it's fine. Does the job."

He seemed nervous again, and his fingers were shaky as he tried to master the catches. I stole a glance at the contents before he shut it. There was a pad of Post-it notes, a phone charger, four or five ballpoint pens bound together with a rubber band, a mobile phone, a comb, and a small cucumber.

"Why two phones? You must have a complicated life."

"Nah, not really—one's for work and the other is just for people who I've given the number to. You know, people I might actually want to talk to."

"Which one am I on?"

"Work one, I think—you know, so I can claim it on expenses as work-related."

"Sounds about right."

"Listen, Gary, sorry about this, but I got a phone call while you were in the boys' room and I've got to rush off. Can't be avoided. I've got to meet this bloke who's a client of ours."

Deep down I was pleased to hear this.

"That's a shame, mate. Still, work is work. I'll be fine. There's probably a match on tonight in the other bar. I can watch it with my mates."

"Yeah, you should do that. Listen, Gary, thanks for meeting up for a drink. We should do this again. I'm sorry I had to cut it short."

"No worries whatsoever," I replied.

"Listen, would it be okay if I popped into your office next week to pick up those documents you're looking after for me?"

"Yeah, just give me a ring beforehand and I'll pop them down to reception for you to collect."

"Nice one. Hey, let me give you my main phone number, the one I always pick up. Give us a buzz anytime you want and let's have a proper drink to make up for tonight."

Brendan scribbled a number down on one of his Post-it notes and slipped it into my coat pocket. He slapped me on the back and made his way out the door. He hadn't laughed once since I returned from the toilets.

I was glad he'd gone. It was a relief. I'd convinced myself that the dark-haired lady might have an interest in me. I ordered another pint and asked the barman if there was a match showing tonight in the other bar. He didn't know. I ordered steak and chips from the bar menu, and as I was doing this, the dark-haired lady got off her seat and walked to the center of the bar, just a few yards up from me, and ordered a white wine spritzer. I felt a shudder of nerves pulse through me and found myself staring at her shoes. They were a beautiful burgundy pair of Doc Martens with dark blue laces. She had tied them with a double bow. The loops of the bows were identical in length and diameter. It was a classy setup. I don't like high heels; they look torturous and contrived. These shoes were a good start. I looked away and took a sup from my pint.

As she watched her drink being prepared, I got a better chance to assess her looks, and in doing so my chances of ever being by her side. She was petite, about five foot six inches, wearing light blue Levi's jeans and a rolltop black jumper. Her messenger bag was still resting against her hip. Her hair was shoulder-length and thick with a clinically straight fringe lying across the middle of her forehead. I couldn't see her eyes but was thinking brown. She could have been a teacher or a restaurant manager, maybe even something to do with pottery. She was even prettier than I had first thought. I didn't stand a chance.

As she left the bar to return to her seat, she took an unnatural curve in my direction. It was a deliberate meander, not a drunken one. I looked down into my beer.

"Your mate abandoned you, has he?" she asked.

"Yeah . . . err . . . yeah, he did. Good spot," I replied with an unfortunate chipmunk grin.

"Well, never mind, it's a nice place to be."

She smiled and walked back to her seat. *Should I try to follow up her pleasantness by approaching her at her booth?* The very thought of this filled me with dread. I've never been good at striking up conversations with strangers, especially the opposite sex. I needed to come up with a suitable opening line. I knew what would work for me if the roles were reversed—something like: *"Do you prefer even or uneven surfaces?" "Do you wish that Sports Direct also sold fresh meat?" "Have you ever needed to use a tourniquet in your work environment?"* I would respond well to that sort of thing because of my excellent imagination. Not everyone does, best to play it safe. I could ask her about her shoes, ask her if she found them viable. Or maybe whether she found the fizziness in her drink helped her to feel young and pertinent. *Ah fuck it, I'll just sit down near to her and put the ball in her court.*

I picked up my pint and sauntered over to the semicircular booth where she was seated. There were two small wooden tables served by the booth, and I placed my pint on the empty one. She looked up at me as I sat myself down, and I gave her a quick smile then looked away. I'd positioned myself about four feet from her, which seemed a polite distance for a stranger to be.

"Were the bar stools too hard for your arse?" she inquired.

I pretended to be surprised—even shocked—that there was someone sat in the same booth.

"Oh, hi. Sorry—world of my own. Didn't quite catch that?"

"I was just saying, was the bar stool getting a bit tough on your arse?"

"No, not at all. Oh, I see . . . well, yeah, a bit . . ."

"You fancied a bit of Dralon luxury . . ."

"Yeah," I said, stroking the material on the bench. "I like to call it velveteen. Makes it sound a bit less bungalow."

"Velveteen. I don't think I've heard it called that before. It sounds a bit like a pudding, doesn't it? A frozen one, but classy."

"Absolutely, nail on the head. I was just thinking that earlier. I don't usually like puddings, but I'd make an exception for a chocolate and orange velveteen."

We both laughed, her somewhat unconvincingly and me with a bit of an unnecessary flourish. There followed a little awkward hole of silence that I felt compelled to fill.

"So, the book you're reading, is it about ducks?"

"I'm not really reading it, to be honest. It's just a prop to discourage people from approaching."

"Shit, I'm sorry, I honestly just needed to park my arse somewhere more benign. I'll shut up."

"No, I don't mean it like that. I approached you, remember. And, actually, I'm glad of the chat. I don't like puddings either."

I was so surprised by her encouragement that I defaulted back to my duck query.

"So, is the book about ducks?"

"No, it's a proper book, so it's not about anything really. Solid prop, though, got a serious-looking cover."

It was a thick hardback, and as she turned it towards me I could see its title. *The Clementine Complex*. The jacket was a golden yellow and in the middle of the front cover there was a bicycle, ridden by a squirrel with a clementine in the wheel spoke. It looked shit.

"There's a squirrel on the front so, you never know, he might have some ducks as friends," I offered.

"Do you want to read it and find out?" She put the book on my table.

"No, that's okay. I'm not much of a reader to be honest, and if it turned out there weren't any ducks, I don't know if I could stand the disappointment." I placed the book back on her table.

At this moment the barman arrived with the plate of steak and chips I'd ordered at the bar. There was a noticeable greasy film on the plate, and the knife and fork both had a little chunk of wood missing from the end of their handles. I thought about asking for another set but didn't want her to think I was an arsehole. That's a risky move if you want someone to like you.

"Sorry, I was starving—haven't eaten since I left work. You don't mind if I tuck in?" I asked.

"No, not at all. I like blokes who enjoy their grub, makes me think their mind is in good order."

"Would you like a chip? Two chips? As many as you like really, as long as you don't take that long one with the burnt tip."

"No, I'm okay, thanks," she replied with a look on her face that suggested she really fancied one of my chips. I ate the long chip hurriedly in case she made a surprise bid for it.

"Hey, that bloke you were with, I saw him put something in your pocket before he left. Is he your drug dealer?" she asked.

"No, my only drugs are pies and Battenberg cake. He was just giving me his most pertinent phone number. He promoted me from 'work contact' to 'friend and family.' So that's like three friends I have now, although I've only got one of their phone numbers."

"Do you think you'll phone him up more often after this promotion?"

"No, I doubt it."

"How do you know him? Is he your lover? Or maybe your chauffeur *and* your lover?"

"No, my chauffeur killed my lover with a powerful blow to the head. I had to sack him."

She laughed, and it felt like a significant moment. The nerves in my stomach disappeared with a tiny tommy squeaker to mark their evacuation.

"So, come on, how do you know him? He didn't seem like a natural companion for you."

"I don't really know him, to be fair. He's just someone I bump into occasionally through my work. Hardly ever see him outside of the office. He had to leave unexpectedly and I'm very glad he did."

"Yeah, me too."

That was a nice thing for her to say.

"Are you sure you don't want a chip?" I asked.

"Yeah, especially now the big one's gone."

As I chomped on my steak, there was an inevitable slowing down in the conversational flow. I was very conscious of it and took a chance with something personal to get the conversation back on course.

"I saw you at the bar earlier and I reckoned you might be a teacher. You know, with the book and the Doc Martens and the fizzy drink. Am I anywhere near?"

"No, not even close."

"Can I have another guess? Would that be okay?"

"Be my guest."

"Does your job involve pottery? You know—making it, selling it, studying it, importing it. Are you in the potting game?"

"Why would you guess that?"

"Mainly because of the fringe. I associate geometric haircuts with the arts. You know—David Hockney, Phil Oakey, Jane Brurier—and the Doc Martens screamed the more crafty end of the arty spectrum."

"Who the fuck is Jane Brurier?"

"I've no idea, but she sounds right."

"And I'll have you know I've worn Doc Martens since I was in my early teens."

"I like them. They take a sock very well and help get over the message that you're serious about things."

"Yeah. My bed isn't covered with cuddly toys, you know."

"Mine neither. So, what do you do for a job, then?"

"I used to manage a restaurant in Brighton."

"I fucking knew it."

"But I packed that in about four years ago. I work from home now selling shit on eBay."

"Duck shit?"

"Not as yet, but if it comes into vogue I'll definitely consider it. I mainly sell vintage clothes, designer clothes, mid-century lamps, ornaments—that kind of thing. Good saleable stuff. I have a good eye for stuff that will sell."

"What sort of a price could you get for what I'm wearing?"

She looked me up and down, taking in the dark gray suit I had bought from Debenhams a few years ago, my Marks & Spencer cotton-rich white shirt, and my brown suede desert boots from Clarks.

"Eight pounds," she declared.

We both laughed, mainly because of the rhythm of things between us.

"It's the first time I've sat in this part of the pub," I announced. "I usually come here when the football's on and watch it in the other bar with my mates. Do you like football?"

"No, but I like watching the blokes watching the football. It brings out the best and the worst in them. Turns them back into little kids, which is something they're usually trying to hide."

A realization hit me out of the blue.

"Hold on, when I came in I noticed a bicycle chained up to a post next to the entrance. It looked like it belonged to the Grinch. I bet that's yours, isn't it?"

"Yes, it is. But how could you know that?"

"I've got a good imagination—just ask me mum—and when I saw the bike I thought about who would own such a thing and it had to be either a fucking juggler or a lass that looked just like you. I'm very rarely wrong about these things. It's a nice bike by the way. Are you happy with what it achieves for you?"

"Yeah, it's perfect. Like tonight, I just fancied going somewhere I didn't know anyone and nobody knew me, so I popped on the bike and found this place. I'm only half a mile away on the Grange estate, so it's perfect."

"*You're perfect*" is what I wanted to say, but, of course, I didn't. We talked on for a few more hours, with me utterly entranced by her every word. I told her about my work and my little flat and the time that my dad took a belt to me for letting a homeless man have a kip in the garage at our house. She told me about the seaside hotel she grew up in and how she once caught her dad trying to have it off with a guest in one of the bedrooms. I told her about the time I took a free kick in a football match and the trajectory of the ball's flight was so beautiful that the referee blew his whistle and insisted on a break for prayers. She told me that when she was a teenager, she and a friend had spray-painted the words "Shit the Fuck Up!" on the boards of Brighton's West Pier. (Apparently you could still see the discoloration in the planks where they had struggled to remove it.) I told her about the landlord of my bedsit in Manchester, where I studied law, who used to collect the rent every Sunday evening and insist that I play a full album of my choice while he sat on the only chair listening and eating peanuts. He wouldn't say a word other than to thank me once the music was finished. She told me about the time she went to the cinema on New Year's Eve to see the Disney version of *Robin Hood*. She was the only person in the screening, and halfway through, one of the staff brought her a free hot dog and a Coca-Cola and gave her a sympathetic pat on the back. She said it was the best New Year's Eve she had ever had.

After I had finished my steak and long chip, she took my empty plate back to the bar on her way to the toilet. I found this overwhelmingly touching and kind. She never took another look at her book, and in the end I was sat with her rather than near her. At around 10:30 p.m. I asked her if she wanted a final drink. I didn't know whether I should ask for her number, offer to walk her home, or just say goodbye and hope that we met again sometime. Getting more drinks was the best way of putting off this choice. She wanted another fizzy wine, and so I pushed my way through the clamor at the bar and ordered our drinks.

As I turned around from the bar to return to the table with the drinks, though, I noticed that she was no longer in her seat. Her book was still on the table, so I assumed she had gone to the toilet. Five minutes later, she hadn't returned, and I wondered if she had maybe gone outside for a cigarette, so I made my way out of the entrance to check. She wasn't there, and the *Wally* bike was gone. I was devastated. I went back to my seat and finished my pint while going over and over our various conversations. What could I have done to upset her? I couldn't pinpoint a moment or any words that would have given her qualms. Then again, maybe it wasn't something I'd said or done—maybe she was just out of my league. After all, that had been my first instinct, and you should always pay serious attention to that. She had left her book on the table, however—perhaps as a farewell gift to me? It was open and facedown. I picked it up, and on the open page she had circled the words "Maybe the ducks knew the secret of the cave." On the top of the page she had written, *"You won't be disappointed—ha!"* I popped the book into my briefcase and left the pub.

As I walked home, it began to rain, and the pavements gave off the smell of pancake batter. I felt dreary and electrified at the same time. I'd met this incredible girl and I was buzzing at that achievement, yet here I was, no further forward and walking alone to my poxy flat. As I entered my estate, I stopped at the play area to see if my bushy-tailed mate was around. I couldn't see him, but I could hear something scrutting around in the leaves beyond the trunk of a large beech tree. I had a quick chat into the darkness.

"All right, Gary. On your own again, mate?" I asked on behalf of my hidden friend.

"Yeah, looks that way. I met a girl, though, and I really like her."

"Did you get her number or arrange to see her again?"

"No, she kind of disappeared on me."

"Walked out on you by the sounds of it. Strikes me you want to think around that and ask what it is you're doing wrong."

"I didn't do anything wrong, except, you know, maybe not looking the part . . . I thought you said that things were looking up for me?"

"They are, Gary, but you don't make it easy. You need to believe in yourself a bit more, think about the positives you possess. Will you think around that for more than a moment?"

"Yeah, I will. How's it going with you?"

"Sweet as a nut. Good night."

"Good night."

3

THE FOLLOWING DAY WAS a Saturday, so I treated myself to a lie-in. Once awake, my mind was full of images of the dark-haired lady. She had a pip of a nose. One of those little button noses that turn up at the end just enough so you can see the nostrils face-on. On some people it makes them look like a werepig, but not on her. She had a lovely quirk where she held the back of her hand up to the side of her mouth when she was about to laugh, and she laughed a lot. She had a little curl of hair on the left end of her fringe at its junction with the main body of her hair, and she even laughed when I suggested the little curl should be called a "Chappaquiddick." She also had the habit of holding the cuff of her jumper in her clenched fist when she was listening.

Ah fuck, man, I would love to see her again. But I don't even know her name. She looked to me like a Sarah, or maybe a Lucy. I should give her a name, I realized, and settled on "Clementine," after the title of the book she left for me. I turned to the page where she had written, *"You won't be disappointed—ha!"* Her handwriting was on the flowery side of frivolous, a little window box of interest at the top of the dreary page. The circle she had drawn in the middle of the text was effortlessly artistic. I wondered if I should buy some Doc Martens. She might like that.

Eventually I got out of bed at around 11 a.m. I was due round at my neighbor Grace's flat in an hour for our regular Saturday lunch snack and chat, so had to get my arse into gear. I took a look around my flat. It looked as miserable as it had every day for the past two years. It has one bedroom with bathroom attached, a lounge, and a kitchen. Being on the third floor, I have a decent view above the gardens and trees through to Peckham High Street at the back. My bedroom has no furniture in it apart from a mattress on the floor, a clothes rail with a missing wheel, and an old Victorian standard lamp. In my living room is a green canvas two-seat sofa, a TV, and a small table with two plastic dining chairs. I'm still living like a student.

I was just about to leave for Grace's flat, when there was a knock on my door. I answered and there, stood before me, were a couple of blokes that looked like off-duty coppers. Turns out they were policemen, but they weren't off duty.

"Hello, sir, sorry to trouble you. Are you Gary Thorn?"

"Yes, how can I help you?" I replied, unable to hide the nervousness beneath my skin. I'm not good with authority, never have been, not since my headmaster at junior school shouted at me so furiously in his office that my nose started to bleed and one of my gloves shrank.

"I'm Detective Cowley and this is Detective Wilmott from Peckham Criminal Investigation Department. Could we come in for a word?"

"Yes, of course, come in. What's this all about?"

I sat down on the sofa. Wilmott and Cowley remained

standing. It was clear from their expressions that they didn't think much of my lack of home comforts. Wilmott was wearing one of those dark green anoraks with a tan corduroy collar, a bit of the countryside in the streets of Peckham. The two front pockets were tainted with greasy marks, and judging from his physique I would guess they were pasty- or sausage roll–based. His face was round, pale, and on the bloated side of full. It was framed by dark, thinning, side-parted hair and, to its south, a pale blue polyester shirt and much-abused tie. He had a barreled chest and a beer belly suitable for sleeping four adult pigeons. His legs, however, were skinny and sticklike, causing his dark brown slacks to struggle to find a patch of skin to rest on. This body shape was a classic example of someone on steroid medication. Rheumatoid arthritis was my guess.

"This your place, is it?" asked Wilmott.

"Well, yeah, I rent it, but it's my place. I've been here about two years."

"Could I ask you where you were last night, Gary?"

"Yeah, sure, I was in the Grove Tavern pub. I went there straight after work to meet a friend."

"And did you come straight home after the pub?"

"Yeah, I walked home on my own, got in about ten-forty-five. Sorry, but could you tell me what this is about?"

"What was the name of the friend you were meeting?"

"Brendan, Brendan Jones. I know him through work."

"And did Mr. Jones leave with you?"

"No, he left much earlier, maybe seven-forty-five. Look, please could you tell me what's going on?"

"We are sorry to have to inform you, Mr. Thorn, but your friend Mr. Jones was found dead last night. We are trying to get a handle on his last movements. It seems from our inquiries that you may have been the last person to have seen him alive."

"Shit, fuck . . . poor bloke. I'm sorry to hear that. What happened to him? Where was he found?"

"You don't need to concern yourself with that. Just answer our questions if you don't mind."

The silent Detective Cowley then sat down beside me. He had very full thighs that stretched the seams of his shiny gray slacks. I could feel the heat of them against my own leg. The move felt both overly intimate and slightly threatening. I decided he was on the weaselly side of the forest spectrum. He had agricultural ginger/blond hair cut to about an inch all over. One of his ears was significantly jugged, and his bottom teeth were strewn around his gum, each and every one of them fighting for the attention of the curious onlooker. I think he had recently had a mustache, because his upper lip was white, in stark contrast to the rest of his pink face. "Smarmy" would be the correct pocket to put him in, and he spoke with a slightly high-pitched inflection. I was desperate for him to retract his hot thigh from mine, but I didn't dare ask.

"Look, Gary—you don't mind if I call you Gary, do you?—in this sort of investigation, the most important thing is to establish a timeline. Do you know what that means, Gary?"

"Yeah, I think so. Could I ask, when you say 'investigation,' has something awful happened? Was he run over or something?"

"Listen, just try to focus on that all-important timeline for the moment. Take us through your evening in as much detail as you can. You say you went to the pub straight from work. What's your job, Gary? What is it that you do?"

"I'm a legal assistant at Tarrants solicitors in the Old Bank Chambers on Peckham High Street."

"I know that firm well—very reliable and established. That must be very interesting work. Is that where you came into contact with Brendan Jones?"

"Yeah, he works for a firm of private investigators, and we use him to track down witnesses, serve injunctions and witness summons—that sort of thing."

"And were you in the habit of socializing with Mr. Jones?"

"No, to be honest, last night was the first time I'd ever met up for a social drink with him. He'd been asking to meet up for ages and I'd run out of excuses. I can't believe he's gone—can't get my head around it . . ."

"Yes, it's very sad, Gary, when you lose an acquaintance. What time did you leave work?"

"Seven o'clock on the dot. I walked to the Grove Tavern on Camberwell Grove and got there at seven-fifteen I reckon. Brendan was already there, sat at the bar."

"So what happened then, Gary? How did events unfold?"

"Well, we had a chat. I think we got on to our second pints of beer. About seven-forty I went to the toilet, and when I returned he explained that he'd received a phone call from a client and had to leave urgently to meet him."

"He definitely said it was a man he was meeting, did he, Gary?"

"Yeah, I'm pretty sure he did. He didn't say his name, but he said it was a bloke."

"You sure he didn't give you a name, or any other details about him?"

"Positive."

"There was no phone on him when he was discovered, but you say he definitely had one in the pub?"

"Yes, in fact he had two, there was another one in his briefcase."

"We didn't find a briefcase either. Can you describe it for us, Gary?"

"Fake reddish-brown leather with brass-effect clasps and handle. Attaché style. A cheap one, maybe forty or fifty quid. Looked pretty new to me."

Wilmott had already searched Google Images for cheap briefcases. He showed me the first couple that came up on the search, and there it was, almost identical, and priced at £49.99.

"Yeah, just like that one. In fact it could be that one. He mentioned that he was very pleased with what it achieved for him."

Cowley's thighs moved slightly away from mine, maybe only a millimeter or two, but enough to let the hairs on my own thigh take a big gasp of air. I took the chance to move my leg slightly away from him. He gave his larger ear a quick twiddle and then exhaled somewhat theatrically. As he did, his thigh pressed more fully against my own, and once again I had claustrophobia of the upper leg. He turned and looked me in the eye.

"And you are absolutely sure that he had this briefcase with him when he left the pub? Think hard about this, Gary. It's very important."

I feigned a quick reflective glance towards the window before replying:

"One hundred percent. I can see him now leaving the pub with the briefcase swinging on the end of his right arm."

"Okay, Gary, very good. Now tell me, what was Mr. Jones's demeanor like when he left the pub? Did he seem anxious or worried or anything of that nature, Gary?"

"No, he was fine. I think he was a bit pissed off that he had to leave early, but no, he seemed his usual self. I don't know him that well, but, yeah, nothing untoward."

"Did Brendan give you anything, Gary? No documents or notebooks or diaries? Nothing like that?"

"No, like I say, we just met up for a drink. It wasn't work related or anything."

"And what did you and Brendan talk about, Gary?"

"Err, I remember at one point he seemed very interested in whether a video recording of a conversation that had copyright music on in the background would need the permission of the recording artist to be admissible in court. We talked a bit of football, a bit about electric vehicles, and he had quite a few questions about the private lives of the secretaries at my work."

"Did he mention any cases he was working on?"

"No, nothing specific. I asked him how work was going and he just said he was doing the usual boring mundane stuff."

"So, what did you do after seven-forty-five when Brendan had left?"

"I got talking to this girl, we chatted, and I had steak and chips. We chatted some more and then suddenly while I was at the bar she disappeared. I guess she was looking for an escape and didn't have the bottle to tell me to my face."

"What was her name?"

"I didn't get her name. I decided to call her 'Clementine' after the event because of the title of a book she was reading."

"Let me guess—would that be *The Clementine Complex* that every Tom, Dick, and Harry is reading?"

"Yeah, that's it. Have you read it?"

"I started it, Gary, but I have to say I found it deeply shit."

"You didn't even like the ducks?"

"I think that's when I packed it in, when those fuckers arrived."

Wilmott chipped in:

"What did this woman look like? Could you describe her?"

"Medium height, about five foot six. Dark, almost shoulder-length hair with a very severe straight fringe across her forehead—you know, like Jane Brurier. She was wearing light blue Levi's jeans and a black jumper, and she had a cute little turned-up nose."

A sly little grin arrived on Wilmott's bloated face. I noticed for the first time that his two front teeth were many shades whiter than the others. This backed up my steroids line of thinking. They can rot the bones that support the teeth. Or maybe Cowley had punched him when he burped on his kebab.

"Sounds to me like you fancied her rotten. Shame she didn't feel the same for you," said Wilmott as his hand reached down and adjusted the lie of his crotch.

"Listen, Gary, as you are potentially the last person to see him alive, we may have to speak to you again. Could I take your telephone number please?"

As I was writing down my number for him, I asked:

"You said 'found his body.' I thought he was run over or had a heart attack or something?"

"No, we never said that, Gary. Like I say, we'll be in touch. Oh, one last thing: Who is Jane Brurier?"

"I don't know what she does but she's famous for her fringe. It's very, very straight and forthright."

"Never heard of her," said Cowley.

"Oh yeah, I know her," said Wilmott. "French woman, rescues big cats and monkeys."

Cowley beckoned his partner to leave with him, and once they were both outside they shut the door behind them without further comment.

I was relieved that they had gone. I noticed that I had a sweat on, so I took a series of deep breaths and had a nice relaxing stare out the window towards the high street to calm my mind. I thought about poor Brendan. It was hard to believe that I wouldn't be seeing him again.

He did me a big favor once, for which I was very grateful. As part of my job I did the occasional house purchase or sale for clients, although I would only be given the very straightforward cases that were really no more than form-filling exercises. Unfortunately, in one particular case I forgot to get the client to sign a very important document—namely, the actual mortgage deed. In effect, this would have meant that the client was under no obligation to actually pay the mortgage. Great for him, but for the firm it would have meant them being sued for the total amount of the mortgage by the building society, and for me it would have meant a certain sacking. I needed to get that form signed without arousing any suspicion from the house purchasers. It was too risky to admit the mistake to any of my bosses at work, so I had a quick chat to Brendan about it.

"Ha ha, you've fouled up good and proper, you slack bastard—ha ha ha!"

"Yeah, I know that, Brendan, but what do you think I should do? You're a bit of a seat-of-your-pants kind of bloke, can't you think of something? You've got to help me out here or I'll lose my job. I'll be out on the streets like a prick."

"What building society is it?"

"The Leeds Permanent."

"And what do money men in Leeds dress like, fucking dungarees or summat? Ha ha ha!"

"I don't know, maybe a trilby and a macintosh? Why do you ask?"

"Because it's simple. I go round to this house looking all formal and say I'm from the building society. I butter them up and ask how they're settling in, are they happy with the service offered, are there any other services we can offer them, and then get them to sign the document as what I will call the 'final formality.' They won't have a clue what they're signing, believe me. Punters just want to get rid of you ASAP—ha ha ha!"

And that is exactly what he did. He borrowed a macintosh and a trilby from his dad and got the thing signed. I could have hugged him till he bled. I did him a free-of-charge will and a cheap conveyance when he moved house in return.

This memory made me feel sad. He still felt kind of "present," like he was stuck to me from last night's meeting. I pictured him bounding into the office reception and spouting off his usual friendly bullshit or sticking his foot through my office door to introduce me to his latest pair of shit socks. My eyes watered and a tear threatened to form. I obviously wasn't the last person to see him, but the police seemed to think that might be the case. Did they think I had something to do with his death? Surely not. *Should I try to track down Clementine in case I need her for an alibi? Should I track her down anyway, just for the prospect of seeing her again?* I needed to talk to someone and think this all through. Fortunately, Grace was just next door, and she was expecting me.

4

WHEN I FIRST MOVED into my flat, I used to call my neighbor Dog Woman. That was the only thing I knew about her, that she owned a dog. My block of flats has a central stairway and lift that serves all five floors. Each floor has a walkway off which the front doors of the flats are situated. On my side of the stairway there are three flats. Dog Woman is closest to the stairway, and then there is my flat, and then an empty flat awaiting refurbishment following a fire in the kitchen that was apparently caused by a very dry naan bread spontaneously igniting. (That's what I believe, anyway.)

On the day I moved in I had to pass Dog Woman's front door on numerous occasions. It was slightly ajar, and every time I passed I could sense that someone was looking at me. Once I'd finished moving my stuff in, I had a cup of tea and a slice of Battenberg and went next door to introduce myself. By this time the door was shut and there was no reply when I rang the front doorbell. I could, however, hear a dog barking inside and the muffled sound of its owner telling the dog to shush itself.

Over the next few months I would occasionally see Dog Woman leaving her flat and taking her dog for a walk on the grass square in front of the building. She was always wearing the same green-and-red checked woolen coat. Her graying hair was tied up in a makeshift bun, and she walked with a slight limp that indicated some confusion within her right hip. She looked to be in her mid-sixties. I got the impression that she wasn't in employment. Her dog had longish hair with black and white patches here and there. From her instructions to it I gleaned that its name was Lassoo. It had a great deal of the sheepdog about it but had long lost its sparkle and intensity. Whenever I saw her walking her dog it was noticeable that nobody would stop and say hello or engage her in a chat. It crossed my mind that she might have a tainted reputation or that there was an unwritten rule that she must not be approached. On the odd occasions that our paths crossed I would say hello to her, but she never made eye contact or responded to my greeting. On one occasion I shared the lift with her, and we stood in silence. She smelt strongly of very old fruitcake. I eventually stopped trying to address her and in time felt quite pleased that I had a neighbor who wished to keep herself to herself. No obligations, no responsibilities.

When my first summer at the flat arrived, however, Dog Woman took to sitting on a chair outside her front door whenever the sun was shining. This wasn't to soak in the rays, I assumed, but rather to escape the intense heat that would build up in the flats due to the three-quarter-height, south-facing windows in the lounge and kitchen. Lassoo would be sat by her with his drinking bowl by her feet. One day, as I avoided her gaze and walked past, she spoke to me for the first time:

"Where are you going?"

Surprised but alert as always, I responded with honesty.

"To get a pie."

"Oh, you like a pie, do you?"

"Yeah, I find them a great comfort. How about you?"

"What sort of pie are we talking about here?"

"I usually make my mind up when I'm at the shop, but savory for sure—probably mince and potato but maybe steak and onion. Depends on the use-by dates."

"Must be nice to be able to pop off to the shop whenever a pie takes your fancy."

"Yeah, I suppose I should be grateful for that."

She then exhaled strongly as if in pain and started to rub her hip.

"You okay?" I asked.

"Yeah, I've got a dodgy hip. It comes and goes. I'm waiting for an operation. So, back to this pie, will you heat it up or have it cold? I like a cold pie, but you look a bit weak to stomach one."

"I'm okay with a cold pie, especially if it's shortcrust pastry with a good crunch about it," I replied.

"Yeah, that sounds nice, very nice indeed."

There was a short silence. The dog had a drink from its bowl. Police sirens complained in the background.

"Would you like me to fetch a pie for you while I'm there?" I asked, mainly on account of the fact that she obviously would.

"That would be great. Steak and kidney please. How long do you think you'll be?" she replied. It was the first time she had smiled at me, and it felt good to receive it.

"Ten minutes or so."

"That works for me. Would you do me a favor and take the dog with you? He could do with a walk."

"Yeah, of course, he seems a nice lad."

"Hold on, I'll just get his lead."

She shuffled into her flat, huffing and puffing from the effort. Once she was inside, I glanced down at the mug she'd been drinking from. In it was either water or vodka. I suspected the latter. She emerged with the dog lead.

"I'm Grace by the way."

"I'm Gary. Pleased to meet you."

"I've been watching you these past weeks. You seem a trustworthy type, not like the usual strays that move in here."

I attached the lead to Lassoo's collar and gave him a few pats and a stroke. He smelt of roast chestnuts with a hint of vinegar. Not entirely unpleasant, but you wouldn't want to bottle it. I imagined, for a moment, that I was stroking his coat with a small Bible. It enriched the moment. As I got out of the lift and walked to the outside of the block, I heard Grace shouting down at me from the third floor:

"Don't tug at his lead. He's a bit knackered, like me. Just let him go at his own pace. See you in ten minutes."

She was right. Lassoo had no pace about him and a definite lack of verve. He had the odd sniff here and there, but I sensed he would be glad when the walk was over. He even yawned a few times, which I thought unusual for a dog on the move in the outdoors. When we got to the play area, however, his demeanor changed. He let out a couple of barks and strained on the lead, begging to be let go. I let him off the leash and he ran straight to the patch where the notorious seesaw had been and had a dump. I didn't have any poop bags and could see an old bloke staring at me through one of the ground-floor windows. Out of fear for my local reputation I approached the dump site, turned my back on the watching pensioner, and mimed the process of unfurling a bag, scooping up the dirt, and placing it in my pocket. Reputation hopefully intact, we carried on to the shops.

On our return, Grace was still sat outside her door. She had placed a tiny circular-topped metal table and a wooden stool next to her. She was making a fuss of looking at her watch.

"Thirteen minutes," she said by way of greeting. "And you said no more than ten. Seems you might be the unreliable type."

"Sorry about that. The dog held me up a bit."

"Yeah, he's a right slouch. Got no oomph left whatsoever."

"He was quite energetic when we got to the play area."

"Yeah, he always gets a rush on when he needs a dump. I sometimes think it's his only pleasure in life. I'm a bit the same. Are you going to join me, then, to eat these pies?"

As a general rule, I like to eat pie on my own. No distractions. No etiquette. Just me and my pie, in perfect harmony. However, the look in Grace's eyes suggested she really wanted my company. Despite her crabby demeanor, she seemed a bit lonely and vulnerable. She also seemed like the sort of person I could easily get to like me—you know, just as an end in itself. She also fascinated me.

"Yeah, I would love to, that's very kind. Would you like me to heat them up?" I asked.

"Not for me, thanks. I find that warmth can bring out the taste of death that you often get from a cheap pie and I can see you've gone budget with your selection."

Eating with Grace turned out to be a great decision. We sat there talking for at least a couple of hours. She fed most of her pie to Lassoo and kept popping inside to replenish her "tea." She was a right talker. She told me about her engineer father who went to Sierra Leone when she was eight years old and never returned but sent a picture of his arse to her mother every year on their anniversary. She told me that she was "in computers" and had worked for the NHS and the Department for Education. Sadly, because of her "crumbly bones," she had ended up flogging computers at the local PC World because it was an easy gig. She told me she got the sack from this job when she told her manager to "Go and fuck a puppet on the moon." She managed to get signed off for disability benefit and claimed that she had never been happier. She did a bit of online computer skills training on the side and eventually admitted that she did like a drink once all of the day's thinking had been done. She hardly stopped talking, and I laughed more than I could have anticipated.

Anyway, we became neighbor friends, and every Saturday, if I wasn't otherwise engaged, I would pop round to her flat and spend a couple of hours in her company.

5

THE LAYOUT OF GRACE'S flat was identical to mine, but the ambience could not have been more different. Hers was filled with possessions she had accumulated over the years. Hardly any walls were visible behind the shelves and piles of boxes and books. Computer hardware and monitors from various decades were stacked at one end of the living room. At the window end was a desk that doubled as her dining table and her workstation. The flat smelt of uncooked sausages and hot electronics.

For our Saturday meetups she would always make an effort to glam herself up. Today she was wearing a flowery Laura Ashley dress and leopard-print slippers. Her hair was tied up beneath a banana-print silky scarf, and her lipstick was bright cherry-tomato red. She was always a little flustered whenever I arrived. As far as I could tell I was her only regular visitor. Lassoo never made a fuss, only glancing up briefly from his cushion when I got there, before licking his lips and falling back to sleep.

"Come in, Gary, I've got the kettle on. What have you brought for the microwave?"

"I've got a shepherd's pie that's described as new *and*

improved and a macaroni cheese that is 'organic and less than three hundred calories.' "

"Oh fuck that, I'll have the shepherd's pie."

She gave me a little motherly peck on the cheek as she took the ready meals off me and strode purposefully into the kitchen.

"Who were those two fellas that just left your flat?" she shouted through from the kitchen. "Looked like coppers to me, or maybe bailiffs. Have you been on the drugs or got behind on your rent?"

"Yeah, they were coppers. When you sit down, I'll tell you all about it."

Grace came back into the lounge, sat down at the table with me, and rested her head on the fist of her hand as if to say, *"I'm all ears."*

I recounted the conversation I'd had with Wilmott and Cowley as well as I could remember. Grace listened in silence, and when I had finished she stepped through to the kitchen and returned with the two ready meals, still in their trays, and plonked them down on the table.

"So what do you think?" I asked as we both struggled to cope with the intense heat of the microwaved meals.

"If this pie is an 'improved' version, then I'm glad I never experienced it in its previous incarnation."

"No, not the pie. About the coppers and my mate being found dead. I mean, if the coppers are sniffing about then maybe he's been murdered."

"What you really want me to say is that you should go and find this woman Clementine. I can tell you've got yourself hot for her."

"Well, do you? Do you think I should?"

"I don't know, Gary, I'm more worried that your mate was found dead. They've probably cordoned off the crime scene. Cordoning gives me the shivers."

"What, because it reminds you of James Corden?"

"The only thing that reminds me of James Corden is folded pizza. Be serious now. They cordoned off Peckham railway station when that wrestler went apeshit. They cordoned off the walkway here when the flat next to yours set fire. This is a serious business."

"Well, obviously, a bloke is dead."

"The thing that bothers me the most, though, is this: How did the coppers know you were the last person to see him?"

"Well, I presume they saw my message on his phone telling him what time and where to meet up."

"But they said they didn't find any phone on him."

"Maybe someone at the pub saw us together?"

"Why on earth of all the pubs in south London would they have chosen to go and ask questions at the Grove Tavern? It doesn't make any sense. He wasn't a regular there or anything. Did they show you any identification?"

"Yeah, one of them gave me his card. Maybe I should give him a ring and ask how I've become involved."

"I think you should."

I rummaged through my pockets, but there was no card. Maybe I had left it in my flat. I rushed back and checked. There was no card anywhere to be found. He hadn't given me one, even though he'd said that he would. I went back to Grace's flat.

"No, he didn't give me a card."

"Are you sure they were coppers?"

"Yeah, I mean, they looked like coppers, they talked like

coppers, and one of them had very authoritative thighs. It all seemed aboveboard to me."

"What were their names?"

"Wilmott and Cowley from Peckham Police Station."

"Make me a cup of tea while I have a sniff around for them on my laptop."

I did as I was told, and when I returned with the tea she looked up from her computer.

"I think you might be in more trouble than you realize," she announced. "You need to track down that woman."

"Why, what have you found?"

"I can't find the names Wilmott or Cowley listed anywhere on the Met Police website. There's a female officer called Cowley in some administrative role at Wembley, but that's it."

"Well, I don't suppose they give out the names of all their detectives willy-nilly. There has to be some sort of confidentiality involved . . ."

"Maybe, but as far as I can tell neither of them pops up anywhere, not in any court reports, press cuttings, social media . . . That can't be right, can it?"

"To be honest, Grace, I shouldn't think detectives are encouraged to fuck about on Twitter and the like. They have to keep themselves behind the curtains. People can have grudges against coppers."

"Everyone is on social media these days."

"Well, apart from me and these two coppers, Grace. Listen, I've got to go. I'll see you when I see you."

"I'm going to keep searching for these supposed coppers."

"I know you are."

The moment I got up from my seat, Lassoo jumped onto it

and grabbed the shepherd's pie tray. He jumped onto the floor with it held between his teeth and started to bang it against the floor until a few stray pieces of gray meat fell out. He ate them up then jumped on the sofa, where he pointed his left rear leg directly up at the ceiling and licked his lips.

6

I WAS SLIGHTLY PERTURBED by what Grace had to say, so I took a little stroll to calm me down. It's something I often do when I feel ill at ease. This is how I use a walk to my advantage: I imagine, for example, that it's a beautiful sunny day and I'm wearing a pair of baggy red corduroy shorts and a magnificent pair of tan yellow clogs. The clogs are massive and important-looking. They are made of a hard, almost translucent toffee. As I walk along, various people of all ages open their front doors or lift up their sash windows to shout out encouragement and admire my magnificent clogs.

"*Those clogs look more than sufficient, Gary!*"

"*Well done, Gary, don't you look the part!*"

"*Amazing, Gary, just amazing. You always seem to get it right.*"

"*You look like you own this place and everywhere else I can think of.*"

At the end of the street, on a day that feels useless, I imagine that I turn around and drink up the applause of the cheering onlookers. If it's a day where I feel more towards the positive, I stop dead still, facing the sun, and slowly look down to the ground. I imagine that my toffee clogs have melted to a sticky puddle around my feet. As I walk onwards, I hear doors and windows being slammed shut and a few lone voices passing comment behind me.

"*Shame about the clogs, Gary. Still, they were nice while they lasted.*"

"*Totally inappropriate material, Gary. But, then, you knew that. You need to get your act together, mate.*"

"*Gary, you fucking wanker.*"

It's all about inviting equilibrium and balance into my life. Today I see the onlookers cheering me, and it helps me come to the decision to go and search for Clementine. The only two helpful bits of information I had were that she lived on the Grange estate in Walworth and that she owned a daft-looking bicycle. I decided to take a drive up to Walworth and have a nose about. First of all, though, I needed to fetch my phone from the office. If you are going nosing, you should probably have your phone with you. I was also hoping that either Wilmott or Cowley might try to contact me. I had new questions for them coming into my mind every ten minutes.

The office isn't open on a Saturday, but I have my own set of keys. On the way there I popped into Wayne's coffee shop to treat myself to a cappuccino and a slice of Battenberg cake to enjoy in the empty office. The coffee shop is called Grinders, and owner, Wayne, was serving behind the counter as usual. He knows me well, and we have a good way with each other. I pop in a couple of times every day and have been doing so for the past two years. He considers me to be his personal lawyer (I helped him with a renegotiation of his shop lease and various traffic offenses) and I consider him a potential friend (although I don't think I would dare announce that to him). He is one of those gym addicts who like to show off their bulging muscles in super-tight white T-shirts. He's about the same age as me, is well over six foot tall, and sports jet-black hair in the bouffant style of Wham!-era George Michael. When he sees me, Wayne offers up a smile as wide as a hippo's toothbrush.

"Hello, Gary, don't usually see you in here on a Saturday."

"Yeah, I was missing you so much I had to come in. It's your muscles, Wayne, they get into your mind, draw you in."

He flexed a bicep and gave it a puckered kiss.

"These guns can make you want to write a love poem or sing a tribute song in the key of muscle," said Wayne.

"That is exactly what they do. You are a sexy man, Wayne, sexier than a cream horn on top of a polished school bell."

"I know, that's why I have three girlfriends."

"Have you actually met any of them?"

"Only one."

"And is that one your mother?"

"No. *Your* mother."

I laughed heartily, but it struck me that the laugh was born in a sad pouch somewhere inside me. I was not being natural. I just wanted him to like me. I want everyone to like me. You have to be adaptable to pull it off, though, and it's a lot of effort. I don't know what my end game is, but I suppose it's better than collecting enemies.

"Slice of Battenberg and a cappuccino to take away please, Wayne."

Wayne fired up his machine and attended to my order.

"Don't you ever take a day off, Wayne?"

"Nah, people need their coffee and I'm the man with the beans. You wouldn't get the lifeboat people taking a day off, would you?"

"You're not an emergency service though," I countered.

"Who says I'm not? You tell that to my regulars. I'm a frickin' lifeline for them, and anyway, if I shut one day the punters might try another place and end up preferring it."

"You're showing a lack of confidence in your product there, Wayne."

"Just being a realist, mate. I'm a one-man band. It's hard to compete."

"That's life, boss," I replied. "Little blokes like us can find it hard to make a mark on the world."

"Fuck off, Gary, you're depressing me. And don't call me little. Save that for yourself, shortarse."

We fixed smiles onto each other for an extended period before he passed me my order. I said my goodbyes and left the shop for the short walk to the office.

The offices are situated in the top three floors of a Victorian bank. It's a warren of corridors and staircases. The walls are white-painted Anaglypta wallpaper, and the individual offices are all decked out with pale green carpet and dark wooden furniture. My office is on the second floor. On a hidden bit of architrave around its door I have written in tiny letters "large bananas." I occasionally take a glance at it to cheer myself up.

My office is furnished with an old mahogany desk and chair, two wooden dining chairs for clients, and bookshelves on either side of a small chimneypiece. The old open fire has been replaced with a two-bar electric coal-effect fire. It pumps out a very directional heat towards any client sat opposite me at the desk. I usually turn it off if they seem the type that might get a sweat on.

My job is deadly dull. Its formal title is "Legal Assistant." I got the gig because I graduated in Law six or seven years ago and then went on to fail my professional qualification exams on two separate occasions. I might take them again one day, but for now this job suits me fine. My work consists of taking initial statements from new clients, attending at police stations, completing legal aid applications, preparing simple wills and conveyances. Any old shit I'm asked to do, really.

I always love being in the office on my own. It almost feels a bit naughty, like you're a burglar or a covert office standards inspector. It takes me back to my teenage years, when I had the family home to myself and could waltz around like Rod Stewart in his Düsseldorf penthouse. I imagine that I am the boss and wander in and out of various offices inspecting the tat on the desks and the photos on the shelves. The silence is unfamiliar and transforms the atmosphere from a workplace to a museum of melancholy. The thought enters my mind that it would be a great place for an assisted suicide.

My phone was on my desk where I left it, and there were no messages or missed calls. I put my feet up on the desk and took a deep bite into my Battenberg. It's so sweet it makes my teeth sting. I thought about Brendan again and remembered that he had asked me if he could pick up his bundle of important documents from work. They were kept in a secure deed box under the bookshelves in my office, so I took them out to check the contents so I could write to his next of kin and inform them of their existence.

The envelope contained a land registry title deed for his home, a simple one-page will leaving all his worldly goods to his ex-wife, and a couple of pension portfolios. Nothing of note.

I was sad at the sight of his name in print and briefly recalled him sitting opposite me with his feet up on my desk displaying a pair of socks with chimps' feet emblazoned on them. I put the documents back in the deed box, picked up my half-empty coffee cup, and headed out of the office to commence my search for Clementine. The Grange estate where she said she lived is only half a mile or so away, but I drove there in my car and was soon parked up and commencing my "nose about." It's a 1950s brick-built London County Council estate. There are eight separate U-shaped five-storey blocks and several small roads with parking that wind themselves around the buildings. Each block has a central stairway with walkways leading to the front doors of every floor.

From where I was parked I had a decent view of the fronts of two of the blocks. One is called "Vaseley House," the majority of its front doors painted pillar-box red, and the other "Drummond House," which has mostly pale blue front doors. The walkways are dark brown brick with white-painted coping-stones on top. A few front doors are painted in different colors, and I assumed these were the flats that had been purchased by the tenants from the council under the Right-to-Buy scheme. If I had purchased one of these flats, I would have kept the door color the same. I felt a tiny frisson of excitement at my situation that faded as the minutes passed.

I wasn't sure what my plan was. I suppose I was hoping that she might suddenly appear riding along on her daft bicycle or pop her head over the walkway wall and shout, "Hey, anyone out there looking for me?" I had no plan. I sat back in my seat and took in the surroundings. There weren't many people about. Some fifty yards ahead of me a bloke in an old boiler suit was fiddling with the rubber seal around the rear windscreen of a car. His arse looked very full and pressurized as he leant over on his tiptoes to reach the farthest corner of the screen. I commenced an interest in the thought that if his heart was actually situated inside one of his buttocks, he would still look exactly the same. His secret would be between himself, his loved ones, and his medical team. Maybe he would have to tell his work colleagues and his insurers. His heart wouldn't have the protection it enjoys by being in the rib cage. That might be a worry, especially, for example, if a farmer was kicking him in the arse for trespassing on his field. The thought faded away, and I spat on my sleeve to wipe away a blemish on the windscreen. I just made it worse.

I picked up the copy of *The Clementine Complex* from the passenger seat. I had brought it with me to use as an excuse for calling on Clementine should I find her—"*Hi, I just wanted to return your book. You left it in the pub the other night. How incredible is that? I'm a wonderful man I hope you agree.*"

I read the blurb on the back cover:

The Clementine Complex is a novel about loneliness, lack of identity, and cultural and moral corruption. Its characters are confused but compelling. A haunting meditation on love and loss and everything in between.

It still sounded shit. I had another quick glimpse at Clementine's message: "*You won't be disappointed—Ha!*" But I knew that I would be if I entered its pages.

I threw the book back onto the passenger seat and poked around in my door pocket to remind myself of its contents.

There were numerous empty sugar sachets and wooden coffee stirrers, an old mint humbug that had escaped from its transparent wrapper and become stuck to a five-pence piece, and a little plastic bottle of nasal spray. I started to unpick the wrapper from the sweet, but my nails just clogged up with sticky goo. I took one of the coffee-stirring sticks and split it down the middle so that I could use it as a nail pick. It worked well, and I was seriously pleased about that. I turned on the car radio; it was tuned in to talkSPORT. They were talking about a boxing match in which one of the boxers hit the other boxer so hard that he fell to the floor. After that revelation an advert for a company that can supply 12mm plasterboard at the drop of a hat started playing. It crossed my mind that if you were to carry a four-foot-by-four-foot piece of 12mm plasterboard with you everywhere you went, you would quickly be considered something of a character. Maybe Clementine would have taken me more seriously.

I changed to a channel that was playing something that might be described as "smooth jazz." It fit the setting well. I lowered the back of my seat and had a good old listen to divert my attention away from the folly of this expedition. *Parp parp parp, dum dum dum parp* insisted the music, and then the trumpet kicked in like a slow pour from a jug of thick gravy.

It dawned on me that I really needed a piss. There was no obvious place to relieve myself outside of the car. Beside me in the central console was my takeaway coffee cup. It was a medium coffee, so I guessed it held just over half a pint. That might just be the exact capacity I was looking for. I checked my surroundings. There was no direct eye line into the car from the block behind me. The block to my left was too far away for anyone to get a clear view inside the car. The two ground-floor flats to my right would be able to see my upper half but not anything below the window line. The only person I could see was Boiler Suit Man, and he seemed fully absorbed in his windscreen shenanigans. *It's worth a shot*, I thought, *even if it's just for the thrill of it.*

I opened my window and shook the last remnants of coffee from the cup onto the grass verge. As I closed the window I noticed that Boiler Suit Man had disappeared, either into his car or into the block of flats. I slowly pulled down my flies as I scanned the area for inquisitives. I placed the cup at an angle and positioned my Douglas on its lip. I pushed out a stream, which immediately warmed the surface of the cup in my hand. I flicked my eyes between scoping for any onlookers and checking the fullness of the cup. Because the cup was at an angle, it filled more quickly than I had expected. I altered the angle, so that it was more upright but in doing so had to thrust my hips and arse upwards so that my Douglas was still over the lip of the cup. I guessed that I was only halfway through the piss.

Suddenly there was a knock on my window. I sat back into the squab of the seat and held the cup over my Douglas. The stream continued for a few more seconds, soaking the front of my trousers. Through the window I could see a swath of French blue boiler suit cotton. *It's Boiler Suit Man.* I wound down the window, flustered and with a sweat on over what he might have seen.

"Hi there," I said, with the most handsome smile I could muster.

"Can I help you, mate? The parking here is actually for

residents only." He said it in a friendly enough manner but with a hint of austerity.

My sweat subsided slightly; he obviously hadn't seen what I was up to.

"Yeah, I know, I'm just looking for someone who lives on the estate. Not sure of their address."

He bent down and placed his head in the center of the window frame.

"Who is it you're looking for? Or are you just up to no good?"

"It's just a girl I met in the pub. She left her book behind and I want to return it to her."

I became acutely aware of the scent of asparagus and peas rising up from my crotch. I saw him glance down in that direction and raise an eyebrow.

"Is that a stock cube drink you're having?" he inquired. "You don't see many people drinking that these days. I used to love one, especially on a Saturday afternoon when the wrestling was on ITV."

He clearly hadn't spotted the dampness around my flies.

"Yeah, I know what you mean—a nice meaty hit to warm you up on the sofa. No, it's just tea, one of them herbal ones— meant to be good for your guts."

"I see you take it without milk. Lot of that about these days. Can't stand it without milk, makes me fucked off."

"Bet you've never even tried it. Do you want a sip?"

"Nah, it's not for me."

"Come on, when was the last time you tried it without milk? Things have moved on. These new blends are designed to taste good without milk."

I raised the cup up to the window, making sure to cover my open flies with my left hand as I did so.

"It's a bit lukewarm but that's how these new teas are meant to be enjoyed. Go on, have a sip."

"All right, go on then."

He retrieved the cup from my hand and started to raise it to his lips. *Shit, he's actually going to drink it.* I came to my senses.

"Actually, mate, on second thoughts you shouldn't try it. I popped a couple of magnesium tablets in there and they can cause a bit of a reaction if you're not used to them."

He handed the cup back to me.

"That's a shame, it smelt delicious; bit pungent, but I like a lot of depth to my brews. That's the problem with herbal teas, they're usually a bit pissy. Anyway, what's the name of this woman? I know most of the people on this part of the estate."

"It's okay, I'll just give her a ring, I should have done that before I got here. Thanks though."

"No worries. Don't hang around though, like I say, this is resident parking only."

As he walked away, I feigned making a phone call, then started up the engine. A squirrel appeared on the lowest branch of a sycamore tree to my right.

"All right, mate?" I asked him to myself.

"Not too bad, Gary. I hear you've been having a piss in your car just now."

"Yeah, stupid of me. Don't know why I do shit like that."

"You want to think around what conclusions people might come to if they saw what you were doing. Why do you do nonsense like that?"

"I don't really know. I mean, I was desperate if that helps."

"I'll tell you why, Gary, because you don't give a care about what people think about you. You don't care enough about anyone to consider it important."

"No, I don't think it's that, mate. I reckon it's because I'm always bending over myself to be someone that people like and, sometimes, I get the urge to do something that feels liberating to me. Yes, I feel terrible now, absolutely mortified if the truth be known, but at least it felt like I was living a little."

"Well, you want to think about what sort of bloke has that inside him by way of motivation."

"Maybe I will one day."

"Yeah, maybe you will."

"I'm full of regret if that helps."

"No, not really."

There was the sudden crash of a door being pushed open then slammed shut about thirty yards in front of me and I guessed a couple of floors above my head. The squirrel jumped off the branch and rushed away. I wound down the window and could hear a man and woman arguing. The man was shouting at full pelt, but I could only hear the odd phrase. It sounded pretty intense. The door slammed again, and that's when I saw it.

High above me, a bicycle had been thrown from the second-floor walkway and was spinning its way down to the ground. It was the *Where's Wally?* bike in all its glory, and it was about to have its spine broken. It landed on the paved area in front of the stairwell. Its front forks buckled, and its rear tire was spinning like a roulette wheel. The seat had twisted full around and was pointing up to the sky.

A man emerged from the stairwell, stamped down on the front wheel with the sole of his shoe, and strode away. He was tall, definitely over six foot, and looked about forty years old. He had a shaved head that he pulled off very well on account of its pleasant shape and his handsome features. He was wearing a blue suit about two sizes too small for him, and the trousers were skinny cut. Big bloke in a teenager's suit—you see a lot of them around these days. He got into a bright red BMW 3 Series and drove off at speed. A couple of minutes after he left, I grabbed the book off the passenger seat, got out of my car, and went to inspect the scene.

As I approached the busted bicycle, I saw Clementine emerge from the stairwell. Her fringe was no longer perfectly set, and her hair was distressed and ruffled. She was wearing a gray dressing gown, and her Doc Martens were untied. Our eyes met. She wiped her nose with the sleeve of her dressing gown and greeted me with a disappointed smile.

"What are you doing around here?" she asked as her eyes furtively scanned the estate.

"Well, err, actually I was looking for you."

"I don't understand. Why would you do that?"

I was stood by her now and could see that she had been crying.

"Are you okay?" I asked.

"Yes, I'm fine. What is it you want? It's not really a great time for me . . ."

"I can see that. Look, are you sure you're okay? Who was that bloke who threw your bike over the walkway?"

"That's not really any of your business."

I was taken aback by her indifference and coldness. This wasn't how I had imagined our meeting would pan out. It shocked me into a more formal attitude.

"I won't take a minute. You remember the bloke I was drinking with in the Grove last night?"

"Yeah, sort of."

"Well, he was found dead after he left the pub and it seems that I was the last person to speak to him."

"Fucking hell, really?"

"Yeah, and the police have spoken to me and I might need an alibi for the time he left the pub to when I got home. I just wondered if you were okay with me giving them your name and address?"

Her response was swift and delivered with a hint of panic and alarm:

"No, I'm sorry, I can't let you do that. It could get me into big trouble and I just don't need that right now."

"Are you on the run or something? Have you been importing faulty vape pens or selling stolen curtaining?" I said, trying to inject a hint of lightness into the moment.

"No, I'm just answering your question. I am not okay with you giving my details to the police."

It was a very clear and certain response, so, being a shithouse, I immediately backed off.

"Hey, no worries, that's fair enough. I had to ask. I don't want to get you into any trouble. Listen, can I help you with the bike?"

"No, please, just go. I'm sorry I can't help. Please don't come looking for me again."

"No, I won't. Don't worry, I'm not a suspect or anything. I'm sure it's no big deal." As she turned away, I remembered the book. "Hey, I've got the book you left in the pub." I held the book out, hoping it might bring her back to me.

"That's okay, you keep it."

She flashed me a weak smile and turned away to drag the bike back up the stairwell. I so wanted to help her, but it wasn't what she wanted. I had written my name and telephone number on the inside flap of the book, hoping she might phone me one day. As I stood there watching her leave, with the book still in my hand, it dawned on me that we would probably never speak again.

7

IT WAS AROUND 3 p.m. when I returned to my flat. Grace had watched me park up and was loitering on the walkway when I emerged from the lift.

"Did you find her?" was her greeting.

"Yes, I did," I replied as she invited herself into my flat for a cup of tea.

"Did you find out anything more about those coppers?" I asked.

"Nothing. So for the time being at least I remain alert and suspicious. Have they contacted you at all?"

"No."

"Hmmm."

She plonked herself down on the settee, and I fetched her a mug of tea and a Viscount biscuit—the minty ones that come individually foil-wrapped.

"Is that all you've got?" she asked as she placed her sage-green slipper booties on the cushion next to her.

"Do you not like a Viscount?" I replied.

"I don't like the foil. Taking it off makes my fillings vacillate."

"You want me to take it off for you?"

"No, the foil is a deal-breaker, Gary, do you not understand that?"

"Fair enough, I'll have it myself, then."

As I walked over to the settee to fetch the Viscount from her, she suddenly raised her hand to indicate that I should cancel my approach.

"Not so quick, lad," she said. "You still haven't answered my question: Is there anything else you can offer me other than the Viscount?"

"I've got a KitKat Chunky."

"Fuck off with your KitKat Chunky. I can't cope with that, not with my teeth."

"I could do you a slice of toast?"

"That's not much of a treat. I have toast every day. I more or less live off the stuff. What about a slice of Battenberg?"

"I've got a couple of those little cardboardy chocolate wafers from the coffee shop?"

"What about a slice of Battenberg?" she inquired with a knowing look on her face.

"How about some Nutella on a cream cracker? That's almost birthday celebration standard . . ." I replied.

"Gary, I can see the Battenberg on the counter and there's a good two inches left. That's an inch each. Having that would feel like passing your driving test and having someone do your ironing *on your birthday*. Come on, let's do it."

"You sure the marzipan won't make your teeth vacillate?"

"Positive."

I sliced the Battenberg and put hers on a saucer. My slice was significantly thicker, but I hid it from her view by eating it from the palm of my hand.

"When are you going to make this place more of a home? Look at it. You're living like a squatter. You've nothing here that you couldn't just run away from and leave behind. It all feels, I don't know . . . temporary."

"It suits me fine. It reminds me that I've got to keep moving on, keep an eye out for opportunities that might arise and entice."

"Come off it, Gary, you're as set in your ways as I am. I see you every day walking out to work with your shitty suit on and your plastic briefcase with nothing in it. You look about as dynamic as an abandoned fridge."

"Thanks, Grace. Anyway, I thought you wanted to hear about the girl I went looking for?"

"Go on, then. And, by the way, this slice is barely half an inch. If I starve to death, it's on you and only you."

I started to tell her about my trip to the Grange estate. After she had finished her Battenberg, she put one of her hands inside the sage slipper beside her and interrupted my flow.

"You are really smitten by this girl, aren't you?"

"Why would you say that? I hardly know her."

"Don't get cutesy with me. Answer the question."

"I haven't even thought about it. She's well out of my league."

"Well, even Lassoo is out of your league, but that doesn't answer my question."

"Okay. I am very struck by her. There is a nice atmosphere around her and she has got me intrigued, so that would be my answer: I am intrigued by her."

"So you've thought about it a lot?"

"Yes."

"You've never spoken to me about your love life. Have you ever had a girlfriend?"

"I thought you were my girlfriend?"

"Fuck off, Gary, answer the question."

Girlfriends are a topic I am never that comfortable talking about. I know I'm not good-looking, but I'm not a full-on spud. I would describe my face as forgettable (certainly many people seem to forget it), and I'm five foot seven-and-a-half inches, which is just one-and-a-half inches below the national average (I've looked this up on many occasions). When I walk into a room, I don't sense that people are thinking, *Hey up, here comes half-pint* or *Danger! A shrimp that walks!* Nothing like that. People only occasionally comment on my height, which I suppose means I've got away with it.

My big problem has always been having the confidence to make that first contact with a girl. As a teenager I had come to the conclusion that I would never meet a girl, and it made me sad. I always reckoned that not having any sisters was the root of my problem. Females seemed like an alien race. By the time I went to university I don't remember ever having talked to a girl other than during the course of some transaction or other. I attempted to explain this to Grace.

"I just find it hard to meet girls and establish a connection. I've had a couple of girlfriends, but the last one ended before I moved here to London."

"Rubbish," replied Grace. "Tell me how you met those two girlfriends if you're so useless."

For some reason—I think maybe it was the presence of Clementine in my thoughts—I decided to open up and answer Grace's question (with a significant spin in my favor).

I told her how I met my first girlfriend in my second week at the University of Manchester, aged eighteen. I was staying in a low-rise student accommodation block that I shared with eight other freshers. For those first weeks I had been generally hiding myself in my room, only venturing into the communal kitchen on the evening when I knew the rest of my flatmates would be out and about enjoying their lives, or pretending that they were. On this particular night I got my timing wrong and came face-to-face with a girl waiting for her toast to emerge from the toaster. I ignored her at first and made a fuss of searching for my bread and, once found, carefully selecting a couple of slices before resealing the loaf in its plastic packing. The slices were extra thick, which is how I like to receive my toast. I fussed about looking for one of my plates (my mum had given me a set of plastic crockery from Home Bargains with a barn owl's face as its motif) and placed it on the counter. I didn't have any butter and had intended to nick someone else's from the fridge. She had scuppered this plan, so I slipped off back to my room to wait for her to leave the kitchen. I returned about five minutes later and she was still stood by the toaster.

"Hi," she said.

"Hello," I replied.

The conversation evaporated, and she turned to face the toaster. I walked over to the counter and noticed that my two slices of bread were no longer on my plate. *She's nicked them*, I thought, and felt an instant admiration for her. It also put me in the driving seat. I could use this to make her like me. She turned around again and spoke to me while looking towards the hallway to my right.

"Listen, I'm sorry it's taking so long. I burnt my first batch. You might want to go back to your room."

"No, that's fine, I'll wait here. I'm Gary, nice to meet you."

"Yeah, same. I'm Layla, I like toast."

"Same. It's very appealing."

"Isn't it."

She turned to face the toaster again, and I noticed her turn the timer control to add a few minutes to the toasting period. I could sense that she had a panic on. She had long, center-parted dark brown hair and a reddish complexion that suggested she had been scrubbing her face with a coconut. She wasn't my type, was my instant assessment. She was wearing beige jogging pants and a light blue sweatshirt with the words "HAPPY NOW" printed on its front. She took a quick glance over her shoulder towards me and delivered an apologetic smile. I noticed she had bright red lipstick on her lips. It hadn't been there ten minutes ago when we first collided. Her incisor teeth were very prominent and confident, perfect for eating any of the meats and useful for opening difficult packaging.

PING went the toaster, and out popped two extra-thick slices of burnt toast. She quickly grabbed them, threw them in the sink, and drenched them in cold water from the tap. She then scooped up the sodden slices and threw them in the bin. "Fucked it up again," she said. "Must be something wrong with the toaster."

"Yeah, must be," I replied.

"They were my last two slices, so no toast for me. I'll just have to eat some butter."

"I'll do you a deal," I said. "You can have a couple of slices of my bread if you let me have some of your butter."

"Sounds good to me."

"You happy now?" I said, pointing at her "HAPPY NOW" top.

"Oh yeah, right, LOL. LAFS even."

"What does LAFS stand for?"

"Layla's awful fucking sweatshirt."

I more or less laughed.

"I like your barn owl plates. Did your mum get you them?" she asked.

"No," I lied, not wanting to appear soft. "I've always loved owls. I love that rotating head thing and the fact that they wear fancy trousers despite leading an outdoor, hunting-focused lifestyle."

"Where did you get them?"

"At a gift shop in a bird sanctuary in a rural area."

"Perfect place to buy some owl plates."

"Yeah, and a great place just generally on account of its ethos and its various stances."

"Did it have a café?"

"Yeah, that's where I first saw the barn owl crockery."

"Did they sell toast?"

"Yes, and the coffee had a barn owl face fashioned into the froth."

"You do like your barn owls."

"Not as much as you love toast."

We spent many hours with each other over the next weeks and months and became a team of two lonely souls against the rest of the world. We relied upon each other for our every need and spent the next three years in a cocoon together. If she left me, I would be in the deepest shit. I did everything

I could to make sure that it was the same for her. We led our lives inside a huge warm watermelon never questioning whether it was for the best, out of fear of what the answer might be. I was very, very fucking comfortable and assumed she felt the same.

Then one night I returned to our flat and she was gone. She left me a note apologizing and explaining that she felt she had wasted three years of her life and it was time to move on. She was right. I wasn't devastated but unsettled enough to return to live with my mum in Leeds in an alternative hot melon. As the pain retreated, I was struck by the thought that I had never really fancied Layla. She had spoken to me, and that had been enough to send us on our wasteful journey. Still, I had been a boyfriend, and I had lost a sliver of my fear of girls.

Grace interrupted my flow.

"Am I meant to feel sorry for you?"

"No, I'm just giving you the facts."

"Just out of interest, why did you stay together that long if everything was so shit?"

"I don't know, Grace, I think I was hoping it would just fizzle out or that she would end it. Have you ever lived inside a warm melon? It's very soothing—makes it hard to leave."

"I would never live inside a large fruit, Gary—especially a warm one. It's obviously going to rot in the end. You just didn't have the bottle to end it. Typical bloke. And you didn't even fancy her. What a prick. So, how did you meet the other girlfriend?"

I told her about my courtship of girlfriend number two: Anne.

I was twenty-four years old and living at home with my

mum in Leeds. I had a job at the town hall processing planning applications. The work was easy, repetitive and dull, which suited my general malaise perfectly. One evening a few of the others in my part of the office were going to a comedy evening at a nearby pub. They asked me if I wanted to tag along. I sensed that the invite was motivated by politeness and not a genuine desire for me to come, but I agreed to go anyway. I'm fascinated by nervous, out-of-their-depth performers. It's like watching myself get tortured without actually having to experience any pain.

The comedy evening was being held in a large function room at the rear of a pub. The stage was at one end, the bar at the other. Above the stage was a banner that read "LAUGH-ABLE!" and there were about twenty tables set out on the function room floor. Our group had prebooked a table that seated six. There were seven of us now, so I grabbed a chair from another table and seated myself between but slightly behind two of my colleagues. One of them was my supervisor at work, called Ian Pepper. Mid-forties and dull as a fucking concrete bell. He turned his head towards me for a chat. "You all right back there, Gary? Can you see the stage okay?"

"Yes, I'm fine, thanks. So, are you a big fan of comedy?" I asked.

"Not really. Don't see the point of it."

"So what do you like to watch, you know, for entertainment?"

"I quite like watching golf on the TV."

"So what's the point of golf?"

"Well, there's an outcome, a winner, an achievement if you like."

"Fair, but if a comedian makes you laugh, then you're the winner as well."

"But they never do. Listen, Gary, do you think you could fetch a round of drinks for the table? Would you be able to do that?"

"Yeah, sure, what does everyone want?"

I took the orders and made my way to the bar. It was empty apart from three girls stood at the center of the counter. They were loud and excited, their minds made jaunty by booze. As I made the order, the tallest one of the group took a step towards me. "All right, shortarse, are all those drinks for you?" she said as she looked down at me and laughed.

"No, they're for my mates."

"What mates? Like you've got any mates." She turned to her friends, and on cue they both laughed along with her.

I got a bit of a sweat on and was desperate for my order to arrive so I could clear off back to the table. The tall one was still looking down at me, sucking her fizzy drink through a straw and giving me exaggerated seductive gurns. I felt hated. She had a pale, round face with straight, jet-black, center-parted hair down to her shoulders. She was wearing a black apron dress, and the overall effect was of a budget Victoria Beckham. I think she was drunk, that or in the first flush of a session.

Her little blond, bird-faced teammate joined in:

"Are you not getting us a drink, then, shorty?"

I just stared ahead of me at the bottles of spirits behind the bar. Sparrow Face repeated herself:

"Are you deaf, mate? Are you getting us a drink or what?"

The first two pints of my order arrived in front of me. I picked them up and made my way back to the table. I asked

Ian if he could give me a hand with the rest of the drinks, and thankfully he obliged. The girls had peeled off and sat at their own table by the time I arrived back at the bar.

After a couple of stand-up comics had presented their wares to the audience, the MC announced the next act, and onto the stage walked the Victoria Beckham lass.

"Hi, my name's Anne Campbell. Why are you all looking at me? Do you fancy me or are you just wondering if I'm any good at doing the Hoovering?"

This was met with total silence. My supervisor, Ian Pepper, was the only person to laugh.

"Ha ha ha. That's VERY, VERY FUNNY!" he bellowed, and it was impossible to tell whether this was genuine or pure sarcasm.

She continued, but I could tell her confidence had taken a hit.

"So, err . . . yeah. I caught a fish the other day and when I cut it open it had a 'Best of Mozart' cassette in its belly. It was hooked on classics."

Silence. This time it was broken by a member of the audience (Ian wasn't listening anymore):

"Tell us a joke, we know you want to."

Some of the audience laughed. They clearly weren't on her side. I could sense a shaking in her constitution. She took the microphone off its stand, and it instantly caused a shriek of feedback through the speakers. A bloke on a front table waded in:

"Here's some more feedback, love: fuck off!"

That line sealed her fate; there was no recovery route that her material could navigate a safe path through. The MC came back on the stage to save her. I felt sorry for her and guilty for the part my colleague had played in her ridicule. I could only partially convince myself she had deserved it due to her earlier behavior at the bar.

At the end of the night my little work group were completely pissed and mostly talking about their memories of tinned foods and frozen ready meals. Only a few other punters remained. I glanced over my shoulder and noticed Victoria Beckham sat alone consoling herself with a blue-tinged fizzy drink. I grabbed a full bottle of beer off our table and walked over to her.

"Hey, here's that drink you wanted me to get you."

"What? Oh yeah. Thanks, but I'm on the blue drink."

"I saw you onstage earlier. I thought you did well to stand up to everyone."

"I'm usually a lot better than that. It's just that some fucker heckled me right at the start and I'm always thrown by an early punch."

"Yeah, I heard him. What a bastard."

"Hey, sorry I called you shortarse earlier . . . I always get into a state when the drink kicks in before I go onstage. You're not that short."

"Yeah, I'm only one-and-a-half inches below the national average. Your joke about the fish was really funny. Even my mate Ian laughed, and he only usually laughs at golf swings."

I looked over to the table and saw that Ian and the gang were leaving. I was glad. Victoria Beckham and I spoke for another hour or so and left together. All her attitude and brassiness had gone. She seemed defeated. I realized that I could easily make this girl like me, and so that is what I did.

We spent the next two years as an item, living in each other's pockets and creating another warm melon for me to tick over in. Then I chanced across her having it off with a policeman behind a dumpster in the cinema car park and that was the end of that.

Grace interrupted me.

"There's a pattern emerging here. Both these relationships turned to shit because all you are trying to do is make yourself comfortable and make it hard for them to leave. What makes you think it will be any different with this Clementine girl?"

"I've played it through in my mind. I think it will pan out into something exceptional."

"What makes you say that?"

"Because I really, *really* fancy her."

"God help the poor girl."

I told Grace about Clementine's reluctance to provide an alibi for me and assured her that if it ever came to it, I would be able to direct the police to her flat. I didn't want that to happen and, of course, given that I had no involvement in this whole thing, assumed that it never would. Grace seemed satisfied with the outcome and advised me to forget all about Clementine for my sake and hers. Lassoo fell off his chair mid-nap, ran a few steps to the side, and spewed up on the carpet.

8

THAT EVENING I WENT to the Grove to watch football. I wanted to try to take my mind away from thoughts of Brendan's death and Grace's worries about Wilmott and Cowley. Most of all, though, I wanted to take my attention away from Clementine and the needling feeling that she might be in some sort of trouble or pain. I joined Nick and Andy at our usual seats at the end of the bar. The match involved two London clubs so was inevitably a dreary affair. After the final whistle I told them about this new girl I had met and lied about how exceptional our prospects were. Nick's advice was very certain: "Don't get involved, mate. All women are a shitstorm, especially the good-looking ones."

Nick and Andy left soon after the match ended, and I walked through to the lounge bar and sat in the booth where I had failed to entice Clementine. Sitting there made me relive snippets of our conversation once again. What had I done wrong? I was a bit rude about her bike, but she had seemed to take it in good spirit. Every other part of our conversation seemed to flow with a good momentum. Why had it not worked?

I needed to stop thinking about her. I looked over to

the bar, where I had last seen Brendan and decided to think about him for a while as a Clementine diversion. I scrolled through the contacts in my phone to find his details and glanced through the five or six messages we had exchanged. They were all just work-related and dull apart from one where he had attached a photograph of his latest sock purchase. A beige pair with a revolver gracing the length of each leg section. The message read "Foot Soldier LOL." I smiled while remembering that I hadn't smiled when I received the message. Our last transaction had been when he placed the note with his "friends list" telephone number in my pocket. I pulled the note out and dialed it. I don't know why; it just seemed the respectful thing to do before deleting the contact from my phone. On connecting it went straight to voicemail: "You have reached the voicemail of Fuzzbox Novelty Socks. Please leave your message after the tone." I ended the call and laughed to myself. Brendan's final joke was a good one.

I decided to try Brendan's usual work number one last time, the one I had always used, and dialed it from my list of contacts. After five or six rings, it was picked up.

"Hello?" I said.

There was no reply, but I could sense that there was someone on the other end.

"Hello? . . . Hello? . . . Hello? Is this Brendan's phone?" I asked into the silence.

Again, there was no reply. I felt a little squirt of adrenaline in my stomach.

"Hello? . . . Is that the police?"

Silence for a few seconds and then the call was terminated

from the other end. Who the fuck had Brendan's phone? My first instinct had been the police, but surely they would have spoken to me. Would my phoning the number get me into trouble with them? I didn't think so. Shit, what if Brendan was actually murdered and I had just spoken to the murderer? Could they trace me from the phone call? Yes, of course they could; I would be in Brendan's contact list. I panicked immediately, then convinced myself that lots of work contacts would have phoned his number these last couple of days. It was no big deal, but, nevertheless, it left me feeling uneasy. I walked back through to the other bar and watched a Spanish football game that was inevitably technically admirable but deadly dull.

On my way home I took the note from Brendan out of my pocket again, gave it a little smile, and threw it in the gutter. As I did so, I felt a small, hard object at the bottom of my pocket. It was a USB stick that had a cover in the form of a tiny corncob. I had never seen it before. It must have been slipped in there by Brendan. I popped into my office as I passed on the way back to my flat and placed the dongle into my PC. A message appeared on the screen stating that the contents of the drive were password protected and demanding I enter the password. I typed in some obvious candidates:

Password
123456
BrendanHA-HA
HAHA Brendan
HABrendanHA

Socks
Sox

None of them worked, and I gave up. I would ask Grace tomorrow if she knew of any way to penetrate the dongle, the contents of which Brendan had obviously wanted me to see.

9

ON WAKING UP THE next day I thought about Clementine for less than ten minutes. *Progress*, I thought to myself. There was no food of note left in the flat, so I decided to go to the coffee shop for my breakfast. On my way out I popped in to see Grace and told her about the flash drive. Her eyes lit up. She very much wanted in on this.

"Leave it with me," she said, with a hungry look in her eye. "Oh, and could you take Lassoo for a quick walk? My bones are not up to it and he's desperate." I agreed to take him with me to the coffee shop.

"Any joy getting information about those coppers on your computer?" I asked.

"Nothing. I got bored to be honest, they must be well off-grid, or maybe you gave me the wrong names. I was actually wondering if they might be journalists. That might make sense. They're always nosing about in someone's misery. This new task sounds much more fun, though. Now clear off and don't tug on his lead."

As usual, Lassoo took his own sweet time and then livened up when we reached the play area. I let him off his lead to attend to his business. As he left, my squirrel mate leapt onto the little wall at the play area entrance.

"All right, mate?" I inquired to myself.

"Yeah, not too bad when I think around that question," I replied on his behalf.

"Your tail isn't so fluffery buffery today. You had a rough night?"

"Maybe you shouldn't be pointing that out, not knowing what state my mind is in. Maybe I'm worried about you. Did you consider that as a possibility before having a snipe at me? I don't think you did. Am I right?"

"Yeah, you're right. Sorry about that."

"So, this girl that walked out on you, I hear you've seen her again. So what's the situation with her?"

"Nothing doing really. I've no right to think she should feel the same as me just because we had a chat in a pub."

"Don't believe you. You hate it that she doesn't seem interested, but what you hate more around it is that you don't think you can make her like you."

"No, you're wrong. I'm not playing that game with her. She isn't interested in me and I'm okay with that."

"So what game are you playing? You wouldn't talk to me unless you had something on your mind."

"Honestly, mate, I will have forgotten her in a couple of days. I've got other matters to address."

"Liar."

"*You are*," I replied.

"*No, you are*," responded the squirrel as it jumped off the wall and disappeared into the distance.

I noticed that Lassoo was in the throes of a deposit, and

once again I didn't have any pooping bags for a clear-up. I walked over to him and went through the charade of miming the collection of the dirt. As I was doing so, I looked up to see Detectives Cowley and Wilmott approaching me.

"Hello, Gary," said Cowley. "What are you up to? Not burying something you don't want us to see, I hope?"

"No, just cleaning up after my dog."

"What, with your bare hands? That's disgusting," chirped in Wilmott.

"No, of course not. I just realized I didn't bring any bags out with me, so I thought I'd have a look at the thing and see if it looked like a dissolver."

"They all dissolve, Gary, unless of course the dog has been eating plastics or grit. I didn't know you had a dog, Gary," inquired Cowley.

"No, I don't, I'm just walking my next-door neighbor's dog for her. She's got crumbly bones and finds it difficult sometimes. Listen, do you mind if I ask to see your ID? You know, just for formality's sake. I don't mean anything by it."

"No problem at all, Gary," replied Cowley. They both took out little black wallets from their pockets. The cover of the wallet was embossed with the Metropolitan Police crest and inside had a plastic photo ID insert. The names and photos were both present and correct. They looked like the real deal.

"Thank you both. So, did you want to speak to me about something?"

"We just wondered if you'd thought of anything new that might be pertinent to our inquiries, Gary. You seem like a deep thinker. Maybe something has popped into your mind?" asked Cowley.

"Yeah, there were a couple of things that I thought you should know but I didn't have your phone number. You didn't leave me your card."

"Oh, sorry about that, Gary. How remiss of me. But we're here now, so fire away. What can you tell us?"

"Well, firstly, for some reason I dialed Brendan's telephone number when I was in the pub last night—you know, just one last time before I deleted his name—and someone answered it. I'm guessing it was the police, but the person on the other end didn't say a word."

"I can assure you that if it was a police officer, they would have spoken to you, and if you remember, we didn't find any phones on Brendan's person. Do you have your phone on you?" asked Cowley.

"Yes, I do."

"Well, why don't you try the number again, Gary? This could be important," instructed Wilmott.

I dialed the number and got the message "The telephone number you have dialed is no longer in service." They didn't seem surprised.

"Well, thank you for that information, Gary. Now, what was the other thing that you wanted to tell us?" asked Cowley.

"It was just that I went into work yesterday and remembered that we were holding some important documents on behalf of Brendan—his will, his title deeds, pension details, that sort of thing."

"Did you have a look at them, Gary?" asked Cowley.

"Yes, they were just in an envelope in the deed box in my office. Nothing that seemed significant, but I thought you should probably know."

"Thank you, Gary, we will look into that, get your firm's permission to take a look. Was there anything else in the envelope of interest? You know—computer disks, diaries, tape recordings, that sort of thing?" asked Cowley with a sudden neediness in his voice.

"No, just the normal documents that anyone might deposit with their solicitor."

I was about to mention the dongle to them, when Wilmott received a telephone call and indicated to his partner that they had to leave. They thanked me for the information and shouted that they would be in touch as they strode away. I was quite pleased that I hadn't had to mention the dongle. I felt I owed it to Brendan to try to look at its contents before telling them. Brendan had made an effort to give it to me personally, and I wanted to do him the service of checking its contents before handing it over. It might be personal stuff, might even be pictures of socks. It was best to wait. They hadn't asked me about my Clementine alibi, which I found strange but decided was probably a good sign. I wanted them to leave us both alone.

I arrived at the coffee shop to find Wayne cleaning one of the four round tables that dominated the interior. He was wearing a tight black shirt that shone brightly under the harsh LED lights of the café. On his legs were a beige pair of what I call Parsnip Trousers, the ones that cling to the leg and taper towards the bottom, gripping the ankle like a vice.

"You again," he said. "On a Sunday. You really must have the hots for me."

"Not so much you, Wayne, as your trousers."

Wayne stood erect with his hands on his hips and his legs

slightly parted. "Yes, they are very cosseting. Are you thinking they look restrictive? 'Cause believe me that is not the case."

"That's good news, Wayne. They do look a bit grippy, especially around your ankles and your balls."

"Absolutely not. It's like wearing a liquid hug. What can I get you, mate?"

"Two medium cappuccinos and two—"

". . . slices of Battenberg," he sang as he waddled off back behind the counter. Lassoo followed him as far as the glass display of cakes and sweetmeats. He put one paw up onto the glass and turned his head downwards to fix his stare on a ring donut. He then allowed his paw to slide down the front of the glass and replaced it with his other paw. He continued to swap paws throughout the visit, never once moving his glare from the donut.

"I met a girl the other night in the pub," I blurted, taking myself by surprise.

"Is she aware that you met her?"

"Yeah, we spoke to each other and made a good connection."

"So, are you going to be seeing her again before she takes a restraining order out on you?"

"Yeah, I saw her again outside her block of flats."

"What do you mean 'outside her block of flats'? Have you been spying on her? Jesus, she needs to get that restraining order pronto like Tonto."

"No, I wasn't spying on her. I was just reconnecting with her."

"And did you reconnect? Or did she just reject?"

"Hard to say. I don't have a great instinct for that sort of speculation."

"Just tell me: How did it go?"

"Shittily. I think I caught her at a bad time. Reckon she had just had an argument with her boyfriend or maybe her landlord."

"Boyfriend?! Leave it, Gary. Take the memory of her and throw it down a shitpipe."

"But she is really beautiful."

"Yeah, and you aren't."

He had a point.

When I dragged Lassoo away from the counter by his lead, he gave me a look as if to say, *"You could have made me happy. Thanks for nothing."* To make it up to him I bought a little pack of dog biscuits from the corner shop, and we made our way home. When I got back to Grace's flat, she was sat staring at her computer screen with the intensity of a Norwegian sniper.

"Hi, Grace, I got you a coffee. How's it going? Any progress?"

"Just put it down and get out. I can't concentrate with you here."

"Okay, but have you got anywhere with it?"

"No, get out."

"But do you think you can crack it?"

"Yes, I'm the best in the business. Get out."

I left just in time to see Lassoo slip off his cushion and bang his head on a magazine rack. He didn't flinch and fell almost instantly asleep on the floor with a satisfied gurgle.

10

THE FOLLOWING DAY WAS a Monday, and I thought about Clementine for about five minutes before I got out of bed and for the entirety of the walk to work. Not too bad. I bought a coffee on the way but was disappointed to find that Wayne was not in work. I asked about his absence and was told that he just hadn't bothered to turn up. That wasn't like him; he was always there come rain or come more rain. Maybe his trousers had caused him a constriction injury.

When I arrived at the office, two uniformed policemen were just leaving the building. The thought crossed my mind to ask them if they knew of Cowley and Wilmott, but I didn't act on it. Once inside, I was greeted by one of the partners, John Blenkingstop. He explained that the offices had been burgled last night and asked if I would check my own office to see if anything had been stolen.

It didn't look disturbed in any way until I noticed that the marks left by the feet of the deed box were visible on the carpet. It had clearly been moved slightly. I opened it up and saw that Brendan's documents were gone. I reported this to Blenkingstop, who said he would pass this information on to the police. I told him the terrible news about Brendan and my vague involvement and was surprised by the sheer indifference on his face when he heard it.

"Come through to my office please, Gary," he requested.

I followed him to his grand office on the first floor. It was designed to intimidate and impress. A huge mahogany desk sat at one end beneath an imposing portrait of the original founders of the firm. Every other wall was covered floor to ceiling with law books. I remembered the first time I entered this room, when I was interviewed for my current job. Our conversation had gone something like this:

"Why do you want to work at Tarrants, Mr. Thorn?"

"Because it's a well-established firm with an excellent reputation that specializes in the type of cases that interest me."

"Bullshit. There are hundreds of firms just like this one looking for staff. What's the real reason?"

"No, really, I took a lot of care researching the firm and it seemed like a perfect fit."

"Last chance, Mr. Thorn, or you are out of here."

"I only live five minutes away and it would be really convenient for me."

"Good lad, I like you, can you start next Monday?"

"Yes."

"Do you want to pretend you have some questions that you are interested in hearing the answers to?"

"No."

"Good lad, see you next Monday."

He was in a similar mood today.

"Listen, Gary, John McCoy, the owner of Cityside Investigations, is a very important client of mine, and as you know,

Brendan was one of his favorite employees. Make sure you cooperate with the police."

"I've spoken to them already. I didn't have anything useful to tell them. I was only in the pub with Brendan for half an hour. He was fine when he left. I'll keep you informed if they contact me again."

"Don't bother. I don't want any conflict of interest arising between this firm and Cityside Investigations. We can't afford to lose them as a client. Keep this as your problem and not mine. If any conflict arises, I'll dump you and not John McCoy, do you understand?"

"Yes, of course, I won't mention it again."

"Correct, and buy yourself a new suit, you look like a carpet salesman."

I had only been back in my office five minutes when the phone on my desk rang. It was the custody officer at Peckham Police Station. A client of the firm had requested that we attend the station to be present when he was interviewed under caution. The client's name was Wayne Moore. *So*, I thought, *that was why he wasn't in the coffee shop this morning.*

When I arrived at the police station, the custody sergeant informed me that Wayne had been arrested on suspicion of possessing class-A drugs for the purposes of distribution and supply. He would arrange for the investigating officer to fill me in on the details. I took a seat in the waiting room, on the hard blue plastic bench that lined one wall of the room. The walls were light gray and empty. The only information being displayed was an "In Event of a Fire" notice. Somebody had written "Drink Lager" on the face of it. Moments later, a middle-aged man in a dark green anorak and blue trousers entered and walked up to the custody sergeant's counter. He had huge feet, and his dirty white training shoes were verging on clown attire. He wore thick-rimmed spectacles and enjoyed an elaborate hair puzzle comb-over which once again gave off the whiff of the circus. He spoke to the custody sergeant with a booming, relatively posh accent.

"Are you in charge here?"

"Yes, I am. How can I help you, sir?"

The sergeant was in his mid-forties. He sported a short back and sides and a large head. He was overweight and had fat luxury fingers, which were manipulating a ballpoint pen as he stared indifferently at the computer screen in front of him. He held an insincere smile as his resting face and had an air of simmering indifference towards his work. A big meat-eater I reckoned, and not someone whose personal space you would invade, on the beach, for example, or in a doctor's waiting room.

"It's my neighbor. I want him arrested and put in the cells."

"And why might that be, sir?"

"I'll tell you why if you'll give me the chance. To put it simply, he has found a way of getting into my attic from his property. He gets in most nights and starts making knocking sounds and huffing and puffing like a small bear. It's driving me mad and is a clear breach of my peace. To make matters worse, he's foreign. It has to stop before I do something I will regret."

"What has him being foreign got to do with the situation, sir?"

"Well, it's obvious, isn't it? In his country it's probably acceptable to scrut about in a neighbor's roof space."

"What's your neighbor's name?"

"Christ's sake, you love to interrupt, don't you? He's called Mr. Dushku."

"And have you spoken to him about this?"

"I was getting to that. No, I haven't, but I've written to him on several occasions and received no reply. He will probably say that he can't read English but that's a lie because I've seen him in his back garden reading the *Sun* newspaper. He can certainly speak English well enough when he's shouting at his feral children."

"So, have you actually seen him in your attic or discovered how he is getting in there?"

"I sit up there two or three nights a week, but he never comes in when I'm up there. No doubt he has a spyhole or something and doesn't come in if the coast isn't clear. I lie down behind the old metal cold-water tank but he still manages to spot me."

"So, how is he getting into your attic? Is there a hole in the party wall or a gap or something?"

"I don't know how he's doing it. There's so much shit up there that I can't inspect the entirety of the party wall. Anyway, what does it matter? I thought I was speaking to a policeman, not a structural engineer."

"Well, I think it will be very important in establishing the facts, sir."

"No, I don't think it will be, because I've got tape recordings of his midnight creeping. Here, have a listen."

Mr. Clown Shoes pressed a button on his phone and started to play a recording he had made. It began with him whispering, "Recording from upstairs hallway 4 a.m., 16th September." There then followed an intermittent scratchy or tapping sound and the occasional baby bear "growl." The sergeant interrupted the playback and inquired:

"Are you sure it's not a pigeon, rather than a baby bear?"

"A pigeon!" barked Clown Shoes. "How could a pigeon make noises like that? Are you fucking serious? Do you reckon the pigeon is using dumbbells or riding a fucking skateboard?"

"Okay, sir, less of the language please. Let's keep it civil. The problem is that if he is indeed entering your property without any intention to steal or without causing damage . . ."

Clown Shoes interrupted: "HE IS CAUSING DAMAGE! Damage to my mental health! I hardly get any sleep and I'm neglecting my church duties. I'm a warden at St. Mary's Church—yes, that's the type of person I am—and yet nobody, and I mean nobody, seems willing to help."

"Okay, sir, I hear you. Listen, I'll get one of our officers to take a statement from you and advise you what action, if any, we will be taking. If you have a seat on the bench over there, someone will be through to get you."

Clown Shoes turned around slowly, his body slightly deflated. He walked towards me with one of his shoes making a breathy squeak. As he looked at me, I gave him the best sympathetic smile I could muster. This stopped him in his tracks. He stared at me for a few seconds with a disturbing intensity, as if he was trying to decide if I was his long-lost son. He then shut his eyes tightly for a moment or two and strode out of the police station.

The sergeant sighed behind his counter and typed something onto his computer.

"Sounded like a squirrel to me," I announced.

"No, definitely a pigeon. I've got one in my attic. Drives you mad," he replied without taking his eyes off the screen.

A young, suited officer emerged from the large security door that separated the public waiting room from the rest of the station. He beckoned me to follow him and introduced himself as Detective Constable Bailey. He was the investigating officer in Wayne's case. He took me to a little interview room halfway down a long corridor of interview rooms and we sat opposite each other. He had Wayne's case file in his hand. Reading from the file, he explained that Wayne and his father had been stopped while driving the father's car in Lewisham. They had agreed to a search of the vehicle, and the officers found a small packet of what was believed to be cocaine underneath the front passenger seat. Wayne and his father were immediately arrested for possession and intent to supply. Neither of them made any comment on arrest other than a straightforward denial that they had any knowledge that the drugs were in the car. Bailey confirmed that the car they were driving was registered to the father. Wayne had asked for a solicitor and I was welcome to see him now. If I waited in the room, they would bring him through.

Wayne arrived about five minutes later. He was wearing a black puffer jacket and skinny ripped jeans, quite severely and randomly sliced, as if to replicate the damage caused by a badger attack. He seemed unconcerned and in good spirits. "They sent *you*! What have I done to deserve that?" he asked as he seated himself gracefully on the chair opposite me.

"What's wrong with me, Wayne? I'm a bona fide hotshot and you know it."

"Nah, mate, you are always high on coffee and Battenberg—enough to make you erratic at the very least."

He fist-bumped me to indicate that he was actually pleased to see me. His first question was the same as that of every other client I have attended to at the police station.

"So can you get me out of here, like now? I've got a coffee shop to govern."

"That depends."

"On what?"

"Well, the severity of the charges, the strength of the evidence against you, whether you are likely to interfere with witnesses, whether you are in employment, whether you have ever jumped bail before—"

He interrupted:

"Listen, I haven't done anything. The coppers put the drugs in the car. They've done it before to my dad. They do it to intimidate him. He used to be a copper. He knows stuff about how they used to carry on and they don't think he can keep his mouth shut. It's just a reminder. The charges will be dropped, just you wait and see. It's a fucking game."

Wayne went on to explain the circumstances of his arrest from his point of view. My best guess was that he was absolutely telling the truth. I had to warn him though that the "planted evidence" defense very rarely convinces a jury. I instructed him to give a "no comment" interview and promised him I would do my best to persuade the officer in charge to grant him bail. He still seemed remarkably relaxed about the whole thing and his interview was a peach. One part will live on in my memory:

DC BAILEY

Why were you in the car with your father?

WAYNE

No comment other than that I prefer
having a lift to walking.

DC BAILEY

Why are you willing to give me that
information but have replied "no comment"
to most of my other questions?

WAYNE

No comment other than that my hatred of
walking is a question of lifestyle and character
and I never want to be misinterpreted
on those matters.

DC BAILEY

Is taking drugs part of your lifestyle and
character?

WAYNE

No comment other than to say I have never
taken any illegal drugs, as my lifestyle and
character are inconsistent with that activity.

DC BAILEY

Where were you driving to when
the police stopped you?

WAYNE

No comment other than that we were going
to the supermarket to buy some cat litter.

ME

Wayne, can I remind you that I have advised
you to reply "no comment" to all questions?

WAYNE

No comment.

DC BAILEY

Why did it need two of you to buy cat litter?

WAYNE

No comment other than to say that it's quicker to
drop one person off at the door and park by the
cash machine than go alone and have to find
a place to park. Also my dad thinks
it's a bit feminine to purchase
cat litter.

DC BAILEY

Did you know there was a bag of
class-A drugs under your seat?

WAYNE

No comment other than to say there is
still a cat at home that is desperate
for a shit.

Once the interview was over, Wayne was taken back to his cell. I had a chat with DC Bailey, who indicated that the custody sergeant was happy to release Wayne on bail pending further investigation. I got the faint feeling that Bailey believed that Wayne knew nothing about the drugs. His father was not going to be granted police bail, so obviously they thought he did have something to do with the drugs.

Before leaving the interview room, I took a chance and asked Bailey if he had any news on the Brendan Jones investigation. He looked at me quizzically and told me he had no idea what I was on about. I explained that I had been visited by his colleagues DI Wilmott and DI Cowley, as I was one of the last people to see Brendan before he was found dead. Again, he looked at me with confusion on his face. "This Wilmott and Cowley, did they definitely say they worked out of Peckham Police Station?" he asked.

"As far as I remember. Said they were CID I think."

"Just hold on here a moment and I'll go and have an ask about."

"That's very kind of you. Wayne is a nice bloke you know, just saying."

"Yeah, I reckon you're right."

Bailey left the room and returned about ten minutes later and informed me that nobody in the major investigation team had heard of Brendan Jones, and there certainly was no ongoing investigation into his death. Likewise, he could confirm that there were no officers connected with the station called either Wilmott or Cowley. He asked me if I wanted to provide a statement or make a complaint against whoever was posing as a police officer. I declined. I instinctively felt that I was best off staying as far away as possible from this business. I was also still stunned by the gradual realization that Brendan might not be dead.

As soon as I got out of the station, I tried Brendan's telephone number again. It was still no longer in service. My next instinct was to telephone DI Cowley, but as soon as this thought crossed my mind I remembered his sudden departure from the play area, which meant they once again hadn't given me their telephone number. Once back in my office, I sent a message to Brendan via his work email.

Hi Brendan

Was great to see you and your socks the other night. Shame you had to leave early. I stayed on and got chatting to a really nice lass, so, to be honest, I'm glad you fucked off! I bumped into her a couple of days later and she didn't seem interested but I'm going to follow your advice and "pursue till it's through."

One bit of bad news . . . those documents that we are holding for you (your will, title deeds, etc.) were stolen from my office on Sunday evening. No need to panic—I have details of them all on my computer and will be able to get replacements.

On a more positive note, could you give me a ring at your earliest . . . got some work I can put your way.

Cheers,
Gary

I received a reply almost by return from John McCoy, the owner of Cityside Investigations.

Hi Gary,

Brendan is working away from the offices and won't be able to take on any new casework for the foreseeable future. Please feel free to contact me directly and I will allocate the work to one of our other operatives.

Cheers,
John McCoy

PS Good luck with the lady.

I took the email at face value and felt suddenly elated by the increasing possibility that Brendan was still with us. I really wanted to see him again. I really wanted to have another drink with him and congratulate him on his Fuzzbox socks joke. This elation was slightly tempered by thoughts of Wilmott and Cowley and their motivations regarding me. Still, all I could do was keep reminding myself that, come what may, I had done nothing wrong.

I knocked on Grace's door when I got home, but there was no reply apart from Lassoo letting out a strange whine that sounded like "Weetabix."

II

AS MY WORRIES ABOUT Brendan subsided, my thoughts about Clementine intensified. By Wednesday evening it became inevitable that I would attempt to see her again. I drove over to the Grange estate after work and stopped in the same spot as last time. The bald man's red BMW 3 Series was parked just beyond the stairwell on the opposite side of the road. Boiler Suit Man was working away replacing the bumper on an ancient-looking Volkswagen Golf about fifty yards in front of me. His vast arse was facing directly at me.

It briefly crossed my mind that if his stomach were actually situated in one of his arse cheeks it would cut down on the amount of pipework required to shift his food intake back into the outside world. The thought soon passed as I began to doubt my decision to visit the estate.

I hadn't really thought it through. The chances of her appearing as I sat there were negligible, and I couldn't really go and knock on her door in case Bald Man was there. From my brief sighting of him he looked a lot older than Clementine, but I hadn't dismissed the idea that he might actually be her boyfriend. In some ways it was a relief to see his car outside. It gave me an excuse not to attempt contact. It made me feel less guilty about the fact that I really just wanted to see her face again. It made me feel one step up from being a stalker.

Boiler Suit Man stood up and arched his back to relieve some distress. He stared in my direction for a few moments and wiped his hands down the front of his cotton romper. He gave his arse a good scratch and started to walk towards me. I opened my window, ready to greet him. He was becoming a problem for me—a right nosy parker. The devil took hold of me, and I retrieved from my pocket the little bag of dog biscuits I had forgotten to give to Grace. I opened them and placed a few on my center console. I put a drop of the eucalyptus nasal spray on each one.

"All right, mate?" I asked as soon as he arrived at my window.

"I thought it was you. What you doing parked up here again without a residents' permit?"

"I'm just picking up my girlfriend. She'll be down in a minute."

"Hard for me to believe you've got a girlfriend, mate. Is she tiny as well?"

"Good one."

He leant down into the window so that his face filled the empty space. He chewed at the side of his mouth as he scanned around the interior of the car. His breath smelt of pork scratch-ings and custard. Eventually he spoke again:

"You know that herbal tea you were drinking?"

"Yeah, I remember."

"It's been on my mind ever since. It was a very unique aroma—incredibly rich and deep for an herbal product."

"I agree—and believe me, it definitely delivers a kick."

"So, I was wondering if you could give me the brand name so I can get some for myself and the wife and kids."

"Yeah, no worries. It's called Deep Balance herbal tea. I get it at the health shop on Peckham High Street. I think the one you tried was rosemary and basil."

I picked up a couple of the dog biscuits from the console. "Hey, you might be interested in these. They're for your gut health, absolutely packed with pro- and prebiotics. Get rid of bloating and keep your movements regular and delightful. Here—try one, they don't taste too bad. If you don't like the texture, you can crush them up and sprinkle them on some yogurt."

He took one of the biscuits from my hand and started to chew. "Jesus, they're a bit fucking hard, aren't they?"

"Yeah, it's best to leave them in your mouth for a while and let your saliva soften them."

He took my instruction and began to swill the biscuit around in his mouth.

"Ah, that's got it. Not bad, quite tart, but not bad at all for something with a health benefit. Would be better sprinkled on yogurt though. Do you get them at the health shop as well?"

"Yeah, they're called Goodboy's Gut Health supplement. Take three a day and your toilet brush will be redundant."

He thanked me for the biotics and waddled away back to his work. As I watched him, I noticed the bald bloke and another man exit the stairwell and drive away in the red BMW. I no longer had my excuse to avoid calling on Clementine.

I climbed the stairwell and knocked on her door. It was

easy to identify it as her flat because one of the wheels from her *Where's Wally?* bike was propped up against the wall next to the door. It was adorned with garish plastic flowers in the spokes.

As soon as she opened the door and saw me, she pushed by me and stared over the walkway wall. I presumed this was to check that Baldy had left the estate.

"You again. What are you doing here?" she asked with a slight smile on her face that suggested she wasn't completely against the idea of my visit.

"I just wanted to see you, check that you were all right, see if you were managing okay without the bike, but mainly just see you. Oh, and to finally give you your book back. Yes, so, how are you?" She took the book off me.

"I'm fine, thanks. I suppose you're really here to ask about me giving you an alibi, aren't you?"

"No, not at all, I promise. That has all gone away."

We stood in silence for a moment. I couldn't maintain eye contact, though I could sense her staring straight down the barrel of my boring face.

"I like your plastic flowers," I offered in order to break the silence. "They have a lovely sheen to them that you only get with plastic. Low maintenance, too, like a nonstick pan. Did you pick them yourself?"

Again, a little hint of a smile, but her body language indicated that my time was probably up. She turned around and made her way back to the front door. "I'll be seeing you, then. Take care," she said as she turned to close the door on me.

"Wait," I said. "I wrote my address and telephone number

inside the book. Please call me if you ever need a friendly chat or fancy a lighthearted drink down the pub."

"I might just do that . . . Cheerio."

"Hey, you might even enjoy it."

"I know," she replied, with just a moment's hesitation.

And she shut the door.

Back in my car I was as high as a kite just from being in her presence and hearing her speak again. I reckoned I had done good. I hadn't said anything obviously offensive. I might've smelt of dog biscuits, but who's to say that's not her thing?

A squirrel jumped onto the hood of my car and stared at me inquisitively.

"I hear you gave that nosy bloke a dog biscuit to chew on. Have you had a chance to think about why you would do that, especially as the poor man has already had to handle your piss?"

"Just me getting my own back on a world of my own making."

"So how did it go with the girl? Did you get her name? Are you an item for ever and ever now?"

"Shit, no, I didn't get her name, but I've kind of made my pitch and handed the decision over to her. Told her to get in touch if she ever fancied a chat and she said she might just do that."

"Maybe she just wanted to get rid of you, have you thought about that for at least a moment?"

"Of course I have, but I'm choosing to ignore that possibility at least until I get home."

"Maybe she's breadcrumbing you. You know, giving you a little morsel to keep you hanging on like a little puppy."

"No, she's not that kind of girl."

"Oh, isn't she? Well, what kind of girl is she, then?"

"A fucking wonderful one."

The squirrel gave me a sympathetic series of blinks and then darted away into the distance.

PART
TWO

12
EMILY

MY NAME IS EMILY. I live in a two-bedroom flat on the Grange estate in Walworth, southeast London. I am twenty-five years old with dark brown hair and a daft button nose. I style my hair with a straight temple-to-temple fringe. I was recently told that it makes me look like Jane Brurier, whoever that is. I'm about to do a runner. Let me tell you how I arrived at this decision.

I am an only child and grew up with my parents in the bed-and-breakfast hotel that they owned on the outskirts of Brighton. Mum didn't like Dad much. In later years she described him variously as "an ignorant shit," "a cold ham," "a farting donkey," and—my personal favorite—"a bongo-playing snake." She left him when I moved out. I think she only stayed with him for my sake, and I often feel guilty about that. She became a different person after she left him—a happy person.

Dad was comfortable having Mum around, but I never recall him showing her any affection. He was a dour and distant man with a foul temper, and I'll be honest, I was scared of him. He never hit me, largely I suspect because he never needed to. One angry look from him was all that was required to make me comply. I never saw him hit Mum, but if I had to guess I would say that he probably did. I remember an incident from when I was about ten years old. The hotel was a four-storey white stucco Victorian house in a crescent of similar imposing buildings. It had twelve guest bedrooms on the first and second floors. The ground floor housed a kitchen, a dining room, and a residents' lounge with ill-matched comfy chairs and a TV. My parents and I lived on the third floor. We didn't have a TV. Between 5 p.m. and 9 p.m. I was required to be out of sight and out of mind while my parents cooked and served dinner for the guests. One of the guest bedrooms on the first floor was immediately above the dining room. If it was unoccupied, I would sometimes take the master key from the cupboard in our hallway and sneak into this room to listen to the chitchat from the dining room below.

On this occasion I was lying on a pillow on the floor of the small en suite bathroom with my ear pressed against the tiled floor. I found that the sound traveled through the ceiling far crisper in this part of the room. Eyes shut, I was just drinking up the laughter and general buzz from below, when the bedroom door opened and in marched my father, hand in hand with one of the female guests.

"What about your wife?" the woman half whispered.

"Oh fuck her, the miserable cow," my father replied, hardly bothering to lower his voice.

Frozen to the spot and praying that they wouldn't look my way, I watched as Dad pushed her onto the bed and started to kiss her face and her chest.

She complained: "Stop it! I don't like it, get off me!"

My father rolled off the bed and marched out of the room. "Fuck you, then, you're all the same" was his parting comment as she followed him out.

The room was quiet once more and my heartbeat gradually slowed. I crept out of the room and never visited it again.

I only remember having one real friend at school. Her name was Louise. She had frizzy ginger hair and bowlegs. She played the violin, and like me, she avoided sports and was wary of every other girl in the school. They called us "the Guppies" because it made us sound ugly. I think a few of them were jealous at just how tight we were with each other. We were the least popular girls in our year. It didn't bother us, though, as we had each other. Louise wasn't allowed to visit me at home and nor was I allowed to go to her house. If I asked for permission, my father would say, "Better to be in the company of those that care for you than those who might be indifferent to your well-being." I never thought of a clever answer to this, and even if I had I would never have dared say it to his face.

One spring term, when I was fifteen, Louise and I took a chance and told our respective parents that they were holding optional revision classes at school on Saturday mornings. My father liked the idea of extra revision and so gave me permission to attend. I wore my school uniform and took a large bag topped up with schoolbooks to conceal the alternative outfit underneath. Louise and I both got on the bus that went to school but stayed on it all the way to Brighton town center. Once there we changed into our jeans and crop tops and paraded around the town trying to attract the attention of boys.

These Saturday jaunts became the best part of my heavily restricted life. We had limited success with the boys, as we both tended to clam up if a member of the opposite sex spoke to us. We did, however, have success at stealing stuff from the shops. Our primary target was cheap makeup.

The best shops to steal from were Boots, Superdrug, and the small independent chemist's. We would target the cheaper makeups, such as Rimmel and Max Factor, as they were subject to less store security. Lipsticks would disappear into our pockets, and eyeliner and eye shadow trays would be dropped into my large bag. We always stole just one item from each shop, in the belief that its presence in the bag or in our pocket could be explained away as a mistake.

I remember on one occasion we were in the large Superdrug on East Street. We huddled together in front of the Rimmel display and dropped a tray of blue eye shadows into Louise's bag on the floor at our feet. I casually walked out of the store onto the street and was immediately grabbed by a female shop detective. She marched me through a staff door and up to an office with gray filing cabinets and a large "conference" table in the center. I was told to sit down while we waited for the police to arrive. The shop detective sat opposite me and stared at me like I was a dog fouling up her perfectly manicured lawn. She didn't say a word.

As I sat there, I experienced fear like I never had before. All of it was focused on the reaction of my father. If I could have ended my life there and then, I would have done so. Fear was circulating through my body like a hot river, and I could feel my heartbeat pumping ten to the dozen in my chest, my head, and even my arms. My forehead was itching and sweating, and my hands and legs were shaking. My mouth was dry, and my stomach felt like a tumble drier full of moths.

A few minutes passed before Louise entered the room with two different shop detectives behind her. I was relieved to see her face. She gave me a little reassuring smile. The male shop detective took Louise's bag from her and poured the contents onto the table. Some school exercise books, a pencil case, and her school uniform spilled out. As the man sorted through it, it became apparent that the tray of eye shadow was no longer there. The female detective asked Louise if she was willing to be searched, and Louise agreed. She was taken to a different room and then returned a few minutes later, flashing me another smile as she did so. The three shop detectives left the room.

We sat in silence. I couldn't speak. I expected a police officer to enter the room any minute. "You okay?" asked Louise. I just shook my head and then rested it on the table as I began to sob. The female detective returned to the room and told us to come with her. She walked us back onto the shop floor and told us that we were free to leave but that they knew our faces and we were never to return. We walked away from the shop and down to the seafront in silence. I still thought that at any moment I would be grabbed by a police officer and taken away.

We sat on the pebbled beach for a while, and in between my sobbing I managed to ask Louise what had happened. She explained that she had seen the shop detective follow me out so had run to another exit, doubled back on herself, placed the eye shadow on a random shelf, and then hung around the shop waiting to be apprehended. "Trust me, Emily. I promise, they didn't find the stuff on me so there is nothing they can do about it. It's okay, nothing is going to happen to us." It made sense to me, and I burst into tears of total relief. I hugged Louise as tightly and closely as I could. At that time in my life, it was the kindest, most remarkable thing anyone had ever done for me.

When I got home that afternoon, I was met by my father

silently reading his paper in our living room. I said hello to him, but he didn't even look up. I thought about how consumed with fear I had been of his reaction as I sat alone in the detective's office at Superdrug. I hated him more than ever.

Our shoplifting trips were otherwise a success and had a positive effect on our school experience. We started to sell the makeup at super-reduced prices to other girls in our year and the year above. It gave us a certain kudos, and we were treated a lot more respectfully for the rest of that school year. Not so many instances of name-calling and not so many occasions when our schoolbooks were strewn onto the pavement and stamped upon. This new status changed dramatically the next year, though, after an encounter with Pete Forshaw, the second-best-looking boy in the school and the boyfriend of the hardest girl in my year, Claire Haslett.

It was a Sunday morning, and I was on my way back from the newsagent's after buying a Sunday paper for my father. As I walked back home along the seafront, I noticed Pete Forshaw up ahead of me, alone on a bench, scrolling through his phone. I had admired him from afar over the years but had never spoken to him. He was wearing his trademark black leather jacket and dark blue jeans. It was his hair that always caught the eye first; it was jet-black with an effortless sheen, parted down the center to perfectly frame his dark brown eyes. He had a flawless olive complexion apart from a small mole to the side of his top lip.

I always got a rush of anxiety whenever I had to walk past a stationary bloke. I didn't like my chest being examined as I approached, and I could always sense their eyes boring into my arse as I walked away. It was worse with Pete, because like most other girls, I fancied the pants off him. He had turned his gaze directly towards me as I approached. I started to become hyperaware of my gait and stride the nearer I got to him. By the time I was within earshot of him, I was walking like a chimp with a leg brace. As I got closer, he stretched out his legs in front of him.

"Hi, Emily," he said. "Have you shit your pants or something?"

"Yeah," I replied, "I like to start the day off with a bang."

"Ha, that's funny, funny and smart. So, what are you doing out and about this early on Jesus's day?"

"Just buying the newspaper."

"I love the news. One day I'm going to be on the front page of all the newspapers. You'll be able to point at the article and say, 'I had a chat with this guy on the seafront once,' and people will take a sudden interest in you. Do you believe me?"

"Yeah, I believe you, Pete."

"Damn right. Come on, have a sit-down for a minute. Let's have a look at the news together."

"No, I'd better get back. My dad is waiting for his newspaper so he can look important while Mum and I do all the cleaning."

"Bad Daddy, he's a lazy Daddy. Come on, have a seat for five minutes. I've always wanted to have a chat with you and find out where you're coming from. Do you believe me?"

He patted the seat of the bench next to him, and I succumbed.

"Go on," he said, "pick out a story that interests you and read it out loud. If it piques my interest, we could have a chat about it."

"Okay, but then I've got to go."

I flicked through the paper and came across an article about how the dog population of a town in India was being terrorized by a maverick troop of monkeys.

"You interested in monkeys?" I asked.

"Maybe, maybe not, depends on the monkey context. Give it a go and I'll tell you."

I started to read the article. After a couple of paragraphs, he interrupted me:

"Nah, I'm not interested, but I am interested in you, Emily."

"What do you mean?"

"Well, I'm told you've been nicking makeup from the shops and flogging it at school, and I must say that sort of behavior intrigues me. Why wouldn't it? Who would have thought that gorgeous little Emily Baker was a pilferer?"

"I don't know what you mean, Pete," I replied, the lie etched clearly on my face and confirmed by my blinking eyelids.

It suddenly hit me that he had just described me as "gorgeous."

Oh my God, I thought, *that felt nice.*

"What would your parents do if they ever found out?"

"Mum would ask me to steal her some wrinkle cream and Dad would chain me to a radiator at best."

"Funny, so funny. Well, let's hope they never find out. Come on, I'll walk back with you."

We walked along the seafront with the bed-and-breakfast in the distance. I wished it was farther away, but it refused to back off. When we arrived at the end of the terrace, he stopped and asked for a photograph of us together. As he took the picture, he gave me a kiss on the cheek. I felt myself turning bright red, so hurriedly grasped my newspaper and said my goodbyes.

"Well, see you around, Pete."

"See you at school. I'll seek you out."

"I might be hard to find, and anyway, haven't you got a girlfriend?"

"Nah, nothing official."

I smiled back at him and waved as I walked away. As soon as I got back to my room I texted Louise. "I think I'm in love" is all I said.

"WHAT!? WHO WITH?" she replied.

"THE BEST-LOOKING BOY IN SCHOOL!!!" I barked back at her.

At school the following week we bumped into each other in the dining hall and agreed to meet up again on Sunday, at the same place and time. I fetched my father's paper early so that I could spend longer with Pete. It was a beautiful cloudless day. We bought ice creams and sat together on the beach with our backs up against a wooden groyne to protect us from the wind. Eventually we had a snog, and before we left he took a couple more photographs of us gurning like clowns in a mirror shop. He asked me if I would consider being his girlfriend, and I told him I would think about it. When I got home for Sunday lunch I was elated and even our tired old dining room and lukewarm lemon meringue pie seemed to possess a magical sheen. I managed to smile so convincingly at one of my father's astute comments that he immediately turned away in shock and surprise.

The following lunchtime I was sat on the school field with

Louise, discussing the situation with Pete. As we chatted, we both noticed Claire Haslett approaching us with three of her friends. I sensed this meant trouble and told Louise to get up off the ground with me. Haslett's message was simple and succinct. She held up one of the photographs that Pete had taken of us and snarled at me, "Keep your fucking hands off my boyfriend, you slag."

"I haven't touched your boyfriend, and anyway, he said that you two—"

I didn't get to finish my sentence, as she struck me full on the cheek and nose with an epic forearm smash. I hit the ground, then looked up to see her leaning over me as she said, "You ugly stuck-up bitch." With that, she spat in my face and walked away, her friends laughing at the sheer excitement of the violence.

Although our paths crossed a few times that week, Pete and I didn't speak, and I assumed that Haslett had frightened him off. I didn't text him in case she was policing his phone. If you were an enemy of hers, then life at school was always going to be a curse. The following Sunday I went to get the newspaper again without any expectation that Pete would be hanging around to see me. On my way back I sat on the seafront bench for old times' sake and watched the seagulls argue with each other over yesterday's seagull football results. Out of the blue he appeared beside me and put his arm around my shoulder. He handed me a long, dusty jelly snake from his pocket. "I got you this—you know, by way of an apology. I should have thrown those photos away. I'm really sorry."

"You said you didn't have a girlfriend, so what was that all about?"

"No, I said I didn't 'officially' have a girlfriend."

"What does that even mean?"

"It means that we act like a couple but for me it's just an informal arrangement."

"Well, she clearly doesn't feel the same. She called you her boyfriend just moments before she punched me full pelt in my face."

"Shit, I'm so sorry about that, but I can't be held responsible for the fact that she's unstable."

"Have you actually told her that you don't consider yourself to be her boyfriend?"

"Yes, but it doesn't make any difference. I think she's used to getting her own way."

"Are you scared of her?"

"Not scared of her as such, but scared of the consequences of getting on her bad side."

"So, you're a coward?"

"Yeah, that would be fair, but a good-looking one."

"Do you think I'm good-looking?" I asked just for the hell of it.

"Ten times better looking than you realize."

We both stared out to sea in silence for a few moments as I tried to drum up the courage to say what I really wanted to. A seagull landed on the post in front of us and stared me straight in the eye. *Who's the coward now?* it seemed to be saying. I took up the challenge and blurted it out:

"Listen, Pete, I really like spending time with you and would love it if we could be open about it and see if we could make it as a couple. But until you sort it out with Claire Haslett, I don't want to see you again."

"I'll sort it out, I promise. Now come on, forget all that. Pick an article from the paper for us to consider."

"You promise?" I asked, with what I hoped was a deadly stern look in my eye.

"Promise," he replied as he stuck one end of the jelly snake into his mouth and started to chew. I flicked through the paper and stopped at a color photograph of a greater spotted woodpecker.

"What do you think of that? It's quite a look, isn't it?" I asked.

"Bit fancy if you ask me, a bit contrived," he replied.

"It's the opposite of contrived! It was born that way. He hasn't put any thought into his look."

"I realize that, but I'm just not drawn to flashiness. Keep it plain; let your words do the talking. You do realize that all those spots and red patches are designed to intimidate? That's a bad opening, don't you think? Where is the love?"

I laughed, grabbed the jelly snake off him, and turned my head towards his to invite a kiss. He responded immediately. It was the first heartfelt snog I had experienced and therefore the most challenging. My lips were dry from the sea breeze and his were sticky and sweet from the jelly snake. I had heard that the tongue should be used and so flicked it in and out of his mouth much like a snake sniffing the air. I had also picked up, from the movies and the television, that a noise of appreciation should be made, and so let out intermittent grunts akin to the noise a python makes when it feels threatened. I took a breath and used the moment to bite the head off the jelly snake to unify the stickiness of the situation. It was too difficult to swallow, and as we reengaged the head slipped out between my lips and fell onto the bench. I kept staring at it as the kiss got more frantic and gloopy. When we finally stopped, both our chins were dripping with green slime. I pointed at him in the style of a cute extraterrestrial and slowly said:

"You. Boyfriend."

He replied with a reciprocating finger:

"You. Girlfriend."

That sounded fine by me.

We never made our relationship public, but of course Haslett found out. In the first term of the following year, she took her revenge.

One day, I was called to the headmaster's office. As I walked up the stairs to his room, Haslett and some of her entourage passed me going down. They were all slightly somber, but Haslett had a curious grin on her face. They burst into a fit of giggles as soon as they reached the bottom of the stairs.

They had told the headmaster about my little cosmetics business. This was serious. He was considering informing the police. I gave a full confession but kept Louise's name out of it. My parents were on the way to pick me up. I was to be expelled. My father never spoke to me with a note of care or friendliness again. I was to be homeschooled so that I could still sit my A-level exams. When not studying, I was required to help run the bed-and-breakfast seven days a week. I told my parents about Louise's involvement in the thieving in the hope that this would somehow dilute the blame. It was a big mistake. My father informed her parents, and between them they agreed that we were not to see each other again. I told my mum that as soon as I had taken my exams, I was leaving home. She told me that she thought it was a good idea.

I would speak to Pete every day at first, but before long the phone calls got awkward and distant. The next time I actually saw him was when I was sitting my exams at school. We smiled at each other but had nothing to say. My father had driven me to school for the exams and waited outside to take me home as soon as they were finished. In August of that year, a couple of months before my eighteenth birthday, I left home and moved into a furnished bedsit room just off the seafront in Brighton. I used the money my grandmother had left me to pay the deposit and the first three months' rent. I took a job as a waitress/barperson at a nearby Mexican restaurant. One night, after I had been there about a month, I saw my mum and dad staring at the menu in the window. They didn't like the look of what was on offer and walked away. It made me sad, but I convinced myself that this sadness was all part of me making a new start and moving on.

Then I met Tommy.

13

WHEN I GOT BACK from my visit to Clementine's, Grace and Lassoo were waiting to accost me on the walkway.

"What time do you call this? Do you not think I've got better things to do than stand here waiting for you?"

"Nice to see you as well, Grace. I didn't ask you to stand out here like the Queen waiting for her liver and onions to be delivered."

"Why are you looking so pleased with yourself?"

"Because my neighbor—that's you, Grace—is an absolute gem. Come on, give us a hug."

I held my arms out and took a step towards her. She crossed her arms and pretended to shiver at the very thought.

"Have you been to see that girl? You have, haven't you? What a dozy prick you are."

My face gave away the truth and Lassoo delivered an exaggerated sigh.

"I'll pop round in fifteen minutes and you can tell me just how much of a fool you have made of yourself. Is that fish and chips in your carrier bag?"

"Yes."

"Well, save some for me."

And off she toddled back into the flat, banging Lassoo in the face with the door as he followed behind her. He looked up at me as if to say, *"That's your fucking fault."*

Grace and Lassoo arrived exactly fifteen minutes later.

"I've just remembered why I wanted to see you," said Grace with a certain joy in her face at the remembrance. She took the corncob dongle out of her pocket and continued:

"I've worked really hard trying to hack the password for this and I'm getting nowhere. I even tried to source an identical corncob memory stick on the internet to see how the password instructions are programmed but couldn't find one anywhere. I found a picture of a similar-looking one from China but nothing for sale. It's a shame. The dongle doesn't even have a manufacturer's name."

"Grace, it doesn't matter anymore. Just forget it."

"Not a chance. The thing is, if it's just a combination of random letters and characters, then I might not have the computer capacity to crack it. The other possibility is that it's something personal to the person who set the password—you know, his birth date, his wife's name, his pet's name, his house name, that sort of thing. You need to tell me as much of that sort of information as you can, then I can have another go."

"Grace, Brendan is still alive and kicking, so I can just give it back to him when we next meet."

"He's alive?! Why didn't you tell me?"

"I was going to tell you last night, but you wouldn't answer the door."

"How do you know he's alive? Have you spoken to him?"

"No, but I was at the police station today and I asked a

detective about the murder. He checked around and told me they had no idea what I was talking about. I can't get hold of Brendan by phone, all I get is that 'phone not in service' message, but I emailed his office and they confirmed that he was working away at the moment. So, yeah, I'm pretty sure he's still alive. Sorry, I should have told you earlier."

"I'm not giving up, at least not until you've actually spoken to him. He gave you that dongle for a reason and, anyway, I'm enjoying the challenge. Don't stop me now. If you do I'll go straight back on the fags."

"You really don't have to, Grace, but if it makes you happy I can't see the harm."

"So, will you get me as much personal information as you can on him?"

"Yeah, I'll see what I've got on file."

"Has he got a wife?"

"Yeah, but they separated a while back."

"Well, why don't you contact her? She might be able to tell you what's going on and maybe she would know some of the passwords he uses."

"That's a good idea, Grace. Maybe I will," I replied, knowing deep down that I wouldn't.

I had divided the fish and chips onto two plates and kept them warm in the oven. We sat at the table eating the grub and drinking some cold lager. I told her about my visit with Clementine. Her interest focused in on the bald man. She concluded that he was probably an overzealous debt collector and that Clementine was likely a wrong 'un who had fallen behind on her rent.

"Maybe I should offer to pay her rent? You don't think he might be her boyfriend, do you?" I asked.

"I doubt it," she said, handing yet another clump of fish and chips down to Lassoo. "From what you've told me she's about twenty-five years old and of an artistic bent, with a daft hairstyle and Doc Martens boots. A bit like Jane Brurier, I think you said. If you reckon he's nearly forty and dresses like a car salesman, then I don't think that passes a compatibility test."

"But he's been there both times that I visited."

"Doesn't mean anything. You would probably call round pretty often if you were owed money. Look, if you're so worried, why didn't you ask her?"

"Dunno. Seems a bit intrusive, a bit forward. Maybe I don't want to know. Do you think me and you are compatible?"

"No," she said, placing her plate on the floor so Lassoo could finish it up. "But you and Lassoo are a good match. By the way, who the hell is Jane Brurier?"

"I haven't got a fucking clue."

We sat in silence for a few beats, enjoying our cold beer and assessing each other's face. I always appreciated the thin lines above her top lip and around the sides of her mouth that revealed she had been a dedicated smoker in her past.

"Why did you pack in smoking?" I asked.

"My doctor said I would go down the priority list for a hip replacement if I was a smoker," she replied.

"Do you miss it?"

"I miss everything about my life before my hip started to crumble and decay. Shame is, I didn't realize I was happy at the time. When the time comes that I can't get out and about anymore, I'll probably just get into my bed and smoke twenty a day until I drop dead or set fire to myself."

"I might join you."

"What, in my bed?"

"No, on the cigarettes. I miss them too."

Another silence while Grace poured a little bit of beer into the plate on the floor for Lassoo to drink.

At that moment my phone rang. It was not a number that I recognized. I answered it anyway.

"Hello?" I recognized her voice immediately.

It was Clementine.

"Hi there, how are you doing?" I replied, my heart skipping a beat and even the longest hairs on my shoulders trying to stand to attention.

"I'm fine, thanks. Just wanted to give you a ring and apologize for being a bit standoffish at my flat. I didn't mean to be rude, it's just I've got a lot going on at the moment."

"Hey, not at all, it was lovely to see you."

From her seat at the table, Grace blurted out, "Oh God, it's her."

I shot her a look of pretend anger and shushed her with my middle finger over my lips.

"Sorry, have you got company? I'll let you go," said Clementine.

"No, no, no," I replied as I walked through to the bedroom in an attempt to get out of Grace's earshot. "Not at all. It's just my neighbor Grace. She popped round to chat about a flash drive I gave her in the shape of a corncob. She's trying to hack the password, so as you can imagine it's far from riveting."

"Are you a spy or something? Or one of those people that

nicks money from online bank accounts? I could do with a bit of that action at the moment."

"No, it's just work stuff. It belongs to Brendan—you know, that bloke I was in the pub with."

"Solicitor stuff?"

"Yeah."

I couldn't think of anything to say. Why the fuck had I started to talk about dongles? I didn't know how to get back on track. In the end, she helped me out, bless her.

"So, did you really like the plastic flowers on the bike wheel outside the flat?"

"Oh shit yeah. It was upcycling using an actual cycle, and that's got to knock anyone out."

At this moment Grace appeared at the bedroom doorway and began to repeatedly mouth the word "boyfriend." I turned my face away from hers, but she stepped further into the room so that I couldn't easily ignore her presence. I continued chatting while ushering her into the hallway and out of the flat, shutting the door behind her.

"That's a nice flat you've got," I continued. "Is it yours or do you rent it?"

"It's rented. It means I can up and leave anytime I want."

"Like Robert De Niro in *Heat*."

"I think you'll find "in heat" only applies to dogs. De Niro is a man, an acting man."

I laughed. "And when he's not acting, he's just a man, like me or my butcher or Harry Styles. Just a man who isn't acting."

We both laughed at the hilarity of our words and the joy of our tempo. Silence interrupted the flow, and I decided to ask her what I really wanted to know:

"Hey, you've never actually told me your name. Is that deliberate?"

"No, you probably just never asked. I'm Emily. Pleased to meet you."

"Strong name," I replied. "Five-letter names have a nice clout about them. Sarah, Grace, Holly, . . . or . . . err . . . Colin. I'm Gary by the way."

Here goes, I thought.

"So, Emily, I have to ask you, are you in a relationship at the moment? Just asking. I don't mean anything by it."

I shouldn't have asked that question was my immediate thought. I got an instant sweat on.

"Nothing official," she replied. "Listen, I'm really sorry for how rude I was the other day. I hope you aren't pissed off with me?"

"No, not at all. I'm glad you rang. Don't forget that invite for a drink if you ever fancy it."

"I might just consider it. I'd better go. See you, Gary."

"Cheerio."

And she was gone. I actually punched the air and barked out "YEEESSS!" *Emily*. Of course it was *Emily*. It had ALWAYS been my favorite lady name. I had her number now, and it was all I could do to resist phoning her straight back just to hear her voice again.

When I walked back into the living room, I was met by the sight of Lassoo sat on my chair finishing up my fish and chips from the table. He jumped down on seeing me, lost his balance halfway down, and banged the table leg, spilling the last of my lager onto the table. As he performed this move, there was a knock on my door. It was Grace.

"I forgot Lassoo," she announced as she walked past me.

"Yes, I noticed," I replied. She beckoned Lassoo and he followed her obediently out of the door.

"How many times have I told you not to feed him?" was her parting remark.

I sat down at the table to reflect on my conversation with Emily. "*Nothing official,*" she had said. Even the odious, clinging cloud of gas that Lassoo had left behind couldn't wipe the smile off my face.

14

THE FOLLOWING MORNING I bumped into my squirrel mate more or less as I exited the stairwell. He jumped down from a tree, ran straight towards me, before stopping abruptly, standing on his hind legs, and giving his whiskers a wash.

"You're very chipper this morning. Still look like shit, but there's a bit of a glow about you," I commented on his behalf.

"Yeah, I made a bit of progress with that lass I fancy last night."

"Pleased to hear it. When you say 'progress,' do you actually mean you might be seeing her again?"

"She said she might consider it."

"Whoops, that doesn't sound good—bit standoffish. You might want to have a think around why she would say something so noncommittal."

"I have, and it's a concern."

"So, you seem to reckon that friend of yours is still alive, then?"

"It's looking that way."

"What's with those coppers that said he was a goner? What was their game? You might want to think around that as well. It's a bit of a worry on the face of things."

"If I had to make a guess, I would say that they weren't coppers, but probably working for someone that Brendan has upset. He mentioned to me that he investigates some dodgy bastards. I reckon they might be after him for money or to give him a kicking. I reckon that's why he's gone underground."

"Why would they tell you he was dead? If you think around that you're bound to find it a bit drastic."

"I think it was just to shit me up a bit, introduce an element of threat to make me cooperate and treat them with respect."

"Sounds like he's in danger to me. You should think around whether he might need your help, mate."

"Well, Grace is trying to unlock the dongle Brendan gave me and I'm helping her with that."

"Might be too little too late, son."

And with that, he leapt away at the sound of a police siren approaching the entrance to the estate. As I walked on past the block that led out to Peckham High Street, I myself received a startle when I saw Boiler Suit Man getting out of a van parked up in one of the residents' parking bays. The writing on the van read "CARFIX MOBILE MECHANIC." He was walking around a brown Citroën SUV, giving it the once-over with another man, presumably the owner of the vehicle. As I approached him, the man handed his keys over and left. Boiler Suit Man placed his hands on his hips and arched his body as if trying to relieve some sort of lower back pain. I stopped beside him and said hello. He gave me a pleasant smile, and I assumed he recognized me from our encounters at Emily's estate.

"Sorry, mate, this is residents' parking only," I said with a charming smile.

"Get out of it, you cheeky bugger. So, what are you doing

here? You got a girlfriend on every estate, have you? I very much doubt it by the look of you."

"No, this is where I live, in that block over there. I'm the king of the estate, so everything has to go through me. You have my permission to proceed with your labor."

"How very fucking gracious of you, Your Honor."

"So, you're a mobile mechanic specializing in council estate breakdowns, are you?"

"I'll work anywhere, mate, but I'm cheap, so yeah, I do get a lot of call-outs to places like this."

"By the look of your stretching and bending I'm not convinced that you are actually as mobile as you claim."

"It's my lower back. It's really playing up today. It's all the bending over I have to do—plays havoc with the spine. The doctors have given me painkillers, but they upset my guts bigtime, so I have to ration them."

I was starting to like this bloke, but the devil got the better of me again.

"Have you tried nettles?" I asked.

"What do you mean? Eating them?"

"No, all you have to do is grab a handful, with a glove on of course, and then rub them on the affected area."

"Piss off. That will sting me right up. Do you think I'm stupid?"

"That's the whole idea. The pain receptors turn their attention away from your spine and concentrate on the pain from the nettle stings. You just have to decide which is worse: the nettle sting, which you soon get used to, or that terrible back pain that's doing your nut in. I've done it loads of times and it's used a lot in the armed forces, especially the Royal Navy."

"Nah, I don't like the sound of it. I've never got along too well with nettle stings. Anyway, I'd better crack on. Thanks again for letting me park here, Your Royal Highness."

"No worries. There's a clump of nettles over there by the garages if you change your mind."

I walked away and stopped out of his sight behind one of the large beech trees at the far corner of the play area. He arched his back again and then walked over to the garages and grabbed a handful of nettles. He returned to the Citroën and undid his boiler suit so that it was resting around his thighs. I lost sight of him for a few seconds as a passerby came along, forcing me to stare at the pavement to avoid looking shady. When my gaze returned to Boiler Suit Man he was slumped over the front of the car with his trouser legs round his ankles, banging on its hood and screaming, "Aaargghh shit! Oh shit! Please, God, help me!"

I felt bad but reassured myself with the thought that my nettle theory might actually have some substance.

I had an appointment at the office with Wayne first thing to take a full statement from him regarding his arrest. About five minutes before he was due, he telephoned me and asked if we could meet in the coffee shop rather than the office. I agreed. Any excuse to get out of the office is always welcome. I sat down at a table with him, and he started talking. In essence, he told me that his father had been a policeman just down the road in Lewisham before he retired four years ago. He worked as a detective with the serious crime unit. The squad was as corrupt as they come, but he had wanted nothing to do with all that. The other members of the squad wanted him out. They considered him a liability and feared that one day he might grass them up to the bosses at Scotland Yard. They made his life a misery at work, and eventually he caved in, took early retirement, and left the force. A couple of years later he was approached by a journalist working for a newspaper or the TV and agreed to an interview talking about corruption in the south London force. Not long after that, he was stopped in his car and the police found a big lump of cocaine in it. It had been planted, of course. Then he was approached by one of his old squad and told that if he pulled out of the interview with the journalist, then the charges could easily disappear. He agreed, the charges were dropped, and he never heard from the journalist again. His theory was that she had been scared off and had made the wise decision to end her investigation.

Wayne was certain that the same thing would happen this time. They were just giving his dad a reminder to keep his mouth shut. He didn't know what had stirred them up again, but he wasn't worried because his dad would do the right thing. He didn't want to waste my time any further with statements and such.

"You'll see, I give it two weeks before they drop charges. Trust me."

I wasn't so sure, but if that was how he wanted to approach it then I had no objection. He still hadn't been formally charged, so there was little I could do in any event.

"How long you been wearing that shitty suit?" he asked.

"Nearly every day for two years."

"You look so cheap, man. Like a carpet salesman or a card-shop owner. It's not fitting with your status. You need to sort it out, get a slimmer fit, a bolder look, like you count for something. You need to look in the mirror and reassess your presentation."

"I'm not flashy like you, Wayne. I'm what they call understated and reliable. It fits my line of work. If I wear expensive clothes, then my clients think that's where their money is going. I've thought this through. I'm not a woodpecker; I'm a little chubby wren or a busy little thrush. You hardly ever even notice me."

"You look more like a parrot with that beak of yours," offered Wayne.

"And talking about thrush, if you keep wearing those tight trousers that's exactly what you'll be getting," I replied.

I finished my coffee and Battenberg and headed straight off to Camberwell Magistrate's Court, where I was applying for a summons against a landlord who was renting out accommodation to a client of mine that was unfit for human habitation. As I sat in the queue, I was surprised to see my old friend Clown Shoe Man standing at the counter. He was still trying to pursue the case against his neighbor. I was sat just a meter or so behind him, so had a wonderful view of his massive shoes. As he shifted his weight from one leg to the other, his left shoe would emit a little damp squeak. I love hearing noises like that in a formal environment. The lady behind the glass had a fixed, patient smile on her face that gradually faded as the conversation developed.

"The thing is, he's foreign"—*squeak*—"and obviously doesn't understand that an Englishman's home is a castle that should never be trespassed upon by a stranger, particularly one of foreign origin." *Squeak.*

"I'm sorry, sir, but I don't see what the gentleman's nationality has to do with anything."

"Then you are not fit for purpose." *Squeak*. "Let me speak to a magistrate or someone who might have a sense of the trauma this is causing me." *Squeak, squeak*. (Double shuffle.)

"You have to fill in this form for the matter to be considered by a magistrate or justice's clerk. At this moment you haven't correctly filled in the part requiring you to outline the alleged offense. Until you do that, I cannot enter the request into the system."

"Yes, I have! There, in box two. Read it for yourself."

"I have, sir."

"And what does it say? I think you will find it's as clear as the nose on your face." *Squeak, squeak, squeak*. (Celebratory shuffle.)

"It says, 'My neighbor is creeping around in my attic at night making noises akin to a baby bear and in doing so is causing me great upset and distress.'"

"There you have it! Let's get this thing rolling and get the bastard locked up."

"I'm sorry, sir, but trespass and noise nuisance are civil matters for the civil courts. This is a criminal court. Unless your application reveals the commission of a crime such as theft or assault, then I can't stamp it and enter it into the system."

"So as far as you are concerned it's okay for some foreigner"—*squeak*—"to enter a person's house and bark like a baby bear without fear of consequence?"

"No, I'm not saying that, sir. I'm just stating that it's not a matter for the criminal courts, and this is a criminal court."

"Where are you from? You don't look like you're from around here." *Squeak, squeak*. (Nervous shuffle.)

"I'm from Deptford, sir. Now, if there's nothing else, I've

got quite a queue building up behind you. Might I suggest you consult a solicitor about what remedies you might have?"

Clown Shoe Man turned away from the counter with a loud sigh of frustration and stared directly at me.

"Are you a solicitor?" he inquired.

"No, I'm a carpet salesman."

"Sounds about right."

And with that he marched out of the room with his shoes pumping out the beat of "Stayin' Alive" by the Bee Gees. After I had issued the summons, I bought a coffee and sat on a wooden bench on Camberwell Green. Brendan came into my mind, and as I had a spare hour before I needed to be back at work, I decided to pop round to his home in Sydenham and leave a note asking him to contact me and explaining that his documents had been stolen but could easily be replaced. I could also check for any signs of him actually being there.

His home was a two-storey Victorian house—yellow London brick with white sash windows and a hedged garden to the front, side, and rear. It was some distance from any other house, and I guessed it might have been some sort of gatehouse many years ago. I entered through the waist-high wrought-iron gate and knocked on the front door. There was no reply. The house had the feel that nobody was home. The curtains were closed to all the front windows, and a flyer for a local restaurant was sticking out of the letterbox. I walked around the back of the house via a paved path that was carpeted with cherry blossom. The back door had a small, circular, frosted pane of glass at three-quarter height. I gave the door a sequence of increasingly bold knocks, but there was no response. The kitchen window to the side of the door had its blinds shut, so there was no way

I could get a view into the house. I noticed a piece of masking tape was flapping from the paintwork next to the keyhole. I looked to my feet and saw a small white square of notepaper lying on the carpet of cherry blossom. The note simply said: "*We need to talk*," with a telephone number written below. I wrote down the number on the back of my hand, then gave the kitchen door one final knock. Again, there was no reply. I scribbled down a note of my own asking Brendan to give me a ring (nothing urgent) and placed it in the front letterbox. I left there with an uneasy feeling regarding Brendan's welfare and whereabouts.

This feeling wouldn't shift all afternoon, so after work I decided to make an unannounced visit to Brendan's workplace, Cityside Investigations, which was just up the road on Denmark Hill. If I talked to his boss, then surely I could finally put my mind at rest.

Their offices were on the first floor of a large Victorian building above a betting shop and amusement arcade. You entered via an anonymous door at street level between the two shops. A small brass plate with "Cityside Investigations" engraved on it and a buzzer intercom marked your arrival. I was buzzed inside and made my way up the stairs to the reception area. The office was mostly open-plan, with two partitioned offices at the far end. It was a busy place, lots of men in shirts of varying tightness staring at their computer screens and speaking confidently into their phones. Probably a banter factory, but who am I to judge?

The receptionist, Sophie, knew me from our work contact and asked me to take a seat while she asked Mr. McCoy if he was free for a chat. I had never met John McCoy, but had been told that he was quite a serious bit of kit. Someone you don't cross, someone who will bite your arse if you shit on his lawn. I was surprised, therefore, when he emerged from one of the offices, to see a rather frail bloke of short stature. A good two inches below the national average height was my guess. He wore a light blue polyester shirt with its sleeves rolled up to his elbows and a pair of baggy dark blue jeans held up with a pair of purple braces. There was a sense of thinness about him. Thin arms, thin face with a thin sharp nose, and thinning hair, combed back close to his head with some sort of product. The skin was starting to droop on his jowls, and his forehead was heavily lined. There was a certain air of menace about him, delivered mostly via his piercing watery-blue eyes. They were too close together for my liking and lacked any hint of emotion or empathy. On the plus side, his dentist had given him the smile of a twenty-year-old, and he smelt like a supermodel's handbag. He beckoned me into his office, and we sat either side of his desk. The first thing I noticed was that there was what looked like a gun of the pistol type on the desk in front of him.

"Is that a gun you've got there?" I asked.

"Yes."

"A real one?"

"What do you think?"

I picked up the gun and was surprised by its weight and heft. It looked and felt real, but surely it wasn't.

"Probably not. You wouldn't have a real gun in the office, and if you did, you wouldn't let me see it."

"Well, then, you've got nothing to worry about, have you? Now, how can I help you, Gary? And let me say that if this goes over five minutes I'll have to bill you for my time."

"Well, that's better than being shot," I said with a hopeful smile on my face.

"Exactly," he replied, without even a hint of lightness in his voice.

"You seem very busy. I didn't realize this was such a big operation."

"Never been busier. I'm taking on new staff all the time. Insurance fraud, commercial fraud, IT security, rent arrears enforcement, evictions, and surveillance—fuckloads of surveillance. I tell you, Gary, the world has gone crackers and we are cleaning up."

"That's great, nice to see a business thriving around here. So, yeah, I've just come to ask after Brendan. His phone has been disconnected so I can't get hold of him. Suppose I just wanted to check he's okay?"

"He's fine. Why are you so interested?"

"Well, because he's a friend, I suppose, but mainly because a really weird thing happened. I had a quick drink with him last Friday night and the following day two blokes, who said they were coppers, called at my flat and told me he had been found dead."

"Fuck off they did."

"No, seriously. I found out later that they weren't coppers and obviously he hasn't been murdered, but it just feels strange being told that just before he goes off-grid."

"I wouldn't worry yourself, mate. This sounds like typical Brendan nonsense. He's obviously upset someone, which he has a knack of doing, and they want a word. They were hoping you would speak to Brendan and in doing so would be delivering a message veiled with the threat of violent retribution. I bet he owes them money or fucked up some job or other. Listen, you don't need to worry about Brendan. He's as tricky as they come. He can look after himself just fine. I'll tell him about what you've told me when he rings."

"So has he been in touch with you?"

"Yeah, every day he phones in to update me on the case I've got him working on. He's doing a good job."

McCoy fiddled with his phone and then showed me the screen. It was a photo of Brendan holding up a pair of socks to his face. The socks were covered in various eye motifs. The message underneath read: "Bought these for you cos I know you love a wink LOL." The message had been sent yesterday at 4:57 p.m.

"So have you got a phone number for him?"

"Yes, I have, but I'm not giving it to you without his permission. Like I say, forget about him and concentrate on your lawyering. Now, that's your five minutes up. Anything else?"

"So, is it a real gun?"

"It's whatever you want it to be, Gary. Now go on, fuck off."

I left the office finally convinced that Brendan was alive and kicking. McCoy was right: I should forget about Brendan and get on with my life. Just as I was enjoying that thought, a red BMW pulled up outside the office and parked itself half on the pavement. Out jumped the bald man I had seen at Emily's estate. He had a bunch of foolscap files under his arm. His shirt was tight and covered in patches of sweat, and he walked right past me without looking my way. In his slipstream, I caught the waft of what can only be described as processed meat. I felt a pang of worry on behalf of Emily. This bloke definitely had the air of a debt collector about him.

Rather than go back to my flat, I decided to go to the Grove and have a drink and watch some football. It was an hour or so before kickoff, and Nick and Andy weren't there, so I treated myself to a sit in the lounge, on "Emily's seat." I flicked through my recent phone calls so that I could have a good long stare at her telephone number. Maybe I should call her and ask if she fancied popping down for a drink. Much as I wanted to, I declined. I had put the ball in her court, and that was the correct way to proceed. I doubted, though, that I could resist for many more days or even hours. The football would be a useful diversion.

At kickoff time I moved through to the bar to take up my usual position at the end of the counter. By halftime Nick and Andy had still not arrived, so I watched the entire match on my own. It was a mid-table championship match, so despite being drenched in effort and commitment, it was bereft of any skill or joy.

At the end of the match, I felt very alone in the half-empty bar, not just for tonight but in the most general sense. I flicked through my phone for a while and supped my fourth pint of lager. I decided to ring the number I had found on the note at Brendan's house. As a precaution, I blocked my number first. After a few rings, it was answered:

"Hello. DI Peterson."

I was too scared in that moment to reply. He spoke again:

"Hello. DI Peterson. Who is this please?"

I ended the call. I was in full sweat. It was hard to be sure, but I thought I recognized the voice. It was the man I knew as DI Cowley. I turned off the phone, downed my pint, and went home.

That evening I found it very difficult to get off to sleep. *Why did I ring that number? Who is this Cowley/Peterson bloke? Is he a real copper (in which case, come the crunch, I shouldn't be in any trouble)? Is he a thug who is after Brendan and thinks I might know more than I've let on (in which case there might be trouble ahead)? Was that a gun on McCoy's desk?* And, once again, *Why did I ring that number? What a prick I am.*

Eventually I drifted off to sleep but would wake up intermittently and hear Lassoo next door whining and occasionally barking.

In the morning when I awoke, I could hear Lassoo scratching at his front door. I had plenty of time before I needed to go to work, so popped next door to offer to take him for a walk. I knocked on the front door and could hear Lassoo pacing up and down the hardwood flooring while letting out the occasional half-arsed bark. Grace didn't answer, so I tried the door and it opened. I called out her name, but there was no reply. Lassoo was acting like a nutcase, running up and down the hallway and climbing on and off Grace's sofa. I knocked on her bedroom door and called out her name again. There was still no reply. I slowly opened the bedroom door and saw that she was not in her bed. She wasn't at home. As I stood in her lounge I noticed that her laptop was gone and that someone had rifled through the drawers of her workstation. Some of the books in her bookcase had been tossed to the floor. It appeared that the flat had been lightly searched. Her smartphone was on the floor, smashed by a heavy boot or some such. I felt an overwhelming certainty that whoever had done this was looking for the corncob dongle. This was my fault.

15

EMILY

I LOVED BEING ON my own and away from my father.

I loved being independent. My bedsit was grimy, with peeling wallpaper and mold spots all over the shower ceiling. The bright crimson carpet literally crunched under your feet, and the windows were painted shut. The hot water tap dribbled rather than flowed, and the cold water tap spewed its contents out like a horse that's been caught short. Seagulls stamped and sang on the roof just above my bed, often waking me up at 5 a.m. The central heating radiator creaked and groaned as it warmed up and cooled down. Despite all its efforts, it never got much hotter than a Labrador's belly.

I had never been happier.

My waiting job at Cactus Barrio Mexican Bistro and Bar also suited me. My shift was from 6 p.m. till 2 a.m., though I often didn't get home until four or five in the morning.

The manager was called Tommy Briggs. He was from Barnsley, not Mexico. He was in his mid-thirties, six foot tall, athletic, and chunky, with long dark hair that he usually wore in a ponytail. Every day he wore a freshly laundered and ironed white shirt, always tight-fitting and always with the sleeves rolled halfway up his hairy forearms. His shoes had a decent heel on them, and his jeans more often than not had a hint of a flare. He was one of those men that spoke very loudly when making small talk, in an attempt to appear confident and amusing. "ALL RIGHT, GEOFF! HOW YOU DOING, YOU DAFT BASTARD?" is how he would greet a person called Geoff. "ALL RIGHT, CAROL! CHEER UP, IT MIGHT NOT ACTUALLY HAPPEN" is how he would greet any lady, whether or not they had any hint of sadness on their face.

I quite liked him. He gave me the job, and he never shouted at me like he did with the other members of staff and some of the customers. He could be brutal. I remember one evening a couple complained about their burrito being too spicy. They were a quiet, mousy couple with little to say to each other apart from to share complaints about the service and the surroundings. They asked to see the manager.

"HI, I'M TOMMY, THE MANAGER. I HEAR YOU'RE NOT HAPPY WITH YOUR FOOD, GUYS. WHAT SEEMS TO BE THE PROBLEM?"

The male mouse did the talking:

"It's the burrito. It's far too spicy. There's no mention on the menu that it's basically a chemical weapon that destroys your tongue and throat."

"THAT, SIR, IS BECAUSE IT ISN'T. IT'S A MILDLY SPICED SALSA THAT IS SERVED WITH NEARLY EVERY DISH ON THE MENU AND I HAVE NEVER RECEIVED A SINGLE COMPLAINT."

"Well, that's as may be, but I would like to swap it for something else please."

Tommy turned his attention to Mrs. Mouse.

"WHAT DO YOU THINK, LOVE? YOU SEEM TO BE TUCKING IN LIKE A PIG IN A CHEESECAKE FACTORY."

The restaurant was by now mostly silent.

"How dare you speak to my partner like that?" blurted Mr. Mouse.

"BECAUSE THIS IS MY HOUSE AND I'LL SAY WHATEVER I WANT TO DEFEND MY CHEF AND MY REPUTATION."

"You won't have a reputation to maintain if you speak to your customers like this."

"THAT DEPENDS ON WHAT SORT OF REPUTATION I AM TRYING TO ESTABLISH."

"Not a very good one would be my guess," offered Mr. Mouse.

"WHAT ABOUT YOUR RELATIONSHIP? IS THAT A GOOD ONE? OR IS SHE A LITTLE BIT TOO SPICY FOR YOU? WOULD YOU LIKE TO SEND HER BACK AND SWAP HER FOR SOMETHING ELSE?"

"Come on, love, we are leaving."

Mr. Mouse made to get out of his seat, but Tommy pushed him back down again:

"YOU ARE NOT LEAVING UNTIL WE HAVE SUNG THE NATIONAL ANTHEM TOGETHER AS AN ACT OF RECONCILIATION AND GOODWILL."

Tommy went down on bended knee so that he was looking directly into the faces of the mice. He started to sing in the fullest volume he could muster:

"*GOD SAVE OUR GRACIOUS QUEEN, LONG LIVE OUR NOBLE QUEEN, GOD SAVE THE QUEEN* . . . COME ON, YOU TWO. HELP ME OUT HERE. WE ALL LOVE THIS

BIT," commanded Tommy as he started to bang his fist on their table.

"*NA NA NA NA, SEND HER VICTORIOUS, HAPPY AND GLORIOUS . . .*"

Mrs. Mouse started to sing along, doubtless fearful of Tommy's bulging eyes and the physicality of his fist-thumping.

"*. . . LONG TO REIGN OVER US, GOD SAVE THE QUEEN.*"

After a few beats of silence and intense staring between the three, Tommy broke the impasse:

"VERY NICE, VERY NICE INDEED, DARLING, AND I THINK YOU'LL AGREE A FITTING END TO YOUR MEAL. NOW FUCK OFF OUT OF HERE."

They got up in silence. Tommy insisted that the whole of the restaurant give them a round of applause as they left.

Tommy lived in the top-floor flat above the restaurant. Swanky and modern with leather sofas and a huge TV. At the end of every evening, certain customers would be invited up there to continue the fun. I soon became one of these privileged few. The drink and drugs were free as far as I could tell. It was Tommy's way of buying company and admiration. I thought he was the King of Brighton, more like a movie star than a restaurateur. I couldn't help fancying him. He didn't seem to care one way or the other about anything. He was shaping his own world, and I was lucky to be part of it. We started sleeping with each other, and more often than not I would wake up in his chrome-detailed king-size bed. I didn't love him, but I loved the life he offered. I was happy.

About a year into this lifestyle, we were partying as usual in Tommy's flat, when in walked Pete with a couple of friends. He was maturing nicely and was even more gorgeous than I remembered. He had moved on from his leather jacket and was wearing a vintage brown corduroy suit and army boots. A very strong look on a thin man. Once his friends had moved away, I sidled up and sat beside him. I was excited and more than partially smitten. "Hi, Pete. How are you doing?" I asked.

"Emily! What are you doing here?"

"I work here. This is my workplace where my living is earned."

"No way. Do your parents know?"

"I suppose so. I haven't seen either of them for ages. They split up after I left home. Mum lives in Leicester now with her dozy sister."

"Just how dozy is this sister?"

"Very, if in fact not totally."

"So did they sell the hotel?"

"No, Dad still runs it. He's changed its name to the Honeymoon. I think it's aimed at the swingers' market, or maybe indoor dogging."

"There you go, funny Emily. So you didn't go to university or anything?"

"No, I've been here since leaving sixth form. I'm assistant manager now and very well respected for what I do. What are you up to?"

"I'm at university in Bournemouth doing Film Studies."

"So, what, you watch films all day and then talk about them?"

"Sometimes they are so good we don't even talk about them."

"Like out of reverence or something?"

"Yeah, something like that, and the fact that we've got better things to do."

"Sounds like a waste of time."

"Yeah, well, most things are, but it's pleasant enough when you're with good people. Are you with good people, Emily?" he asked.

"Things are pleasant enough, as you would say, thanks for asking. Hey, have you had your name on the front of a newspaper yet?"

"Yes I have."

"Well, go on then, what for?"

"I bummed an otter at a holiday camp."

I laughed and we talked some more until I was beckoned over by Tommy. He didn't like me talking to other guys and gave me the cold shoulder before telling me it was time I went home. Pete must have seen me leave, because about fifty yards up the road I heard footsteps behind me and turned to see him waving and smiling as he caught up with me.

"So, do you think you'll actually ever make a movie?" I asked as we walked side by side.

"No, that's not what I'm about. I just want to believe that I might make a movie one day. That's enough to keep me ticking over. Can I walk you home?"

We went back to my bedsit together and listened to some music and chatted about the good old days. I wasn't surprised when he told me that Claire Haslett had given birth to twin daughters but was surprised to find out that the father was our old music teacher, Mr. Andrews. I always thought he was gay. As we lay on the bed chatting, there was suddenly a loud banging on the door.

"YOU IN THERE, EMILY? ANSWER THE FUCKING DOOR."

Fuck. It was Tommy and he didn't sound happy. Pete jumped off the bed and stood by the window.

"Shit the fuck up, who is it?"

"It's okay, Pete, it's just my boss from work. Calm down," I reassured him as I answered the door and let Tommy in. He wasn't doing the loud speak anymore, which was not a good sign. He walked over to Pete and stood in front of him with his face only six inches away from Pete's.

"Who the fuck are you?"

"It's just an old mate from school, Tommy," I told him. "We were just catching up."

I put my hand on his shoulder by way of reassurance, but he pushed me away without taking his gaze away from Pete's face. I fell onto the bed.

"I wasn't talking to you. Come on, Army Boots, tell me what's going on here."

Pete was visibly shaking but managed a softly spoken reply: "It's like Emily said. We were friends at school and we were just having a catch-up."

Tommy placed his open hand on top of Pete's head and started to massage his scalp.

"I saw you having a catch-up in my flat and then I saw you follow her out. Did she invite you over here?"

"Err . . . no. It just sort of happened. We're old friends . . ."

"So you came here uninvited, is that what you're saying?"

I didn't like where this was going and intervened again: "Listen, Tommy, I said he could come in. Nothing happened or was going to happen. We are just friends."

Tommy took his hand off Pete's head and gave his cheeks a quick pinch. He kept his finger pointed at Pete as he came and sat down on the bed next to me.

"If you are such good mates," he said, "then tell me, Emily, when was the last time you spoke to each other? When did you last communicate to nurture and progress this great friendship?"

"We haven't spoken since school," I replied. "Look, what is your problem, Tommy? I'm telling you the truth. Nothing happened."

"Did you arrange this little cozy-up when you were in my flat? IN MY FUCKING FLAT!"

Pete interjected: "Listen, mate, we didn't arrange anything. I just happened to leave at the same time as her and we bumped into each other. Nothing more to it. I'll leave now. I don't want any trouble."

Pete took a few steps towards the door but was halted by Tommy.

"No, why don't you stay for a while? Maybe we can become good friends and then catch up again in two or three years and have a nice chat on a bed?"

"Look, I don't know what's going on here," said Pete. "I think it's best if I just go."

"You know what? I think you're right. I'll come along with you and we can have a catch-up on the street." As he pushed Pete out of the door, he turned and said, "You don't work for me anymore. I hope it was worth it. You only have yourself to blame."

They left, and of course, I feared for Pete's safety, but instead of following them out I just lay back on the bed and wept into my pillow. I knew I would never see Pete again.

I stayed in bed feeling utterly miserable and scared for the next few days. My grandmother's money was all gone, and without the job I couldn't pay my rent. I missed my work colleagues, I missed the buzz of the restaurant, and I hated having to think about an uncertain future. I missed the partying afterwards, which always lifted my mood. I wanted things to be "pleasant enough" again.

When I eventually peeled myself out of bed, I made my way to the restaurant to pick up a few of my things and to say goodbye to the staff. I went at 6 p.m. sharp in the hope that I wouldn't bump into Tommy. As it happened, he was the first person I encountered when I walked in. He was carrying a tray loaded with glasses to be placed on the tables. As soon as he saw me, he walked over, handed me the tray, and walked away into the back kitchen without saying a word. I took it as a cue to finish placing the glasses on the tables. A few minutes later he appeared beside me and threw a white blouse on the table in front of me. Again, he walked away without comment. The blouse was the restaurant uniform, and so I went into the toilets and put it on. It seemed that my job was still available, and if that was the case, it was something that I very much wanted.

The staff seemed totally oblivious to my "sacking" and simply inquired about my health and hoped that I was feeling better. I worked my arse off that night, and after a couple of hours the sickening feeling I had had in my stomach those past few days simply disappeared. Tommy made sure that he never caught my eye, and at the end of my shift I went straight home, still not having said a word to him. This standoff continued for the next couple of shifts, until one evening, just before I was leaving, he came up behind me at the bar and put his hands around my waist. He leant around me and gave me a kiss on the cheek.

"You've made the right choice," he whispered into my ear. "Why don't you stay here tonight?"

I turned around and kissed him. I was so happy. In that brief moment, it felt like love. Later that night, we were on his bed taking coke. He smiled at me, placed his hand over my head, and began to give it a massage. I smiled back at him. I think this was the moment I realized that my life was no longer mine to control.

My next big mistake came a year or so later. I still had my own flat (a slightly larger one in the same building as the bedsit), but spent the majority of my time at Tommy's place. One Monday morning, when I had actually slept in my own bed (the restaurant no longer opened on Sunday evenings), I received a phone call from Tommy at about 4 a.m. He was in some sort of panic and told me he was coming round to see me.

When he arrived, he explained that something had gone wrong with a drug deal he was doing. The police had swooped in, and he had managed to run away and evade them. It was really important, he said, that if the police got in touch with me, I should tell them that I spent the whole night with him. He told me a simple timeline that I was to adhere to and then we spent an hour cleaning every area of my flat that we thought might have any evidence of drugs. I was to go to the restaurant at 7 a.m. and do the same for his flat. He had already been there to clear out the stuff he knew of, but he wanted me to go over the place with a fine-tooth comb. I, of course, agreed. He needed to get some sleep.

The police arrested him at work around lunchtime and then called at my flat to take a statement from me. I stuck to the story, and later that evening Tommy arrived at work a free man. He was smiling like a horse and hugged me so hard that my bra came off. For the next three months he treated me like a princess who was number one in the charts. The late-night after-hours drinking at his flat stopped happening, and we actually lived like something akin to a married couple. I made a concerted effort never to flirt with anyone in Tommy's presence, and he often bought me little gifts of jewelry and fancy clothes. It really was pleasant enough. I even persuaded him to cut his hair and lose the ponytail. Once removed, I saturated it with hairspray and mounted it above the bar in the restaurant. It had a small plaque underneath that read "Tommy's Tale."

Eventually, though, the lock-ins returned, and Tommy became less attentive. His mood swings seemed more frequent, and managing them became hard work. He started to become paranoid that the dealer who was busted was out to get him. Apparently there were rumors of this circulating around town, largely based on the fact that Tommy had got away scot-free and the dealer had ended up with an eighteen-month prison sentence. We will never know for sure if the two things were linked, but one Sunday evening the restaurant was set on fire and completely gutted. Tommy managed to leave via the rear fire escape and declared, that very day, that we should leave Brighton for good. It wasn't safe for us to stay. I didn't openly oppose the decision, but when we drove out of town for the final time, we passed my parents' hotel and for the first time ever it reminded me of happier days.

Our destination was south London. Tommy had an old

friend from Yorkshire who put him in touch with a company called Cityside Investigations. They always needed trusted and verified blokes to help with rent collection, document serving, surveillance, and the like. I don't think Tommy really fancied the job, but it came with the promise of a nice two-bedroom ex–local authority flat on the Grange estate in Walworth that was owned and rented out by the boss of the business. He took the job as a stopgap but has ended up working there for these past four years. He didn't like the idea of me having a job, but as his workload increased, I occasionally helped him out when it was felt a job required the female touch. If a summons or injunction needed to be served, the door was much more likely to open when the visitor was an innocent-looking lady in her mid-twenties. Some jobs, such as honeytraps, absolutely required a female. These are cases where a wife is certain that her husband is cheating on her and wants to test out his faithfulness by setting a trap in the form of a pretty and seemingly willing female lure. I only ever participated in two of these, and on both occasions Tommy was nearby to keep an eye on things. The one I remember most fondly took place in a wine bar on Camberwell New Road. I was told that the client was a suspicious wife who had contacted Tommy's boss and told him that she suspected her husband was out on the pull that very night. The husband had telephoned her with some lame excuse about possibly not being able to make it home that evening. She was convinced that he would be at this particular wine bar and would be out to grab himself a lady.

Tommy fitted me up with a tiny buttonhole camera disguised as a brooch that I wore on my lapel. He also chose me an outfit that he considered appropriate—a white blouse with the top button undone, a gray trouser suit jacket, and a pair of skinny jeans. He allowed me to wear my Doc Martens. We arrived at the wine bar separately. Tommy took a seat at the bar, and I sat near the back in a "cozy corner" ideal for courting couples. I would usually read a book when sat on my own, to discourage unwanted approaches, but tonight I needed to look available.

The Chump arrived about ten minutes after us and actually struck up a conversation with Tommy at the bar. Tommy later told me that his first words were: "Not a lot of fanny in here tonight." The Chump would occasionally stare over at me, and when he did I would try to encourage him by smiling back and acting fidgety, hoping to give the impression that I was uncomfortable being sat alone. Eventually he walked over to my table with a bottle of plonk and a couple of fresh glasses.

"You on your own?" he inquired.

"Yeah, I think I've been stood up, I was just about to leave," I replied.

"Oh, don't do that. Come on, let's drown our sorrows together," he suggested as he took the seat next to me and started to pour out two very large glasses.

The Chump was around forty years old and worked at a bank in central London. You would have guessed that without my help. He wore a dark blue suit, white shirt, and a very thinly knotted light blue tie. His complexion was piggy pink, and his lips were nonexistent. His hair was sandy brown, brushed back over his crown and his ears, and held tightly in situ by some sort of hair grease. He smelt of Windolene and spearmint. Not unpleasant after the initial hit had faded. His accent was posh and nasal.

"So, what fool of a bloke has stood up such a sweet thing like you?" he asked.

"Oh, just some guy from work. It wasn't a definite arrangement or anything," I replied.

"My name's Laurence, by the way." (It wasn't. His name was John. John Bell.)

"Pleased to meet you. Is that really your surname? 'Bytheway'?"

"Oh no, not at all. I should have said, 'Incidentally, my name is Laurence.' Ha ha, that's hilario. My surname is Romano. My father was Italian, you see. Owned a canning factory on the outskirts of somewhere or other. Massive place. Produced over a million tins per annum—pasta, peaches, and fuckloads of peas. Do you like a tinned pea? I prefer to do it in the toilet, ha ha, hilario. This is the greatest of fun."

"Do you mind if I swap seats and sit opposite you?" I asked. "I think it makes for a better chat."

"Absolutely not, all the better to drink in your shameless beauty."

I shifted to the seat opposite him so that my camera had the best chance of catching the action. It was also a relief not to have Tommy directly in my vision.

"Ah, that's better. So, have you just popped in here for a quickie before you head home?" I inquired with an interested look on my face.

"A quickie would suit me just fine, ha ha ha, but no, I'm out for the night. I work hard and I play hard. Some people think because you're not doing physical work that it can't possibly be exhausting, but it is. I shifted millions of pounds of currency between large pension portfolios today and the pressure of those decisions literally bleeds you dry. So, yeah, I'm out for the night, abso-bloody-lutely yah. Fuck it."

"Do you live in this neck of the woods?"

"Not a chance. Bloody shithole. I live out in the sticks near Reigate." (He didn't. He lived just up the road in Kennington.) "Live on my own. The wife died of the big C a couple of years ago." (She didn't. She ran a 10K last weekend.) "No kids, sadly. Would have been a great legacy." (He had two children, aged three and five; neither of them looked like him.) "So, no, I don't live in this neck of the woods, but when I have to be here for work I stay at a little bijou hotel near the Elephant and Castle." (It's called the Grand Saffron, forty-four quid a night, no TV, no minibar, and no pillow chocolates.) "I do get lonely, though, so having your company tonight is really special for me."

He reached out and gave my hand a squeeze. I had to hope that Tommy was remaining calm. I was enjoying this challenge. I was enjoying punishing The Chump.

"What about you?" he asked. "You local? You got a lucky fella to keep you warm and sated?"

"No, I haven't had a relationship for years. Well, apart from with my cat and occasionally the cat's vet."

"You have a veterinary friend, how fabulous. I love vets. They get themselves very involved with animals and I adore animals. I have a couple of cats at home—a ginger one and a not-so-ginger one." (They had no pets. He hated animals. It was one of the reasons his wife mistrusted him.)

"No, I don't have a relationship with the vet. I just see him from time to time when I have to take the cat in for her injections. It was a joke."

"Oh my word, hilario! You were just being frivolous. What a joy you are. Really, you're a total delight. Would you excuse me a moment or three while I make a phone call?"

"Of course. I'll fill these glasses up, should I?"

"You bet."

The Chump went out onto the street to make his phone call. I would guess it was probably to the Grand Saffron booking a room for the night and then one to his wife confirming that he wouldn't be home tonight. While he was outside, Tommy came over and told me he had to leave for fifteen to twenty minutes. He asked if I would be okay and told me I mustn't leave the bar till he got back. I confirmed this to his satisfaction.

When The Chump returned, he had a strange, lipless grin on his face, which confirmed to me that he had probably secured a room at the hotel. "Sorry about that," he said. "I have to be available 24/7 in case some underling overstretches or puts a cock-up into the machine. So, where were we? Ah, that's right, I was saying what a joy it was to share your company."

He downed his glass of wine in one and replenished it with what remained in the bottle. I was beginning to enjoy this even more now that Tommy was gone. I hadn't flirted with anyone for years, and was surprising myself with my abilities. I decided I should try to move things on.

"You're nice-looking, quite a catch I would say, what with your house in Reigate and your general importance. I can't believe you haven't found someone else to share your life with—you know, obviously still respecting your wife's memory, but two years is a long time."

"It's simple, I've never met anyone like you before." (His

wife reckoned he went through about three or four a month.) "Listen, the bottle's wept its last tear. Why don't we go and get something to eat? There's a superb little place right next to my hotel. I just know that you would love it all the way to next month."

"Lovely." (In my mind I spewed up a thousand tinned shrimps.) "Hey, I hope your wife isn't watching down on us."

"Ha, yes, hilario. She really wouldn't mind. She would want me to be happy. So, shall we make a move?"

"Err, could we just give it another twenty mins or so in case my friend turns up? I've texted him a few times but he hasn't replied. Would that be okay? I'll get us both a cocktail, shall I?"

"Not for me thanks. So, what do you do for a living?"

"I design posters and flyers and all sorts of print work. I suppose you would call me a graphic designer, but I'm not trained or anything."

"Sounds deadly dull. I hated art at school—always seemed totally pointless. You don't look the arty type—well, apart from your shoes that is."

"What type do I look like?"

"Hmmm." He looked me up and down and gave my hair a repulsive stroke. "A check-out assistant . . . Ha ha ha, hilario! Only joking. Tell me, this bloke you are meant to be meeting, what is it about him that appeals to you?"

"Well, he's good-looking, got a nice way about him, and he makes me laugh. He showed an interest in me, so I suppose that's the main thing."

"Better looking than me? I doubt it. I'm only joking, but listen, I'm not buying the graphic designer line. Not with that gray jacket and that awful fucking brooch."

He grabbed at the brooch and tugged it towards him. It came away from the jacket, revealing the wire to which it was attached.

"What the fuck is this?" he exclaimed. He pulled some more until at least a foot or so of the wire was revealed. "Are you fucking filming me? You little fucker. My wife sent you, didn't she? Piece of fucking shit."

He stood up and began to pull as hard as he could on the wire. I felt the little black box at the other end of the wire unclip from my belt. He gave it a harder pull as more of the wire emerged from my lapel. I yelped in pain as the box was forced upwards around my waist and then got trapped under my bra, through which it was threaded. I stood up and grabbed the wire. He clawed at the front of my blouse, trying to get a grip on the box. I couldn't scream. I couldn't speak. I let go of the wire and just stared straight into his eyes.

"Give me the fucking camera. You are not leaving here until I have that fucking camera," he barked.

I reached inside my blouse and started to unscrew the housing that attached the wire to the box. He was looking around at the five or six other customers in the bar, offering them a reassuring smile.

"Sorry about this, just a wardrobe malfunction," he offered to the concerned but docile onlookers.

I stopped what I was doing and dropped my arms to my sides.

"Why don't you just leave her?" I asked.

"Just give me the camera," he replied.

"I'm not going to do that. You will have to rip it off me and, like I say, why don't you just leave her?"

"If you give her the footage then it will be her that fucking leaves me."

"Well, maybe that would be easier for you."

He let go of the wire, picked up my glass of wine from the table, and downed its contents in one. He stared me dead in the eye for a short while and then sucked the last dregs from the glass.

"Fuck it," he declared. "Tell the wife I'm sorry," and he marched out of the bar. I slipped back down into my chair, retrieved the box, and rearranged my blouse. The barman came over and asked me if I was okay.

"Yes," I replied. "Could I have a look at the cocktail menu?"

Not long after, Tommy returned to find me sipping on my drink, the camera sat on the table in front of me.

"Hi, babe, how come he's gone? Did you get the footage?" he asked.

"Yeah, it's all on there. Job done I reckon. He asked us to say he was sorry to his wife."

"I'll put it in the report. Doubt it will make any difference."

"It might," I replied, not really believing that it would. As we left the bar, Tommy placed the glass from which The Chump had drunk into my handbag. It was something he was always told to do when on a surveillance job, collect something that the "subject" had handled.

Tommy hardly spoke to me for the next three days. Just seeing me sat with another man had turned him sour. *Just leave*, I kept saying to myself, but the thought eventually faded and hid itself under the carpet for a year or so. It came back with a bang last week, though, when I was doing a surveillance job for Tommy. This was one of those jobs where I get told nothing and I ask no questions. The subject of the job was a workmate of Tommy's at Cityside Investigations. His name was Brendan. All I had to do was watch him closely during a meeting he was having with someone at the Grove Tavern pub in Camberwell. My job was to identify the person he was meeting and more specifically watch to see if Brendan handed any documents, or in fact anything at all, over to that person. Tommy was not happy with me going there on my own, but his boss required him to be elsewhere.

I got there about fifteen minutes before Brendan arrived, took a seat at the end of the bar, and ordered a lemonade. I had never met Brendan before, as Tommy didn't allow me to go to the office or any of the social events that flowed from office work. Tommy had provided me with a photo and told me that he was impossible not to spot as he had a face like a potato crisp and socks that scream "wanker." He was right. The first thing I noticed about Brendan when he walked in was his fluorescent pink socks with yellow wrenches embossed on them. He sat at the center of the bar and ordered a pint of lager. He had a cheap brown leather briefcase with him and was fiddling nervously with the handle as he drank.

Not long after, a shortish bloke wearing a cheap dark gray suit and an open-necked white shirt joined him at the bar. He looked like a carpet salesman or maybe a clerical assistant at the town hall. I took a book out of my bag and pretended to read it. I occasionally picked my phone up and pretended to scroll while taking photos of the pair of them. They chatted for a while, the carpet salesman went to the toilet, and while he was away Brendan fiddled about with the contents of his briefcase and took a phone call. When Carpet Salesman returned, they continued chatting for a while. I could hear most of what they were saying, and it was perfectly banal and dull. At one point Brendan wrote something down on a piece of paper and popped it into Carpet Salesman's pocket. After about half an hour had passed Brendan left, and Carpet Salesman stayed seated at the bar.

I decided that I needed to find out what information had been handed to him on the note, so I walked past him and made some comment or other to him in the hope it might encourage him to strike up a conversation with me. He took the bait and joined me at my table. He was a nervous type but very amusing. He reminded me a lot of Pete but without the bluster and immaturity. He seemed very present and eager to inquire about me. He was a very easy bloke to like. Our conversation flowed naturally, and I remember he took a particular interest in the book that I had been pretending to read, *The Clementine Complex*. It turned out he was simply a work acquaintance of Brendan's and that the note he had been passed was just Brendan's non-work phone number. I could have made my excuses and left, but I found myself still sat chatting to him two hours later. At some point he had gone to the toilet or to the bar, when Tommy phoned me.

"Where the fuck are you?" was his opening line.

"I'm just about to leave the pub. The guy Brendan was talking to has just left. I thought I should stay in case Brendan returned."

"I'm just around the corner, I'll come and fetch you."

"No, it's all right, Tommy, I'm on my bike, I'll just—"

He had hung up. I have never left a pub as quickly in my life.

When I got home, Tommy was waiting for me. It was clearly hurting him that I had been in the pub so long on my own. He was unable to find any holes in my explanation, though, and therefore just sulked. The next day he took his anger out on my bicycle and threw it over my balcony.

"From now on, if you need to go anywhere, then ask me for a fucking lift," he shouted as he threw the bike to its demise.

A few days later he brought a bloke home with him who he claimed was a policeman friend. They wanted me to go into fine detail about what had happened in the pub between the carpet-salesman guy and Brendan. I repeated my story and, I think, convinced them that the meeting was entirely innocent and that the carpet-salesman was just a casual acquaintance of Brendan's. Tommy was extremely agitated by the fact that I had stayed so long in the pub after Brendan had left. I told him it had taken that long to get carpet guy to reveal that the note was simply a telephone number. Tommy was agitated, and I could tell that he didn't believe me. Just before he left, he gave me a kiss on the cheek and whispered, "You are fucking dead." I'd heard it many times before, and it had long lost its power to intimidate me. It just made me sad.

Not long after, Gary actually appeared at my front door claiming that he was anxious to return the book I had left in the pub. He made a decent joke about the plastic flowers that I had used to decorate one of the buckled bicycle wheels. I could tell he fancied the pants off me. Those couple of hours we'd spent together in the pub felt like a glimpse into a happier place.

When I flicked through the book later that day, it opened where Gary had folded a page in half. Reading a passage that he had himself recently read made him feel closer to me than when we had stood together on my balcony:

She was numb to the loneliness. It had become familiar and reassuring. She was exhausted from thinking about her fate. Her blood flowed slow and heavy with sadness. She was certain that outside the cave there was grave danger. The old blind man who had brought her here had told her so. He still came every day with food and water and would tell her, "The crocodile is outside and he is hungry; you must never venture forth."

Then one day a mouse entered the cave and asked her why she lived in this awful place when so many riches were just at her door.

"I can't leave. I'm scared of the crocodile that sits outside the entrance waiting to feed on me," she explained.

"Don't be silly," said the mouse. "Follow me."

The mouse guided her through a maze of small tunnels and narrow openings until they reached another exit blocked only by a thorny bush.

"There you are," said the mouse.

She could smell orange and lemon blossom spilling into the cave. She could hear birdsong in the distance and a gently gurgling river just beyond the bush.

"Go on," said the mouse. "Just leave and discover the world outside."

She declined. "Thank you, little mouse, but I think I'm happy to stay here for the time being. The blind man who feeds me has been so kind and I fear he would miss me terribly if I left."

"Suit yourself," said the mouse. "In that case I'll leave you to find your own way back. The blind man will have to be told of our meeting."

The next morning the blind man brought her berries and nuts as usual. She died that evening from the poisoned food.

16

MY FIRST INSTINCT ON finding Lassoo apparently abandoned in the burgled flat was to call the police. They simply asked if I was able to secure the premises and look after the dog. I explained that I considered Grace to be vulnerable, but they insisted that I was to wait for forty-eight hours before phoning them again. They gave me an official crime number and explained that a community police officer would visit, hopefully within the next forty-eight hours.

I phoned in sick and took the day off work, then went out in the car with Lassoo to search for Grace. He sat on the back seat and seemed to grow confused by the sounds and the motion of the car. He decided to force his head into the gap between the passenger headrest and the seat. The gap was so tight that it dragged his rear gum backwards, revealing his dirty yellow teeth. Saliva started to dribble through the opening in his mouth and slowly make its way down the front surface of the seat. There was a real danger that it would start to pool and soak into the cushion. I tried to push his head back through the gap while still driving but found my hand getting covered in the warm mouth gloop. I wiped it off onto my trouser leg. This motion caused a majority of the gunge to collect in the spaces between the fingers of my left hand. I held the hand out in front of me and slowly separated the fingers. As the fingers spread, it gave the effect that they were actually webbed.

"Quack quack," I said to Lassoo.

He stuck out his tongue, allowing another dollop of the stuff to fall onto the seat. I decided to pull the car over and attend to releasing Lassoo from the headrest trap. By the time I had got out of the car and opened the rear passenger door, Lassoo had already freed himself, and he ran right past me into the grounds of St. Giles' Church.

The churchyard fronted straight onto the main road, separated only by a low flint wall. The grounds were mainly laid to lawn with a few fruit trees dotted here and there. It was a favorite haunt of the local homeless, and a couple of groups of them were sat around boozing and chatting. Lassoo was on the lawn making to produce a number two but failing in his efforts. I shouted his name, and one of the homeless blokes started copying my call. Lassoo ran over to the bloke, who started making a right fuss of him before walking him over to me on his lead.

"Thank you," I said. "He just ran out of the car when I opened the door."

"You should be more fucking careful, then, shouldn't you?" he replied.

"Yes, you're right. Anyway, thanks again." I held out my hand as if to request a transfer of dog possession.

"No, I think I'll keep him," said the bloke.

I tried to quickly assess what I was dealing with here. He was about my height, maybe a couple of inches taller, but a lot skinnier than me. He had prison-style tattoos on his hands and forearms and a large scar on his left cheek. I think one of the tattoos was of a helicopter landing on a banana. He wore a light brown bobble hat and a red-and-black hooded jumper. He was wiry, with a lot of bent and pointy teeth. I suspected he might well be a biter, or at least a gnawer, and he was certainly equipped for those tactics. Fighting him would not be an option.

Lassoo was looking at me as if to say, *"Your move, mate."*

"Listen, it's not actually my dog," I offered as an opening gambit.

"Oh, well, in that case it's not a problem, is it?"

"I'm looking after him for a lady who lives on her own. He's her only friend and companion."

"Well, send her down to fucking fetch him. I'll be here all day."

"Come on, mate, he's not your dog. You can't just steal him."

"You going to stop me, are you?" He gave me an exaggerated smile, fully revealing the arsenal of pain that his mouth contained.

"What about if I was to pay you—you know, for catching him and looking after him? Would that work for you?"

"Well, I went to a lot of fucking trouble for this hound so it's not going to be cheap."

"Yeah, that's fair enough, I was thinking maybe a tenner would cover it?" As soon as I said this I knew I was in trouble. He knew I was scared, and he could smell my panic.

"No chance. Fifty quid and you're getting a bargain."

"I don't have fifty quid on me," I said as I pulled the contents of my pocket out to reveal that I had about seventeen pounds in total. "This is all I have."

"Well, then, I'll take that as a down payment and you can go and get the rest for me. Like I say, I'll be here all day."

"Maybe I'll phone the police and see what they think?"

"Doubt it. I'll make sure the dog is long gone before they get here, that's if they even bother coming. Look, mate, get me my fifty quid or don't bother coming back." With that he turned away and began to walk back towards his mates.

Suddenly from behind the low wall I heard someone call Lassoo's name. Lassoo immediately broke free from his captor and rushed towards the wall. I turned to see Grace stood there kissing Lassoo and making a general fuss of him. I walked hurriedly to join her and then ushered her towards my car as quickly as possible. As we drove away from the church, I could see the dog kidnapper stood defiantly in the middle of the lawn. He had dropped his trousers down around his ankles and was singing the Status Quo song "In the Army Now."

Grace was quite rightly confused by her abrupt removal from the scene.

"What's going on, Gary? Am I in trouble?" she asked.

"No, Grace, but Lassoo very nearly was. Some bloke tried to kidnap him," I replied.

"What, that bloke in the churchyard?" she asked.

"Yes, the wiry one with the military teeth," I replied.

"Well, why didn't you clip him around the earhole?"

"Because I didn't want to get my head kicked in by him and his gang."

"Jesus, Gary, you're such a shithouse."

"Too right I am. And anyway, what were you doing leaving Lassoo alone in the flat? You never do that."

"I had an emergency."

"Well, you've got another one now, because when I went into your flat to check on Lassoo, it looked like someone had been in there and nicked your laptop and made a bit of a mess of your drawers and bookcases."

"That was me, actually. Like I say, I had a bit of an emergency."

Once we were back in her flat, she insisted that before we tidied up I sit down and listen to what she had to say. She seemed upset and slightly nervous as she pulled my hand across the table and held it tight.

"Gary, I've done something terrible and I'm so sorry," she said, looking me in the eye like a naughty puppy.

"I'm sure it's not that bad. Come on, spit it out."

"I've lost the corncob dongle." She let go of my hand and bowed her head. "I've looked everywhere but I just can't find it."

I sensed that she was about to cry, so I got up from my seat and gave her a hug.

"Don't be upset, Grace. It really doesn't matter. Brendan is fine. I'll tell him I mislaid it and he can make another copy if he wants to. Don't be upset."

"I got so angry that I threw my phone at the screen of my laptop and broke it. I took it to the repair shop this morning and they said it might be beyond repair. [*Sniffle.*] I can't afford a new one and I think I might have broken my phone as well. [*Sniffle.*] I don't know what I was thinking. I'm lost without my laptop. It's okay for you out at work all day, but I'm just here on my own. [*Extended sniffle with nose wipe.*]"

It was the first time I had heard her admit to being lonely. It was a topic I had never raised, and hearing her mention it made me panic. It wasn't something I wanted to address, probably because I was lonely, too. I ignored the moment and started to rally her round:

"Hey, come on, you've got me, you've got Lassoo, and I've got a Battenberg next door. Let's get this place tidied up and then we can destroy that cake."

Grace stayed seated while I started to tidy up the mess. After a few minutes she got up from her seat.

"I'm going to bed," she said in a very despondent tone.

I finished up as best I could and phoned the police to tell them I had found Grace. I looked in on her before I left. She was fast asleep and Lassoo had his chin resting on her shoulder. He gave me a look as if to say, *"Look what you've done, you nasty bastard."*

17

THAT AFTERNOON THERE WAS a knock on the door. I opened it to see Detective Bailey and a uniformed officer stood there.

"Hello again, Gary. Detective Bailey from Peckham CID, and this is Constable Dhawan. Can we come in please?"

"Yes, of course," I replied.

Bailey was the officer in charge of Wayne's case, and I immediately assumed he was calling about that.

"Sorry to bother you at home, but I telephoned your work and they said you weren't in today."

"Must be something urgent, then?" I replied.

"Yeah, you could say that. It's actually about Brendan Jones. You remember you told me at the station that two police officers had informed you that Brendan had been murdered? Well, I was wondering if you could take me through that story again?"

We all sat down, and I repeated my tale about Wilmott and Cowley. I was also able to add the details of my conversation with John McCoy and my visit to Brendan's home. Something in the back of my mind stopped me from telling him about the missing dongle. Bailey listened intently and then hit me with a bombshell:

"The thing is, Gary, there has been a significant development. Brendan was found dead behind a warehouse in Peckham early this morning. It would appear that he was stabbed to death sometime within this last week. It could well be that you were the last person to see him alive. It also strikes me that either you or this Wilmott and Cowley had a premonition about this happening or, alternatively, you are all somehow involved. What do you say to that?"

I got an accelerated sweat on and began rubbing my hands on my thighs. Constable Dhawan noticed this and looked at me with a note of disdain on her face. I looked down at my thigh and saw that the gloop from Lassoo that I had rubbed on there earlier had now dried and left a controversial stain. "It's just dog saliva," I said, and then immediately regretted it as her expression turned to disgust.

"Of course I'm not involved. You need to speak to John McCoy, Brendan's boss at Cityside Investigations. He reckons that this Cowley and Wilmott are two people that have fallen out with Brendan, maybe over a debt or a job that had gone wrong."

"We've tried speaking to him this morning but he's not cooperating, says it's bad for business. Look, I'm going to pass this information on to the detectives handling the case and I'm sure they will be in touch with you. In the meantime, if this Cowley or Wilmott contacts you, please inform me immediately. We really need to talk to them."

Bailey handed me his card.

"Don't worry, Gary, I'm sure this will all go away if you cooperate," he said as he left. He seemed to be on my side. PC Dhawan took a final glance at my trousers and shook her head in disbelief.

I was back to where I had been a week ago, sad at the loss of Brendan and worried about my involvement in it all. I convinced myself that an alibi for the evening I last saw Brendan might still be important and gave Emily a ring. It went straight to voicemail, so I left her a message asking her to ring me as soon as she was free.

About an hour later my phone rang, and I saw that it was Emily's number. As I answered, there was a knock on my door.

"Hi, Emily, thanks for ringing," I said as I walked to my front door.

"Hello, Gary," came the reply. "This is John McCoy. Do you mind if we have a word?"

I opened my front door, and there he was with Emily's phone to his ear. He was with the bald man who smelt of processed meat, and they pushed past me and into the flat. McCoy sat down on the sofa, and the other bloke made a quick inspection of each room in the flat.

"Sit down, Gary, and promise me one thing: that you won't mess me about."

"Yeah, of course, why would I?"

"First thing, where is Emily?" he asked as Mr. Processed Meat shook his head to indicate to McCoy that she wasn't here in the flat.

"I haven't got a clue."

"The thing is, Gary, my colleague here, Tommy, is her common-law husband and he's missing her terribly. She hasn't been home for two days and we want to know where she is."

So, bald bloke *was* Emily's boyfriend. I think maybe I had suspected this all along. I immediately assumed that the purpose of this visit was to warn me away from Emily and probably to give Tommy the opportunity to deliver unto me a beating. By phoning her number I had put myself in a significant amount of shit.

"Honestly, Mr. McCoy, I have no idea," I said in the manner of a pathetic and undercooked Harry Potter actor.

"WHY WERE YOU PHONING HER? WERE YOU HOPING TO ARRANGE A HOOKUP?" growled Tommy.

"No, no, no . . . The police called here earlier and told me that Brendan had been found dead and they think I might know something about it because of the two fake coppers I told you about, and I wanted Emily to confirm to the police that Brendan left the pub hours before me that's all. I was in a bit of a panic," I blurted out, sounding like a naughty child trying to cover his tracks.

"OH, SO YOU WERE SAT IN THE PUB WITH HER, WERE YOU? SOUNDS VERY MUCH LIKE A LIAISON TO ME," Tommy said with a crooked grin enhancing the left half of his mouth.

"All right, Tommy, turn it down," interjected McCoy. "Just let me handle this. So, when did you last see her?"

"Two days ago, I think. I called at her flat to return a book to her that she left in the pub that Friday night."

"HAS SHE EVER BEEN IN THIS FLAT?" asked Tommy with a lopsided gurn on his face that made him look both angry and thoughtful.

"No, absolutely not," I replied, thinking I could actually hear the sweat popping out of my pores.

Tommy took a couple of steps towards me.

"SO YOU KNEW WHERE SHE LIVED, DID YOU? THAT'S NICE, ISN'T IT? BUT TELL ME: WHY DIDN'T

YOU POST THE BOOK? WHY DID YOU HAVE TO GO
SNIFFING AROUND MY HOME?"

I couldn't think of a suitable reply but was saved by McCoy.
"Leave it, Tommy, I'm sure he won't be seeing her again and
I'm sure that if she ever did turn up here Gary would inform
me immediately. That's right, isn't it, Gary?"

"Yes, of course," I said, while thinking, *Like fuck I would.*
"It's terrible news about Brendan, isn't it?" I said, trying to
change the drift of the conversation. "I told the police about
our conversation—you know, about how he maybe owed
someone money or . . ."

"Can I stop you there, Gary? For your own sake and
everybody else's, including Emily, stop talking to the police.
You should know that, working for a solicitors' office. Come
on, start behaving yourself."

"Yeah, good idea. I agree. Won't say another word," I said,
desperately hoping that they would leave and I could phone
the police.

"One more thing," said McCoy. "Where is the corncob
dongle?"

"I don't know what you mean, Mr. McCoy."

"Oh, is that right? Perhaps you should ask him, Tommy."

Tommy walked over to me and placed the flat of his hand
on top of my head. He started to gently massage my scalp with
his fingers.

"RELAX, YOU LITTLE PRICK, AND GET YOURSELF
GOOD AND PRESENT IN THIS VERY MOMENT. WE
KNOW YOU HAVE THE DONGLE, SO HAND IT OVER
AND LET'S MOVE THIS THING ON."

I knew that I was probably heading towards a beating if

I didn't come clean. I felt fear rushing around my body like maggots in a bait box, and I think the stubble on my chin started to retract into its housing. My mouth was dry and sticky, but I managed to say, "Listen, I do know about the dongle but I haven't got it now. If you could stop rubbing my head, I can explain."

"THAT IS NOT GOING TO HAPPEN. IT'S TO HELP YOU RELAX," said Tommy. "I'LL STOP WHEN YOU TELL US THE TRUTH."

So that is what I did.

I told them how I came across the dongle and how I was unable to read its contents because it was password protected. I had asked my neighbor who used to work with computers to try to hack it, but it had proved impossible. She had subsequently lost the dongle and, if it helped, was very upset indeed about the loss.

"Where did you last see it?" asked McCoy.

"In this very room. It was on that table there and my neighbor took it back to her flat. She can't find it and I promise she has searched her flat high and low, corner to corner, ashes to ashes—"

"FUCK OFF WITH THE LIGHTNESS, YOU WANKER," barked Tommy.

"I guess you didn't search hard enough, Gary. Come on outside with me and let Tommy do a proper job on your getup first."

Tommy lit up a cigarette and held it in his mouth before searching the clothing I was wearing. I got the feeling that he was deliberately allowing the smoke to infect my eyes and taking pleasure in keeping the hot end of it dangerously close to my forehead. He then allowed me to join McCoy on the walkway, leaving him free to search my place alone. Almost immediately, Grace emerged from her flat.

"Hiya, Grace, you feeling better?" I asked.

"No, not really. I still can't find the thing and the computer shop has phoned up to say a new screen will cost two hundred quid."

McCoy butted in:

"Oh, hello, Grace. My name is Brendan. I'm the chap who gave Gary the dongle to look after. He was just telling me that you have mislaid it."

"Oh, yes I have, Brendan, I'm so so sorry. I've turned my place upside down but I just can't find it. I had it yesterday. Honestly, I'm getting so useless these days. Do you need it urgently? I'm still looking. You can help me if you want? You've probably got better eyes than me . . ."

"Yeah, that's a good idea, and Gary can help as well. Listen, Grace, don't you worry. It might not be the end of the world."

Under the supervision of Grace, McCoy and I went through her flat with a fine-tooth comb. Eventually he seemed satisfied that the dongle was not to be found. Before he left, he got her to confirm again that she had not been able to open the files on the dongle and as a parting shot pulled a wad of notes out of his pocket and gave Grace two hundred pounds "for her troubles." She made a fuss of rejecting it but caved in more easily than I would have thought.

We returned to my flat, and Tommy confirmed that the dongle was nowhere to be found in there either. McCoy asked Tommy to go back to the car, and he addressed me with his steely eyes fixed on mine.

"Listen, Gary, that dongle is very important to me and therefore, by default, very important to you. If you should find it, you will immediately hand it over to me. If you mention it to the police, I will find out and you will regret it. We wouldn't want Grace or little Emily to suffer, would we?"

"No, of course not."

"Take care, and might I suggest you clean that dirty mess off the front of your trousers? It's very off-putting."

As soon as he left, I felt physically sick. I had been in the presence of a potential murderer, and the thought really shook me up. I was scared, and the fear was tingling throughout my body. To be honest, all I wanted at that moment was a hug off my mum.

I sat down at my table and tried to sort out in my mind the current state of events. It seemed to be something like this:

1. Brendan is dead.
2. Don't panic . . . you didn't kill him.
3. Emily is missing.
4. The dongle is very important to McCoy. Maybe it contains evidence against him or financial details he wants to get hold of.
5. The real police are going to question me.
6. McCoy will hurt me, Grace, or Emily if the police find out about the dongle. This might not be an empty threat. Brendan may well have been killed by McCoy or Tommy.
7. Emily is missing, and she doesn't have her phone.
8. Don't panic; you haven't done anything wrong.
9. Best bet is to tell the police everything.
10. Or maybe not.

I went next door to see Grace. She was still searching the flat. I sat her down and gave her the news that Brendan was dead.

"But I was just speaking to him," she insisted.

"No, Grace, that was a man pretending he was Brendan so that he could get you to confirm the dongle was lost," I replied.

"Well, why did you let him deceive me like that?" she asked in her disappointed voice.

"Because he's a scary bloke and I don't want either of us getting into any trouble."

"Jesus, Gary, you really are such a shithouse. And what do you mean Brendan is dead? You only just told me he was alive and kicking."

"He was found dead somewhere in Peckham early this morning. I don't know anything more about it."

"That is just so mad. Just a few days ago you were told he was dead and it turned out he wasn't. Now it turns out he is actually dead. Are you in trouble?"

"I don't think so. The detectives investigating his death are going to want to speak to me, but my conscience is clear. Listen, if you do find that dongle, tell me straightaway."

"So, who was that bloke, then?"

"It was the bloke that Brendan works for—sorry, *worked* for. I think the dongle must have something incriminating or valuable on it because he wants it very badly."

"If I find it, will you give it to him?"

"No. I think I will give it to the police."

"Good lad."

I stepped over and gave her a great big family-style hug. For the first time ever, she reciprocated. I could feel a small slice of worry and fear leave my body. It wasn't Mum but it was as near as dammit.

"That's enough, you're going to crumble my bones," she said as she released her grip. "Is it okay for me to use the money he gave me?" she asked sheepishly.

"Yeah, I reckon."

Grace perked right up and handed me a twenty-pound note. "Well, go and buy a couple of large pies and some wine and beer. I could do with a boost. Take Lassoo with you. He needs a bit of fresh air. Oh, and take a poop bag. He didn't go this morning when I took him down."

As I left the estate, I noticed Boiler Suit Man still working under the hood of the Citroën. He looked up just as I was passing the play area and shouted over to me:

"Hey, the nettle thing worked a treat. I should employ you as my personal physician. Good on you!"

He gave me a thumbs-up and went back to his work. I was noticeably pleased with myself.

Lassoo did his usual trick and ran over to the bit of the play area where the seesaw used to be. He did his business and then started nosing around the walls of the opposite block of flats. Just then, my squirrel mate rushed down the trunk of a tree and gave me the stink eye.

"Oh, so you are in the shit now, isn't it though?" I asked on his behalf.

"Maybe I am, maybe I'm not," I replied to myself.

"Oh, so John McCoy, who we both know is a dangerous bastard, has made threats around and towards you and is telling you not to speak to the police."

"Yeah, but I am going to speak to the police."

"I would think around that decision a bit deeper than you obviously have. What about Emily and Grace? Don't you think they should have a say around that course of action?"

"Weird part of it is that Emily seems to have disappeared from her home. Well, at least that's what McCoy said."

"I'm so sorry to have to say this, but you need to ask if McCoy is actually telling you the truth. You might want to think around that for a good long while."

The squirrel suddenly rushed away, and I walked on to attend to Lassoo's poop. As I grabbed the lump, I felt something hard caught between my fingers. I released the mess from my grip and let it fall onto the grass. And there it was, the corncob dongle.

18

I ABANDONED THE IDEA of fetching the booze and pie and took the dongle straight up to Grace's flat. She cleaned it up and dried it thoroughly with her 1970s hairdryer, which sounded like it was powered by a moped engine.

"There you go: Good as new. All ready for the coppers," she declared.

"Do you think the police will be able to hack the password?" I asked.

"Maybe. Depends on how clever Brendan was with the password."

"Well, at least it won't be my problem."

Grace stared out the window for a moment, then spoke to me in a very deliberate tone:

"It's always struck me as strange that if Brendan wanted you to have the dongle, he didn't also want you to have the password. I mean, he might as well have just hidden it or put it in a bank vault or something."

"I know what you mean, but all he gave me that night was the dongle and a scribbled note with his "friends only" telephone number on it."

Grace flicked her head round towards me, her eyes wide and anxious:

"And where is that note now?"

"I threw it away, on Camberwell Grove. It's long gone."

"Are you sure it was a phone number?"

"Yes, I am. I actually dialed it and it went through to a company that sold novelty socks. It was just one of Brendan's little jokes."

"So, you'll still have the number you dialed on your phone?"

"Yes, I guess. Hold on, do you think the shop number could be the password?"

"It's worth a try."

I ran next door to fetch my phone and scrolled through the recent calls. There it was: the number that Brendan had given me. Grace and Lassoo had followed me into the flat. I grabbed my old laptop off the top of the kitchen-wall cabinets and opened it up. It needed charging, so we sat and stared at the screen waiting for it to come to life. When it did, the usual box appeared: "Enter password." I hadn't used the laptop for months or even years and had no idea what it was.

"Try the one you use at work," suggested Grace.

So I typed in:

PASSWORD1

It didn't let me in, so I tried some others that I had used in the past:

PassWord
LetMeIn
SOILSCIENCE

68TallAnts
ChinDoctor

None of them worked. Grace grabbed the laptop off me and placed it on the table in front of her. I noticed on the back of the lid a sticker that depicted a bunch of bananas with a knife and fork either side of it. I had written something on the corner of the label: "Fruit999." I took the laptop back off Grace and typed that in. The screen came immediately to life, and I put the dongle into the USB slot. Its name appeared on the screen so I clicked on its icon and the "password protected" box appeared. I typed in the phone number of the sock shop and handed the laptop to Grace for her to click "enter." She clicked on it, and a document began to load. Grace leapt off her seat in celebration.

"We did it! We fucking did it!" she yelled. Then she walked around the table and gave me a great big kiss on the top of my head. "I knew it. I knew we could do it. We are shit-hot, Gary. Do you realize that? Literally shit-hot."

"Yeah, I guess we are."

"Listen, I'm going to go and fetch that pie and booze. You can tell me all about what's in that document when I get back. What are we, Gary?"

"Shit-hot, Grace."

Grace left the flat while Lassoo stayed with me. I turned my attention to the contents of the document:

"STATEMENT OF BRENDAN JONES CONCERN-ING CORRUPTION WITHIN THE SOUTH EAST

LONDON SERIOUS CRIME SQUADS WITH
PARTICULAR REFERENCE TO THE ACTIVITIES
OF CITYSIDE INVESTIGATIONS."

I immediately wished I had never opened the file, but it was impossible to resist reading on. It started with a list of police officers' names and members of staff at Cityside Investigations. It then went on to detail at least twenty cases in which Brendan was alleging that the police had obtained information illegally via Cityside Investigations and/or had used them to pervert the course of justice by planting evidence, losing evidence, making false statements, intimidating witnesses, protecting drug dealers for payment, etc. etc. On and on it went, and it was made all the more compelling because Brendan himself was involved in a good percentage of the cases. There were a number of audio and video files attached throughout the document. If the contents were true, it was seriously incriminating.

I had an instant desire to destroy it right there and then and leave the country to start a new life as a boatbuilder in Newfoundland. I desperately wanted this corncob dongle out of my life. I wanted to take it down to Peckham Police Station immediately. I felt that I could trust Detective Bailey, so I gave his number a ring, but it went to voicemail. I didn't leave a message. It was bothering me that John McCoy had told me not to speak to the police about the dongle. He had even threatened me with the words *"We wouldn't want Grace or little Emily to suffer, would we?"* I was certain that McCoy didn't make empty threats. Maybe I should take it to McCoy? Maybe I shouldn't tell another soul that I had found it? I settled on a course of action that would at least see me through till the end of the day. I would bury my head in the sand and get moderately pissed.

When Grace returned, she had two bottles of wine and one massive family-size steak and potato pie. She hadn't had enough money for the beer. I didn't want her to have any further involvement with this Brendan business, and so I told her that the document was just a set of impenetrable accounts. She seemed a little bit disappointed but was easily distracted by the pie and the wine. It turned out to be a very solid pie—thick, crispy shortcrust pastry and a very rich gravy that Grace described as having "just the right amount of clout." Lassoo sat at Grace's feet and watched intently as every single bite went into her mouth. When Grace had finished her half of the pie, she announced that she needed a lie-down and left with Lassoo in tow. As they walked out the door, Lassoo turned his head back towards me and gave me a look as if to say, *"Don't worry, I'll get my own pie, mate."*

I returned to the document and started reading through some of the examples of corruption again. The first one that caught my eye and simultaneously raised it was a case involving a Mr. Derek Moore. Cityside Investigations had been instructed by a detective called Peterson to plant a significant amount of cocaine into the vehicle of Mr. Moore, who was subsequently stopped by the police and arrested for possession with intent to supply. It was Brendan himself who had planted the drugs. This was surely my client Wayne's father. It would seem that Wayne had been telling the truth; his dad was the victim of police intimidation. It was the name Peterson, however, that really rang alarm bells, as it was DI Peterson who had picked up the phone when I rang the number on the note left on

Brendan's door. Peterson's name came up again and again in the document and was also the second name highlighted at the start of it. The note left on Brendan's door by Peterson had read "*We need to talk.*" This message could open up any number of possibilities, all of which I declined to consider at this moment. Instead, I clicked on one of the video links. Emily's face jumped out at me. She was sat at a table in some sort of bar talking to a posh-looking bloke and drinking wine. The footage was being filmed by someone seated away from her and to the rear, but there was no mistaking it was Emily. The link to the video included the name Stephen Coldbeck.

I searched for his name in the main body of the document and soon found the details of the case. Stephen Coldbeck was a key witness in a trial involving a drug dealer who was under the "protection" of the Lewisham Serious Crime Squad. Cityside Investigations had been instructed by Peterson to make sure that he either changed his evidence or was a no-show. They had set him up in a honeytrap with an operative called Emily. They then threatened to reveal the video footage to his wife unless he modified the evidence he was going to give in court. The possibility suddenly dawned on me that she had actually been working for Cityside Investigations the night we met, presumably keeping an eye on Brendan. If that was the case, though, why didn't she leave when he left the pub? I doubt very much she had been Instructed to Investigate Gary Thorn. My memory was that we had made a genuine connection that evening. Perhaps she was just very good at her job.

It was all a bit too much for me to get my head around, especially as the booze was beginning to fuzz my mind up. I needed to put my head even deeper into the sand, so I went for an afternoon nap. Before I drifted off, I came to the decision that I should get the dongle out of the house and hide it somewhere for later consideration. It would also make sense to get rid of my old laptop, which might now have some sort of fingerprint from the dongle deep inside its hard drive.

19

I WOKE UP A couple of hours later to find that a greeting card had been posted through my letterbox. It had a painting of a duck on the front and the words "WHAT THE DUCK ARE YOU UP TO?" The message inside read:

"Fancy a chocolate and orange velveteen tonight 7:30?"

It wasn't signed, but because of the velveteen and duck references, I instantly knew it was from Emily and that the meeting place was the Grove Tavern. I was so excited by the prospect that I decided to have a bath. I have always preferred a bath to a shower—much more of a sense of occasion and indulgence. I'm drawn to its quiet warmth whenever I am either under stress or joyful with anticipation. Given the events of today, I suppose it was a twin-purpose grief and euphoria tub session. I made it into a forty-minute experience, shaving my face, ears, and shoulders, cleaning between my toes, topping up with hot water every time the temperature faded, cleaning under my nails, reading the ingredients of my shampoo and toothpaste, squeezing the blackheads on my nose, cleaning the sealant between the bath and the wall, floating the cap from the shower gel on the surface and then sinking it by spitting a stream of bathwater from my mouth, lying slowly down to gradually fill my eye sockets with water, polishing my kneecaps with shaving foam, shining the taps with my big toe, throwing the soap up in the air then dipping my head underwater to hear its reentry into the swill, and making spirals from my chest hair so that it resembled a Mediterranean garden. It was a good bath and a welcome break.

It occurred to me that Emily had never seen me in any outfit other than my shitty work suit. My go-to smart outfit was a blue shirt, mid-brown corduroy jacket, and a pair of slim-fit blue jeans from Tesco. The problem was that my jeans had the inconvenient dried saliva stains from Lassoo's dribblings. I washed the affected area with water and soap in the bathroom sink. They emerged wetter than I'd hoped, so I turned up the bedroom radiator and placed them on it to dry. Just before leaving for the pub, I sprayed some cologne on my neck and the front of my jacket. The cologne was a Christmas gift from Grace that I had never had the occasion to use. It was called "Electricity" by Sebastian Longcoq. I suspect she bought it from the local corner shop. Its aroma reminded me of a ripe banana with a hint of hot concrete. I should have tested it out on a sock before committing, but no matter; I reckoned it would fade quickly on account of its cheapness. The jeans didn't dry completely, but they would be fine by the time I got to the pub.

I left my flat around 7 p.m. with a spring in my step and my stomach pleasantly excited at the thought of seeing Emily. I made my way over to the play area and buried the corncob dongle in a muddy crack at the base of the plinth that had once supported the seesaw. As I stood there assessing the quality of the interment, my squirrel mate hopped up onto the plinth and gave me the once-over.

"Hold your horses, mate, what's with the fancy clobber?" I asked myself on his behalf.

"Just going to the pub. What's it to you anyway?" I replied.

"What's with the attitude? And why are you hiding things? You got some scheme on the go?"

"I'm meeting Emily. You know, the girl from the pub."

"Whoa, you want to think around that for a decent period, mate. You've just found out she's shacked up with that Tommy bloke and you intend to show her your face?"

"Well, yeah, I mean, he's not going to be there, is he?"

"Isn't he? Maybe she's just luring you out so he can confront you. A bloke like that isn't going to rest until he's given you a good kicking. Have you thought around that?"

"I think she might have left him, so it's got to be worth a gamble. If he is there and he kicks me in, then at least it's over and done with."

"Nah, if you nick his woman off him, he'll make your life a misery. It's not worth it. Sorry to have to say, but that is what it is."

"Well, I'll sit in the other bar for a while and make sure she's on her own."

"Sure you will. Have you thought around whether she's just been sent by John McCoy to butter you up and keep an eye on you?"

"Yes, I have, and I think I would be able to suss that out pretty quickly."

"You going to tell her about that dongle you just buried? I bet you've thought around that and decided it might be a bit risky."

"Of course, and I'm not going to mention it. Listen, I just

want to see her and find out what the situation is with Tommy and hear what she has to say about McCoy. If it seems dodgy then I'll run a mile, and that's a promise."

"I hope you are not making promises to yourself that you can't keep. I promised myself that I would stop bothering the lady squirrel with the long eyelashes, but I keep giving her my nuts and as you can probably see I'm getting dangerously thin. I wouldn't want to see you waste away."

"Whatever the outcome, mate, I will still be eating pie, don't you worry about that."

"What's that smell on your clothes? Have you been hanging around in a banana factory?"

"It's perfume—'Electricity' by Sebastian Longcoq. Grace bought it for me from the corner shop. It's a bit on the heavy side, isn't it? But I reckon it will fade."

"Or maybe it will deepen and linger, have you thought around that?"

"Yeah, well, sadly there's nothing I can do about it now. Where are you taking that nut?"

"None of your business. Have a good night and if I don't see you again it's been nice knowing you."

And with that he rushed away and disappeared behind a large beech tree. As I made my way onto the road, he appeared again on the low wall surrounding the play area:

"One last thing," I said on his behalf. "How did McCoy know about the dongle?"

"To be honest, I don't know. Maybe one of his mates in the police?"

"But you haven't told anyone in the police about it, have you?"

"No, you're right, I haven't. The only people who know about it are me and Grace, and I think I mentioned it in passing on the phone to Emily."

"You might want to think long and hard around that, mate. See you around sometime."

And then he was gone. He had made a good point: there had to be a chance that it was Emily who had told McCoy about the dongle. This evening out was going to have to be handled with a large dollop of caution.

When I arrived at the Grove, I used the side entrance and took up my seat at the bar where I usually watch football. There was a match being shown later, so if Emily didn't turn up I could still have a few drinks with Andy and Nick. From my seat I could just about see through the bar to the entrance to the lounge room. After half an hour there was no sign of Emily (or Tommy), so I went through to the toilet to have a go at drying off the remaining damp on my trousers with the hand dryer. I didn't make much progress, and by the end of my attempts the whole room smelt of warm bananas and even hotter concrete. I arrived back at the bar just in time to see Emily enter the pub, thankfully on her own. She was wearing a light green zip-up running top and baggy black trousers. She had her tan messenger bag slung on her hip and a large rucksack on her back that had some small tartan details but wasn't overly Scottish in its attitude.

I ordered another pint, waited for fifteen minutes, then walked through to the lounge. She gave me a beaming smile and a childish wave. I fancied her so much I suspect it made me blush. As I approached her, she put a finger to her mouth to shush me and mimed the motion of using a mobile phone.

She wanted me to turn my phone off was my guess, and so that is what I did.

"Sorry about that," she said, "you never know who might be listening. How are you? It's lovely to see you."

I took this reference to people listening as her way of acknowledging that there was something untoward going on in our lives. I noted it but didn't comment. She got up from her seat and gave me what felt like a very genuine hug. I took this as an indication she wanted me to know that she was "on my side." "Same," I replied as I sat down beside her.

"Did you get caught short?" she asked, pointing at the crotch of my trousers.

"No, not at all. I washed them before I came out and they didn't have time to dry."

"Did you only wash the crotch area?"

"Yes. There was a lot of dog spit on it."

"I won't ask."

"Thank you."

There was a small hole in the conversation. Truth is, I had no idea what was going on or what I was trying to achieve. I think maybe she felt the same, and we found ourselves dancing around each other and reaching for subjects to connect us.

"You smell nice," she said. "What is it you're wearing?"

" 'Electricity' by Seb Longcoq. It's on the banana-y side of roadworks, don't you think?"

"Yeah, with a hint of damp balaclava somewhere in the background. You look different in your casual clothes—less carpet salesman and more like an architect or university lecturer."

"It's the brown corduroy. It gives me a certain gravitas, much like driving a Volvo or carrying a vintage briefcase."

"My dad drives a Volvo and he's a very serious bit of kit, but very much of the odious kind."

"Do you still see your dad? You know, to say hello and catch up on his latest irritations?"

"No, I haven't seen him since I left home when I was eighteen. We never had much going on between us."

"My dad died when I was little, about seven or eight years old. He drank too much salt one day and fell into a coma. Never woke up."

"You're kidding me?"

"No, honestly. He drank a whole bottle of soy sauce after a hike in the Cotswolds."

"Really?"

"No, I'm just kidding. It was the Lake District."

She laughed, and I noticed that she wasn't wearing any makeup. It suited her perfectly. Her skin was radiant enough without any enhancement. Her fringe was still as straight as a die with its Chappaquiddick curl at one end and a little kink where it fell over the ears. Her eyes were still friendly and kind and her little button nose in perfect alignment with its surroundings—so much so I felt compelled to comment:

"Your nose is looking excellent. Is it something you appreciate yourself?"

"Get out of here. I hate it; makes me look like a hedgehog. Your nose is on the big side, but it suits you. Have you got a cold by the way? It's very red."

"No, I was just doing a bit of blackhead gardening in the bath and as usual I went at it a bit too aggressively. Do you want to get something to eat? The steak and chips I had here last time were very satisfactory."

"Yeah, that would be great. I'm starving. Only problem is I haven't got enough cash on me to pay for anything."

"No worries. It will be my treat on account of it being lovely to see you. So, how are you doing?"

"To be honest, not great actually. I left my boyfriend and my flat a couple of days ago and it's been tough."

I didn't know whether to mention that I had already been informed of her departure or whether to tell her that I had already doubted if it was in fact true.

"Wow, that's quite the upheaval. You must be feeling pretty jittery. To be honest I wasn't absolutely sure that you even had a boyfriend. I think the term you used was 'nothing official.' "

"Well, I'm officially single now, for the first time in years. I thought it would feel liberating but it just feels sad and a bit shit."

"I think that's to be expected. You just need time and distance and plenty of booze."

"Are you speaking from experience? Have you walked out on someone before?"

"No, they always walk out on me, but I imagine the principles are the same. Do you still have feelings for him?"

"Do you know what? I'm hoping that I don't, and I have to say that since the moment I walked out of the door I've only thought of myself. That's a good thing, don't you think?"

"Yes, I do, bang on the money."

I took a little kick of pleasure in the fact that she *had* thought about someone else, and that person was me. Then again, if she was still working for McCoy, she would, of course, have had to contact me. Tricky.

She continued. "There was this song that my dad used to

play really loud after Mum had upset him, where the singer repeated the line 'I've got six things on my mind and you're no longer one of them' over and over again. I keep saying this line in my head as a way of blanking him out. I don't know if it helps but it's a nice tune anyway so why not?"

"And have you got six things on your mind?"

"Let me think. Well, I need somewhere to live, I need a job, I need a bath, and I need a new phone. That seems to be it at the moment, so it's four things."

"Well, you're also hungry, so you need a bit of grub—that makes five—and you wanted to meet me for a drink, so let's add booze as the sixth thing."

I was pleased to have again confirmed, albeit obliquely, that I was one of the things on her mind. I wondered if she knew that Tommy was actively looking for her.

"How is your boyfriend taking it?" I asked.

"I don't know, to be honest. I made the move when he was out of the flat. I just left a note saying that I was leaving."

"How come he has your phone, then?" I blurted out, and instantly realized I had made a big mistake. I was going to have to admit that he had visited me that afternoon.

"How do you know that he's got my phone?" she asked.

"I'm sorry. I didn't mean to bother you with it, you've got enough on your plate, but he came to my flat earlier today and he had your phone with him. From what he said and the way he was acting, I think he thought that you might be staying at my place."

"Why on earth would he think that? We hardly know each other. That's ridiculous."

"Well, I'm assuming he checked your phone records, saw

that you'd telephoned my number, and used his contacts at Cityside Investigations to find out the address that went with the number."

"He took my phone from me on the day I left. It's something he often does if he's feeling vulnerable. He must have seen something in my demeanor that morning that set him off. I'm sorry you had to get involved with him. Did he threaten you or anything?"

"No, not really. I had to promise to inform him if I found out where you were, but I would never do that of course. He was with his boss, John McCoy. Do you know him?"

"I know who you mean—thinks he's a bit of a gangster. What was he doing there with Tommy?"

This was a question I was not going to answer. As far as I was concerned, and certainly until the playing field changed, I was not going to talk about the dongle to anyone.

"I think they just happened to be together, on their way to a job or something. It was all fine, not a problem. I have to say, I wouldn't really have thought Tommy was your type. He seems a lot older than you and a bit—if you don't mind me saying—a bit unpredictable. I wouldn't have put you together in a love match—or any match to be honest. Not even Ping-Pong."

"I know what you mean, but let's just say he was a very different man when we first met. Listen, I'd rather not talk about him if you don't mind."

"Okay. Let's talk about you, then. Your lime-green jacket— are you happy with what it achieves for you?"

"Yes, very."

"Okay, moving on to your baggy trousers. Are you happy

with how flappy they are? Could be quite a distraction in windy circumstances."

"I wish they had slightly less billow, but I'm happy with the freedom they gift me, especially when I'm having a sit-down."

"Good answer. Now, I know you are happy with your DMs and your hairstyle, so I suppose that's you covered and concluded appearance-wise."

"I've got a few other bits of clothing in my rucksack. Do you want to give them the once-over?"

"No, that's okay. My mum always told me you should never look inside a lady's bag, even if they give permission."

"I like your mum."

"Why aren't you wearing any makeup? As I remember, you always have a bit of paint on your face."

"I'm not actually that keen on it. Tommy used to insist I wore it all the time. I've had a checkered history with makeup ever since I was at school."

"You look nice without it. Shall we order some food?"

We both chose steak and chips, and Emily added side dishes of cauliflower cheese and onion rings. She explained that she never turns down the chance of an onion ring as she has loved circular food ever since her granny used to give her spaghetti hoops as a treat when she was a child. I told her I had a liking for the long foods such as hot dogs, asparagus, and seaside rock candy.

"Rock isn't a food," she responded.

"Fair enough," I replied. "In that case I'll exchange it for another hot dog, but an even longer one."

After we had eaten, I bought another couple of drinks, and as we sat back to enjoy them everything seemed charming and snug. I felt increasingly reassured that she wasn't still working for McCoy, and a part of me didn't care anyway. She told me how she had met Tommy and how they came to be in London. I casually asked her about Tommy's work and if she ever got involved. She shrugged her shoulders and said, "Occasionally." I didn't sense any nervous reaction to my question. Then I asked her where she was staying at the moment.

"I've spent the last two nights in this hotel at the Elephant and Castle called the Grand Saffron."

"Is that where you're staying tonight?" I inquired.

"No, you see, that's the thing, Gary. I've run out of money and I was going to ask if maybe I could stay at your place till I get myself sorted."

I wanted to say, *"Yes, you can stay forever, rent free,"* but resisted.

"Have you not got family or friends you could stay with?" I asked instead.

"Not really, and anyway, Tommy will be keeping an eye on them. It's not good that he found out about you. Maybe I should see if my dad would put me up for a bit in Brighton."

"I thought you and your dad had fallen out big-time?"

"Yeah, but I don't think he would turn me away."

The possibility of her deciding on another option rather than staying with me caused me to panic.

"Listen, I would love you to come and stay at my place. I've got three locks on my door—*yes, three*—and my next-door neighbor has a ferocious dog that I'm sure she would let us borrow for a few days. Honestly, I'd be very happy to help."

Emily's eyes began to water. I hadn't realized just how exhausted and desperate she really was.

"Would you like to do that?" I asked.

She nodded her head and placed her hand around my forearm.

"Thank you," she whispered with a sniffle and a smile.

"Is it okay if I finish my pint?" I asked. "It's a very refreshing one."

"You can have as many as you like. I love it in here," she replied and gave me the most pleasing smile I had ever been subjected to.

We stayed for a couple more hours, and not once did she raise the subject of Brendan or dongles or anything to do with "the case."

When we got to my block, we approached from the Peckham High Street entrance so that we emerged at the western end, away from the parking and the stairwell. I told Emily to wait while I went up and checked that the coast was clear. It was, so I beckoned her from the bottom of the stairwell to come and join me.

Once inside, Emily was very complimentary about my shitty flat, which was kind of her. Most visitors took great joy in telling me what a dump it was. I made a fuss of finding my sleeping bag and swapping it for the duvet on the bed.

"You can have the bed. It's probably best if I use the duvet— it might be a bit muggy."

She yawned apologetically and then gave me a whole-hearted hug. Her hair smelt of marzipan and freshly dug soil, pleasant enough but definitely due a wash.

"Do you mind if I go straight to bed?" she asked. "I think there's a chance I might get my first decent night's sleep for three days."

"Fill your boots," I replied as she slowly yawned her way into the bedroom.

I didn't sleep well that night. I kept thinking that Tommy might arrive at the door any minute. It was also very distracting having the girl of your dreams under the same roof but beyond your reach. The sounds outside were different from the back part of the flat—more traffic noise, more human activity, and an owl occasionally hooting somewhere in the distance. Worst of all, Emily had left the light on in the bathroom, meaning the electrical air vent was whining away like a faulty edge trimmer. I didn't have the heart or the courage to knock on her door.

At around 2 a.m. I made myself a hot Bovril for the avoidance of caffeine and to receive its meaty punch. As I sipped on it the thought occurred to me that I should delete the references to Emily contained in the dongle. Only Brendan knew what was in the document, and he was dead. My reading of things was that Emily must have been an innocent participant in the shenanigans, unaware of the greater scheme at play.

I crept outside in my dressing gown to retrieve the dongle from its muddy tomb, and as I emerged from the stairwell and took a few steps across the paving, I noticed a lone figure leaning on a tree by the low fence, staring intently into the play area. They were holding a lighted candle in one hand while shielding the flame with the other. It wasn't particularly dark—the street and estate lights provided a dusky glow across the area—but because of the shadow of the tree it was hard to make out the cut and identity of the midnight creeper.

I stealthily maneuvered myself around a couple of white vans to get a better view, and in doing so accidentally kicked a discarded can of beer, which rattled and clanked as it rolled under a van. I turned my gaze towards the stranger just in time to see them extinguish the candle with one sharp breath. I stood stock-still with all but my head obscured from the creeper's view by the body of one of the vans. I could sense the stranger's glare upon me and wondered if I should just sprint back up the stairs to my flat and safety.

After a minute or so, I saw the figure light the candle again and shuffle away from the tree and into the open. I took the chance to hide myself fully behind the van. Crouching down, I made my way along the row of parked vehicles, then emerged about fifty feet farther up the service road. The creeper was now bent down next to the plinth where the seesaw used to be, and I was now near enough to hear their voice almost chanting the words "I'm sorry, I'm so sorry. Please forgive me."

It was Grace, and I could tell from her voice that she was sobbing.

I stayed hidden away until I saw her walk back to the stairwell and disappear into the block. It had seemed like a private moment that I had no right to disturb. I retrieved the dongle and went back up to my flat. Eventually sleep took hold of me. In my dreams, Tommy beat me to within an inch of my life with a large watermelon while Emily and Lassoo stood watching on.

20

IT WAS A BEAUTIFUL sunny Saturday morning when I awoke, so I walked down to Grinders to get Emily some coffee and treats for her breakfast. I replaced the dongle in its hidey-hole and then found a secluded spot behind a row of garages where I could destroy the laptop unseen. I threw it against a brick wall Frisbee style a few times at full welly, and it soon fell apart. I put the debris in a nearby bin, apart from the piece I guessed might be the hard drive, which I popped through the bars of a gully drain in the road.

It was still early when I arrived at the coffee shop, and Wayne had no customers. He was wearing a tight yellow T-shirt with the slogan "DON'T ASK" on its frontage.

"Hi, Wayne, how are you doing? Or am I not allowed to ask?"

"You are allowed to ask, and I'm doing just fine, thank you. Why are you looking so pleased with yourself?"

"Do you remember that girl I told you about that I met in the pub?" I replied.

"Vaguely."

"Well, she spent the night at my flat. Can you believe that?"

"Not really, Gary. Not unless she was under duress or off her tits on something."

"It's true, no word of a lie, and hopefully I'm going to spend the rest of the day with her."

"Who's to say she will be there when you get back? She might have come to her senses and made an escape."

"No, I think she might be falling for me, just like you have, Wayne. You should have made a move on me earlier; I'm increasingly looking like an unavailable. Has your dad heard anything from the police yet, by the way?"

"No, but he will, don't you panic."

"You know what, I'm beginning to believe you."

I didn't tell Wayne about the contents of the dongle. It didn't feel like the right time. I didn't want to get his hopes up when the whole thing was so up in the air and uncertain. I ordered two coffees, two almond croissants, and a couple of skinny blueberry muffins. While Wayne prepared my order, I was surprised to be joined at the counter by Mr. Clown Shoes. He was wearing his usual clothes and carrying a plastic carrier bag bulging with eight-and-a-half-by-eleven documents and letters. I looked away as soon as I caught his eye, but I was too late. He poked me on my shoulder.

"Hey, I know you," he growled. "You were the bloke hanging around in the police station and at the court. What's your business with me? Are you working for my neighbor? Are you his spy or something?"

Wayne had taken note of Mr. Clown Shoes's attitude and told him to calm it down and keep things civil. Mr. Clown Shoes gave Wayne a defiant glance but realized that Wayne was not someone to be disobeyed. He lowered his tone.

"So, why did you happen to be at those two places at exactly the same time as me? Are you going to suggest that it was just pure coincidence? Because I very much doubt that."

"It is just a coincidence, but not that big a one, because I work for a firm of solicitors and I'm often at the court and at the police station."

"Liar. You told me you were a carpet salesman, and by the look of you I would say that's just about right."

Wayne interrupted on my behalf:

"Listen, mate, the guy is a lawyer. He represents me as it happens. So let it go, will you, or get out of the shop."

Mr. Clown Shoes looked me in the eye as he stroked his chin and made a humming sound from his throat:

"Would you like to represent me? You've probably heard the outline of my complaint from your eavesdropping. It's a big case—could be worth thousands in damages."

I didn't want Mr. Clown Shoes to like me, so the devil took a tug on my shoulder.

"Sorry, but it's not the sort of work I take on. I have got a suggestion for you, though. There's a firm of private investigators in Camberwell Green called Cityside Investigations that specialize in gathering evidence for neighbor disputes. You should call in on them in person. I think they will be able to help you make some real progress."

I loved the thought of Mr. Clown Shoes and his bulging bag of bullshit clogging up their offices. I wrote down their address for him, and he thanked me profusely. As I was leaving with my coffee and sweetmeats, I turned back to Wayne and asked him exactly what it was that people were not allowed to ask him.

"How I became so gorgeous" was his reply, and I think he was telling the truth.

When I got back to my block, I had a good look around to see if Tommy was lurking, but everything looked familiar and correct. Once inside the flat, I closed the latch on all three locks and secured the chain. Emily was sat at the dining table staring out of the window. I gave her the coffee and treats and sat down opposite her. She smiled, then leant over the table and gave me a kiss on my cheek.

"Listen," she said. "I think I should go down to Brighton and speak to my dad. Maybe he will have a room that's not being used and I can look for a job down there."

Her expression suggested that she knew I would be disappointed, but I tried my best to give the opposite reaction.

"It's a good plan, a solid plan, better than just being holed up here wondering if Tommy is going to turn up. What about we drive down there today? If your dad doesn't come good, you can always come back with me."

She instantly agreed. The prospect of a day by the seaside with Emily filled me with joy. As she was getting her stuff together, my phone rang. It was an unknown number, so I let it go to voicemail. When I listened to the message, it was from a colleague of Detective Peterson. He wanted me to phone him as soon as possible to arrange a chat about Brendan's murder investigation. I decided immediately that I wouldn't be calling back anytime soon. No one was going to rob me of my day out with Emily.

As we left the flat, we found Grace and Lassoo waiting for us outside her door.

"Hello, Gary. Who's this lovely young lady with you?" she asked.

I explained as briefly as possible that Emily was just a friend who needed a place to stay for the night.

"Is that right, Gary? Just a friend. How kind of you," said Grace with a sliver of sarcasm. "I wanted to grab you because I've had some good news. I got a letter from the NHS saying I could go in for my hip operation on Monday if I am able to do so at such short notice. Do you think I should do it? I have to phone them immediately if I want to take up the offer."

"Yes, of course you should," I replied. "There's nothing stopping you, is there?"

"Well, I was just a bit worried about Lassoo, I have to stay in overnight. Would you be able to look after him?"

I looked down at Lassoo, who was being made a fuss of by Emily. He gave me a look as if to say, *Okay by me if this lady is staying.* I told Grace that would be fine and that I would pop in to see her when I got back from Brighton later this evening.

"Oh, Brighton, is it?" remarked Grace. "That's where people used to go to fall in love. Be careful."

21

WE DROVE DOWN TO Brighton in my six-year-old tan Renault Clio. We took turns to choose tracks to play on the sound system as we motored around the M25 and down the M23 to the South Coast. I chose the likes of the Kings of Leon, Steely Dan, Eminem, and Hot Chip. She chose the likes of Drake, Kendrick Lamar, and Taylor Swift. We gelled, however, over an old boy band track called "Keep on Movin'" by the band Five. I had always been slightly embarrassed that I liked it but took a chance. I could always pass it off as irony if it didn't land. I got lucky. She loved it too. We played it over and over again and sang our hearts out along with the track.

> *So get on up when you're down*
> *Baby, take a good look around*
> *I know it's not much but it's okay*
> *We'll keep on movin' on anyway*

I felt like a teenager after his first bottle of cider and wanted the journey to last forever. I hadn't felt like this in a long, long time.

When we arrived in Brighton, Emily took me on a tour

through her town. She was in her element; her whole body came alive and relaxed as she rushed me from street to street recalling places and people from the past. She would hold my hand to speed me through the tour and occasionally link her arm with mine and rest her head on my shoulder.

"This area is known as the 'back parallels.' Years ago, back in the 1970s and '80s, it was a bit of a dump full of secondhand clothes shops and junk shops. See that shop there? It used to be a laundrette, and one night my dad got arrested because he kicked the huge glass window and it smashed to smithereens. He was angry with Mum about something. It went to court and he was fined fifty pounds. He made my mum pay off the fine by taking money from her housekeeping every week for a year . . . See that chemist there? It's been here since I was a kid. My friend Louise and I used to steal little bits of makeup from the racks and sell them at school . . . That's the Theatre Royal, we would go to the panto every year as a school trip. One year a lad called Eddie Bryson took all his clothes off and ran down the aisle singing the theme tune to *SpongeBob SquarePants*. We never saw him again after that . . . This is Churchill Square. It's where all the teenage girls and boys used to come and eye each other up on Saturday afternoons. Louise got off with a boy called Callum once and they went down to the beach for a snog. I just watched on from the promenade up above. I was really jealous, to be honest. He had very good hair. Louise told me afterwards that I hadn't missed much. He kept his eyes wide open as they kissed, and as the kiss developed his eyes started to move around his eye sockets as if trying to count a swarm of midges."

"Do you still keep in touch with Louise?" I asked.

"No, haven't heard from her in years. I often wonder what she's doing. Something cool I expect."

Eventually I had seen all she wanted me to see, and we drove a couple of miles out of town and parked up on the seafront. Emily ran straight to a small newsagent's shop that also sold buckets and spades and all manner of seaside tat. She told me to stay by the car till she returned. When she emerged from the shop, she beckoned me to follow her to a wooden bench overlooking the English Channel. She had a paper bag of goodies for me: a stick of rock, some foam bananas, and a jelly snake.

"Hope the rock is long enough for you," she said before biting the head off the jelly snake and chewing on it like a softhearted Labrador.

She pointed to a terrace of grand houses and hotels farther up the seafront.

"That's my dad's hotel up there, second from the right. He's had the outside repainted and it didn't have those red-and-white striped awnings when I last saw it. Really fucks me off that he's dolled it up. Mum was always asking him to get it done but he never did while she was around."

"Do you see much of your mum?"

"Not as much as I would like to. Tommy wasn't keen on me visiting her by myself. We went up to see her a couple of times but it was just awkward. Tommy wanted to leave more or less the moment we arrived. I've met Mum and her sister in London a few times when they've been up for a day out, but mainly we just text each other or speak on the phone. I hope that's going to change now."

"I hope so too. Is there any chance you could go and stay with your mum and her sister?"

"No, their flat is tiny and her sister is on her last legs. It wouldn't be fair."

I picked the cellophane off the end of the rock and took a series of long and concentrated licks. Emily rolled the jelly snake head around in her mouth.

"I used to come and sit here every Sunday morning on my way back from buying Dad his newspaper. I actually had my very first proper kiss on this bench."

"Wow. It should have a plaque on it or something to mark the event."

She put her head on my shoulder and turned her face to look up at me. "Why don't we mark it with our first kiss?" We kissed in a slightly jokey, ironic way. It could have just been mates having a snog, but it will forever remain in the list of top kisses that I have benefited from. After the kiss, she stood up.

"I guess it's time for me to go and see the old shit and beg for his charity. Do you want to come or do you want to stay here and eat your long rock in peace?"

I opted to stay put and admire the sea and the gulls frolicking and arguing on the beach and on the promenade. I watched her walk away, thinking to myself how much I hoped her father would have no room at the inn. I was convinced that she liked me and genuinely intended to leave Tommy. I had abandoned all thoughts that she might still be in league with McCoy and Cityside Investigations. Maybe I did have a chance with her. While I waited for Emily to return, I decided to call Grace to check in on her.

"Hi, Grace, how are you doing?"

"Oh, it's you, is it? Mr. Lover Boy . . ."

"I'm just checking in to see if you are okay."

"Yes, why wouldn't I be?"

"No reason. Did you sleep okay last night?"

"Yes, like a baby."

She was lying, but I didn't have the balls to pick her up on it.

"Have you gone ahead and booked the operation?"

"Never mind that. Aren't you going to ask me what I think of her?"

"Wasn't going to, no, but I expect you're going to tell me."

"She's too good for you and then some. But you looked cute together and Lassoo liked her so that's good enough for me."

"Well, thank you, Grace, I value your opinion above everyone else's apart from, of course, the local butcher. So, have you booked the operation?"

"Yes, it's all done. If I don't survive it, you can have Lassoo and whatever is left in the fridge."

"You'll be fine. I'll speak to you later or in the morning."

"Oh, in the morning, is it? You mean if you get lucky tonight?"

"I'm lucky every day, Grace, because I have you to watch over and harass me."

"That's true, that is."

"Has anyone called at my flat since I've been gone?"

"I did hear someone knocking on your door an hour or so ago, but I was on the toilet so I didn't get out quick enough to see who it was. Hate it when that happens."

"I know you do."

Emily returned about half an hour later, giving me the thumbs-down gesture as she approached. She slumped down next to me on the bench and told me what had occurred.

22

EMILY

THERE WAS NOBODY ON reception or in any of the public rooms when I got inside the hotel, so I made my way up to the family flat on the top floor. I knocked on the entrance door and opened it slowly and politely while continuing to gently knock. My father was sat reading a newspaper on the same winged easy chair he was sat in on the day I left home. I was shocked to see how much weight he had lost and how pale and drawn he seemed. His skin was paper-thin and his breathing loud and uncomfortable. He clearly wasn't well. I stood in the doorway for a moment. He didn't look up.

"Hello, Father," I said as I walked a few feet into the room.

Nothing much seemed to have changed about the décor or ambience of the place. The only thing that stood out was a large table lamp to one end of the sideboard in the shape and design of a clementine. The room had never had to accept such a splash of color when I lived there. Mum used to wear bright orange and yellow dresses and skirts and would shine like a peacock whenever she sat in this room. Perhaps the lamp was some sort of token to her absence.

My father turned his head towards me.

"What do you want?" he replied without a hint of famil-iarity, affection, or surprise.

I was overcome with the weight of the sudden transfer-ence to past times of sadness and fear. It warned me that this encounter would not go well. I briefly wondered if I should just walk out the door and leave it at that. This had been a big mistake. I replied to him but couldn't summon up any warmth or emotion in my voice.

"I'm in a bit of a fix, Dad, and I wondered if you could help me out?"

"You want money, I suppose. I've often wondered when this day would come—you knocking on my door, having failed in life like you failed me as a daughter."

"No, I don't want money, I just need somewhere to stay, and I didn't fail you, Dad. I did everything you asked of me."

"Yes, and you hated me for that. You hated me for trying to guide you into adulthood when that, my precious daughter, was my duty as a parent."

"I didn't hate you. I just hated the way you treated Mum and how little you actually wanted to be with me. Everything in this home was designed to make life bearable for you whatever the cost to me and Mum. You don't have to help me if you don't want to. You know I wouldn't ask unless I was desperate."

"Why would I want to help you? I lost your mother because of your behavior and lack of responsibility."

"That's not true. She left because you treated her like shit. Did you know that she's happy now? Did you know that hap-piness started the very moment she stepped out of this place?"

A slight tremble of pain crossed his face before he stood

up and said, "I'm pleased for her, but not as pleased as I am at your obvious misery."

This was the moment that, as a child, I would have burst into tears and begged him for forgiveness, but not today.

"Do you know what, I don't need your help. I don't think I ever did. Why don't you just fuck off and rot just like this miserable place."

Father smiled at me, which was a rare occurrence usually accompanied by a sarcastic remark or a barbed comment. Not this time, however.

"That's more like it," he said. "Maybe there is hope for you yet."

I delivered a final "Fuck off" before slamming the door behind me and leaving the hotel. As I walked down the steps, I thought about the moment my mother had done the very same thing. Just like her, I knew I would never see my father again. It felt good.

23

"WOW" IS ALL I could think to say.

"So, I guess I won't be staying here," Emily concluded.

"How are you feeling?" I replied.

"Liberated, hungry, and a little bit sad. Hey, that's quite a sharp point you've fashioned your rock into."

"Yeah, quite a weapon, isn't it? Do you want to borrow it and plunge it into your dad's chest?"

"No, that would be pointless—he hasn't got a heart. I would stick it right up his arse; that would hurt him more."

"Don't worry about finding a place to sleep. You can stay at mine for as long as you want."

"Thank you. I worry about Tommy, though. He's bound to turn up again."

"I don't think you should. Remember, I've got three locks—*yes, three locks*—AND a chain, an actual chain."

Emily laughed and gave me another friendly kiss.

"Shall we stay here tonight?" she asked.

"Yes, I think we should."

We booked into a small hotel just off the seafront. It was a twin room with separate beds. Neither of us made a move on the other, but it did feel like our first night together as a couple. As we sat watching the TV and eating a bucket of KFC, I received another message from Peterson's lackey asking me to arrange to meet him. I was more than happy to make him wait.

● ● ●

In the morning we drove back to London slightly giddy at our blossoming connection. I didn't ask her if we were now boyfriend and girlfriend, but it felt like we were. We arrived around midday and approached the flat with military-style caution. Once inside, we went straight to bed for a nap. An hour or so later, we were disturbed by a loud knocking on the door. We hid under the covers until we heard the visitor walk away. Emily guessed it wasn't Tommy, because he would have ranted and raved and probably tried to break the door down. My phone rang again, and I let it go to voicemail. It was Detective Bailey, advising me to report to Peckham Police Station to give a statement regarding Brendan's murder. He apologized for the fact that if I didn't attend, then the investigating officers would have to call at my house to interview me.

I needed to talk this over with someone, and as I no longer had any worries about Emily's motives, I decided to unload on her. I told her about Cowley and Wilmott and about McCoy coming round in search of the dongle. She asked me where the dongle was now, and I told her it was safely hidden away from the flat and as far as I was concerned would remain forever "lost." I didn't tell her that I had seen the contents of the document and that it mentioned her name. She didn't need any more worry in her life. We concluded that the best course of action was to stick to the lost dongle story.

"You're not involved in Brendan's murder, so you have nothing to worry about," she reassured me. "My guess is that their only interest is in following up about the two fake coppers. Come the crunch, you can still give them the dongle. You would just have to say it turned up again, in some long-forgotten pocket."

I telephoned Bailey, and we arranged for me to attend at the station at 3 p.m. that afternoon. Emily and I had an hour to kill, so we both popped into Grace's flat for a cup of tea.

"Oh, it's you, is it?" was how she greeted me. Her attitude changed immediately when she saw I was with Emily. "Oh, hello, Emily, how nice to see you. I love the color of your jacket by the way. It really suits you. I've got a trouser suit in the same green. Come through into the bedroom and I'll show it to you."

Grace ushered Emily into her bedroom, and I went through to the kitchen and put the kettle on. On the counter was a tin of peaches in light syrup that Grace had obviously tried to open but had failed. She had managed to get an inch or so of the lid open and then cut herself trying to prise it. There were a few drops of blood on the counter and a smear of blood on the abandoned tin opener. There was a crust of bread sticking out of the electric toaster that was toasted and had been left there to harden. I got the sense that Grace's spirits must be low. Something was wrong. I was worried about the meaning of her lonely vigil a couple of nights earlier, and I felt a pang of guilt at leaving her alone the day before she was going to hospital for her operation.

I made the tea and waited on the sofa. I could hear Emily and Grace chatting and laughing in the bedroom. Grace was always one for putting on a brave face, or maybe it was simply that she preferred Emily's company to mine. Lassoo lay down on the hallway floor immediately outside the bedroom door, his eyes fixed on me and with an expression that said, *"I don't think you're needed here."* When they came back through to the lounge, Emily was wearing Grace's lime-green trouser suit. She looked stunning, and I could tell from her smile that she thought so, too.

"You must keep it," said Grace. "It's no good to me anymore, and it's probably four sizes too small. I would love you to have it."

Emily made a decent fuss of refusing, but Grace was not to be knocked back, and eventually she accepted the gift.

• • •

An hour or so later, I left the two of them chatting and made my way to the police station. After waiting ten or fifteen minutes, I was greeted by Detective Bailey and taken through to an interview room. He gave me the usual spiel about not being under arrest and that I was free to leave at any time I wished. He then explained that he would not be carrying out the interview himself and that the officers from the unit investigating Brendan's murder would be through to speak to me shortly. As I waited, I reflected on the fact that if I were one of my own clients I would be advising myself to give a "no comment" interview. Maybe I should heed my own advice and do the same.

The door opened, and there they were in all their dreary glory, Detectives Wilmott and Cowley. Cowley was on the phone as he entered, finishing a call.

"That is very interesting indeed, and perfect timing if you don't mind me saying. I'll get back to you as soon as this is finished" were the final words of his telephone conversation.

As before, it was Cowley who did most of the speaking,

Wilmott seeming more interested in his burger and milkshake than in me.

"Hello again, Gary. My name is Detective Peterson from the Lewisham Serious Crimes Squad, and my colleague here is Detective Rowlett. Forgive us for our late arrival but we are not familiar with the layout at this station and took one or two false turns."

"I thought you were Wilmott and Cowley?"

"Yes, we are from time to time, but that needn't concern you, Gary," said Peterson (née Cowley). "It's just an operational peculiarity that's employed from time to time. It sometimes helps us catch the bad guys, and you would want us to do that, wouldn't you, Gary?"

"So, when it suits you to do so, you use false names and ID? It sounds dodgy to me but, yes, I want you to catch the bad guys. So, how can I help you?"

Peterson continued:

"Gary, we want you to understand that this investigation is very complicated and very sensitive. We really need your cooperation. Are you willing to cooperate, Gary?"

"Yes, of course, I've got nothing to hide."

Rowlett (née Wilmott) barked out a laugh and in doing so spat a chunk of bread and burger onto the surface of the table. He reached his hand over and grasped the morsel between his finger and thumb and placed it back in his mouth.

"Are you not going to caution me and read me my rights?" I asked.

"No need for that yet, Gary, this is just an informal chat. We value your cooperation greatly, so let's just keep it nice and relaxed," replied Peterson.

"Okay then, fire away," I replied, pretending that I didn't have a care in the world.

"Are you good at hiding things, Gary? Are you like a little squirrel that hides his nuts away from sight then returns to them when the time is right? Would that be you, Gary?" asked Peterson.

"I don't know what you mean."

"Where's the dongle, Gary?"

A sweat pulse rushed through my body and dampened my skin in places it had never done so before.

"No comment," I replied.

"We know you have that dongle and that you have hidden it away for what you think is safekeeping, but believe me, Gary, you and your loved ones are not safe until we have that dongle. Now, where is it?"

"No comment."

Rowlett chirped in, his mouth laden with gray meat and damp bread.

"Stop with the 'no comment.' Hiding evidence from us is a serious offense, pal. Just tell us where it is and this whole thing just goes away."

"No comment."

"Have you opened the memory stick and read its contents, Gary?" asked Peterson.

"No."

"Is that 'no I haven't opened it' or an attempt at another 'no comment,' Gary?"

"No comment."

"Listen, Gary," continued Peterson. "We know with absolute certainty that you have hidden the dongle somewhere outside your residence. Do you want us to have officers and dogs search the entire estate? Is that what you want, Gary?"

"No comment."

They kept on asking me about the dongle for the next ten minutes, and I continued to answer "no comment." At one point Rowlett took two photographs out of a file and placed them on the table. One was a photograph of Brendan with dried blood all around his neck and chest, and the other was a photograph of a knife in a plastic tube. The knife seemed vaguely familiar to me, but I couldn't fix on where I had seen it before. They didn't comment on the photographs or ask me any questions relating to them.

Eventually they seemed to accept that I was not going to cooperate. I asked if I could leave.

"That's your prerogative, Gary," said Peterson. "But next time it might not just be us you're dealing with. It could get a lot worse. I sense you don't appreciate exactly who you are dealing with, which is reassuring, as it means you probably haven't opened that memory stick. We will see you soon, Gary, and might I suggest you have a rethink before that happens."

I left the police station feeling shaken and afraid. Peterson and Rowlett were not interested in finding Brendan's murderer. In fact they probably already knew who the culprit was. I wasn't a suspect; their only interest in me was concerning the dongle.

I popped into Wayne's coffee shop, mainly, I think, to catch sight of a friendly face. He looked up at me from behind his counter and immediately picked up on my suffering.

"What's the matter, mate? Your harvest been ruined by pests or flood?" he asked.

"Yeah, something like that. Two coffees please and a couple

of slices of Battenberg," I replied, not wishing to get involved in a to-and-fro.

"Blimey, you have got a carp on. You're fully turgid."

"Thanks, Wayne. Hey, has your dad heard anything from the police?"

"Why don't you ask him? He's sat over there in the corner by the window."

I turned round to see a man well into his sixties with thinning hair wearing a well-worn gray wool suit and a shirt and tie. His face was gaunt with large bags under his eyes. He kept licking his lips to moisten them. The suit was hanging off him slightly, and his gaze was fixed up towards the ceiling. It looked like his batteries might be on the blink. I walked over and introduced myself.

"Hi there, are you Wayne's dad? I just wanted to say hello. I'm Gary, Wayne's legal beagle. You mind if I sit down?"

He gave me a silent shake of his head to indicate he had no objection.

"If you insist, and by the way I think it's legal eagle, not legal beagle," he said as I took my seat.

"Yeah, it usually is, but I occasionally do work for the Queen so I'm allowed to use beagle." He looked at me as if I was an advert for a donkey sanctuary.

"How can I help you, Gary?"

"Well, your son seems to have got mixed up with your ex-colleagues at Lewisham Serious Crimes Squad. My problem is that I also appear to have become involved with them and, in a word, I'm frightened."

"Which ones are we talking about?"

"Peterson and Rowlett."

"That sounds about right. Have they planted evidence on you? Are they trying to bribe you? Are they trying to get you to perjure yourself?"

"No, I've got a document that they want very badly. It kind of blows the lid on everything they have been up to."

"And I expect you're thinking of giving it to a journalist, or the police, or even your MP?"

"Yeah, all of those have crossed my mind."

"Have you got any family here in London?"

"No."

"Close friends?"

"No."

"Then my advice is just give them what they want and leave town. If you don't, your life will change forever. Years ago I made the mistake of challenging them and I have regretted it every single day since. I hardly ever even leave my house. I might as well be in prison. If it weren't for my medication, I wouldn't even still be here. Don't fuck your life up, Gary."

"Well, that is certainly the easiest option, but it doesn't sit well, letting them get away with it, letting them continue with the corruption and harassment."

"You need to think about yourself and nobody else. They will kill you if need be. Do you know a bloke called Brendan Jones?"

"Yeah, he was found murdered last week."

"Well, he was digging up dirt on Peterson's activities and look what happened to him."

"Do you know why he was thinking of spilling the beans on them? I mean, he worked with John McCoy, and from what I can tell was right in the middle of it all."

"I've heard a few different explanations. I was told that he wanted to become a partner in McCoy's company but McCoy refused. I've also heard that McCoy's sidekick Tommy Briggs was hooking up with Brendan's ex and he wanted to give him a kick in the balls. Maybe he just got a conscience, a bit like you. Either way it hasn't worked out how Brendan expected. Don't do a Brendan. I wouldn't want Wayne to be without his legal beaver."

"Beagle."

"If you insist."

"Have the police been in touch with you about the drugs charge? It's getting close to the first court appearance."

"Not yet. They like to keep me sweating. Maybe this time they will go through with it. To be honest, I can't say I'm bothered either way. Main thing is to keep Wayne clear of it. If they go ahead, I'll plead guilty so long as they drop the charges against Wayne. They will do that, no problem. I'll serve my time, probably five years, and like I say, I might as well be in prison, so what's the worry?" He gave his lips a good licking and got up to leave. "Right, I'm done. I might as well get off back to my cell."

"Nice meeting you. Have a good day," I said with a decent amount of sincerity.

"If you insist."

I didn't want my life to be like Wayne's dad's. I felt a certain lightness from the thought of handing the dongle over to Peterson or McCoy.

24

WHEN I RETURNED TO my flat, a note had been pushed through the letterbox.

"We need to talk. I'm at my office."

It was from John McCoy. I called out Emily's name, but there was no response. I assumed she was still next door with Grace. I ate my slice of Battenberg and took the other slice next door in the certain knowledge that it would end up in the mouths of Grace and Lassoo and not Emily. When Grace answered the door, she had obviously been asleep and was in the process of shaking off her nap haze. "Hi, Grace, sorry to wake you up."

"I wasn't asleep. Why do you always think I've been sleeping?"

"Is Emily there?"

"No, she left just after you did. Has she done a runner or something?"

"Not that I know of. Did you notice if anyone came to my flat while I was out?"

"How would I know? I was fast asleep. Come in and make me a cuppa."

I did as I was told. The milk was on the turn and formed a greasy film on top of the tea. Grace didn't seem to notice.

"Are you okay, Grace?" I asked.

"As well as can be expected. Why do you ask?" she replied.

I decided to grasp the bullet and admit to Grace that I had seen her strange little vigil in the play area the other night. I knew she wasn't feeling okay, and I felt it my duty to offer a friendly shoulder if it was needed.

"It's just that a couple of nights ago I couldn't sleep, and when I went outside for some fresh air I saw you on the play area and it looked like you were crying."

"Well, that's none of your business and I'll thank you not to spy on me in future."

"I wasn't spying on you, Grace. Come on, tell me what's going on with you."

Grace looked me dead in the eyes, then slowly rose out of her chair to fetch something from one of the boxes on her shelves. She threw a photograph onto the table in front of me as she sat back down. It was of a lady with shoulder-length dark brown hair stood on the walkway outside Grace's front door. She was wearing the green trouser suit that Grace had gifted to Emily that morning. Beside her was a young girl, around five years old, licking on an ice-cream cone. They looked happy.

"It's a nice photograph. Who are they?" I asked.

"It's my daughter, Mary, and my granddaughter, Lizzie."

"Shit, Grace, you've never mentioned that you had children."

"*Child* not children, and no, I have never mentioned it to you."

"Why not?"

"Because it breaks my heart when I think about her."

"I don't understand. Has she passed away or something?"

"No. She hates me, and I haven't seen either of them for the past three years."

I could see that she was close to tears. She slowly got out of her chair again and turned her face away from me to stare out the window and beyond the trees towards the high street.

"Mary used to live only a couple of miles away from here, in East Dulwich. About once a month, or whenever she was in a fix, she would drop Lizzie off here for me to look after her for the weekend—Friday night through to Sunday morning. I would take her for a day out on the Saturday, maybe to the zoo or to see the *Cutty Sark* in Greenwich, and every Sunday we would go to East Street Market to buy her a little present for being a good girl and have an ice cream or a glass of sarsaparilla. The rest of the time we would spend in the flat watching the TV or playing on the computer. She had a real talent for computers, just like her grandmother. She adored Lassoo and would demand that we took him out for a walk four, sometimes five, times a day. She always slept in my bedroom even though her mum had given me a little fold-out bed to put in the lounge. Her favorite bedtime story was called *Billy's Bus*. It was about a fat black-and-white cat that used to drive his bus around town so that cats could go and visit each other. I had a little handbell on my bedside table and she would ring it every time the bus stopped to pick up a passenger."

I noticed Grace swallow hard and wipe a tear from her eye. I decided not to interrupt.

"It was a Saturday evening, three years ago, and Lizzie wanted spaghetti hoops on toast for her supper. I didn't have any in the cupboard so decided to pop out to the corner shop on Havill Street to get some. Lizzie was already in her pajamas and pink dressing gown and a bit grumpy due to tiredness. As the shop was only five minutes away and she was pretty responsible for a seven-year-old, I didn't feel too worried about leaving her in the flat on her own. I told her I would be back before she knew it and that she must stay on the settee with Lassoo and rub his tummy until I got back.

"When I got back to the flat the door was wide open and Lizzie and Lassoo were nowhere to be seen. I looked over the walkway towards the play area and could see Lassoo wandering around without his lead. I rushed down the stairway shouting Lizzie's name, and when I emerged from the stairway Lassoo was already there to greet me. He had what looked like blood on his nose. At the far end of the play area I glimpsed three or four teenagers riding away at full speed on their bicycles. As I ran towards the play area, I could see the crumpled-up figure of Lizzie lying facedown on the mud beneath one of the arms of the seesaw. When I reached her, I turned her over and could see that her little jaw had been smashed to smithereens and blood was streaming from her nose and mouth."

Grace was sobbing. I was lost for words. I stood up and placed my hand on her shoulder.

"I stayed with her in hospital that night. She had to have her jaw wired back together and have an operation on her tongue. When her mother arrived and found out what had happened, she threw me out of the hospital and told me I would never see either of them again. I miss them both so much, every day."

"I'm so sorry, Grace," I said. "Why have you never told me this before?"

"Well, you know, I have good days and bad days, but I've

always thought that if I talk about it then it will take me back to square one."

"You seemed in such good spirits this morning when you and Emily were trying on clothes together."

"I'm good at pretending. It's what I do every day."

"Blimey, your daughter really looks like Emily, especially in that trouser suit."

"I know, I think that's what might have set me off again."

"So do you have any contact with your daughter at all?"

"I tried and tried for a year or so, begging for forgiveness and asking for updates on Lizzie, but she never responded. I used to take the bus down to East Dulwich to see if I might get a glimpse of Lizzie, but I bumped into Mary one time and she threatened me with the police and solicitors and all sorts. I've stopped going there now. I heard she's moved down to Kent. I just have to hope that one day she'll forgive me or that Lizzie might seek me out when she's older. I'm running out of time, though."

I stayed with Grace for half an hour or so, until her spirits had appeared to lift. When it felt appropriate, I gently mentioned that she had the right as a grandparent to apply for visitation rights to Lizzie if she wanted to. She seemed surprised but declined to pursue the conversation. When I left her flat, she gave me a hug.

"Maybe it's no bad thing to talk about it. I feel a lot better for a chat and a cry. Thank you," she said.

"Anytime," I replied.

25

BACK IN MY OWN flat I went into the bedroom and noticed that Emily's backpack and messenger bag had both gone. I could only think of two possibilities. Either she *had* done a runner, or she had left with McCoy. If she had left with McCoy, then she was either still working for him or she had left with him under duress. I decided to visit the offices of Cityside Investigations and to take the dongle with me.

I made my way to the play area and sat on the plinth of the dismantled seesaw. As I poked around in the muddy crack to retrieve the dongle, it was hard not to imagine how Grace must have felt on that terrible day. It crossed my mind that maybe the accident was the reason that people on the estate seemed to shun Grace. Though it was probably more likely that she shunned other people on account of her guilt and shame. She had reached out to me after I arrived on the estate, though, and that made me feel both special and very lucky at the same time.

Out of the blue, my squirrel mate appeared beside me. His tail looked limp and greasy, and his eyes lacked their usual brightness.

"What's going on with you? You look well shabby. Have you been in a fight?"

"As a matter of fact, I have. A bloke was bothering my girlfriend so I tore into him, made him think around his behavior, and warned him off."

"Oh, so she's your girlfriend now, is she? Does she know you're calling her that out in public or are you just hoping it's the case?"

"Well, put it this way, me and her have decided to have kids together, so if you think around that you would have to say it was pretty serious, wouldn't you?"

"Fair enough. Are you injured anywhere? You look a bit sullied."

"I've got a bit of a sore head, but I've chewed on some willow bark. It works like aspirin—I'll be right as rain when it kicks in. So, why are you digging that dongle up? What's your plan?"

"I'm going to hand the dongle over to the people that want it and be rid of the whole business."

"And where does that girl fit into this calculation? Because I know you will have thought around that."

"You're right, and one of the reasons I didn't want to hand it to the authorities was because it implicated her. I've dealt with that. If I hand it to McCoy, my guess is she will be safe. I thought before today that Peterson and McCoy had bought the line that I had lost the dongle, but they haven't and they know I've hidden it."

"How do they know that?"

"Maybe they've been watching me."

"If that was the case, they would have dug it up themselves. Have you told anyone else? That batty woman you hang around with, for example. She seems a bit tricky to me."

"No, I've only told Emily, but she's on my side. She wouldn't put me in the shit."

"Oh, is that right? Funny that she should leave the flat without any explanation or even a light farewell. You might want to think around whether you're being played here, mate. Maybe she was just sticking around long enough to complete her assignment."

I thought about the phone call that Peterson was having just before my interview with him. The image of Emily phoning McCoy and then McCoy alerting Peterson seemed to fit the moment. Fuck, I'd been played, and worse than that, it was by Emily, the lady that I adored.

"You need to give them the dongle. It's the only way to find out what her true intentions are. Maybe she will stick around, maybe you will never see her again. Best find out either way and cleanse your worrying."

"Should I take it with me now?"

"Take it into the lion's den? I don't think so, mate. You need to hand it over on your own terms, out in the open and after getting some reassurances about your future involvement."

"Yeah, you're right," I said as I pushed the dongle back into its muddy purse.

"Anyway, it was nice talking to you. Got to get back to the wife."

"Oh, 'wife' is it now?"

"Don't tell her I said that."

And he was gone.

I got in my car and drove to Camberwell Green, and this is where you joined me at the beginning of my story, stuck at a zebra crossing, waiting for some bloke to retrieve his spilled onions that are strewn across the road. No Emily and no friends to speak of apart from Grace. Life does indeed feel shit. I am both scared and exhausted by the whole affair. Hopefully my meeting with McCoy will be the beginning of the end.

I park up in the loading bay a few yards from the entrance to Cityside Investigations. I give my name to Sophie via the intercom and am buzzed straight inside. I'm greeted by McCoy at the top of the stairs and follow him through to his office. Emily is nowhere to be seen. DI Peterson is already seated in the office at the end of McCoy's desk, examining McCoy's gun as he speaks.

"Hello again, Gary, I'm glad you've come. We need to move things on a bit more quickly. I'm sure you're as tired of all this as we are and hopefully it's dawned on you that you have more to lose than we do. Have a seat," says Peterson, clearly enjoying the moment.

I sit down and notice that a sweat hasn't arrived. I'm feeling strangely numb. I think it's the idea of Emily's betrayal that has made me feel this way. I ever so slightly don't give a fuck.

"Gary," says McCoy as he sits down and fixes the stare of his watery eyes directly on me. "Can we stop fucking about with each other? Where is the dongle? Tell me now or things might start to get drastic."

"Where's Emily?" I ask, my voice lacking any emotion even before the words leave my mouth.

"She's with Tommy, or at least she was last thing I heard. That's of no importance to me, though. Just tell me where the dongle is."

"Was it Emily who told you I had hidden the dongle?"

McCoy glances over to Peterson, and it's Peterson who answers:

"No comment."

"Is she working for you still?" I inquire.

"No comment," says McCoy. "Except perhaps to say that she has been very useful to our cause so maybe you should think more about handing over the dongle and less about that little floozy."

I'm crestfallen, and it must show on my face. McCoy's expression changes to one of pity and then pleasure at my anguish. There must have still been a tiny sliver inside me that believed Emily was genuine. I thought I could make her like me, but she played the better game.

"I'm happy to hand it over, but there is something I want in return," I blurt, as if to suggest I still have some room for negotiation.

"And what might that be?" asks McCoy with a degree of impatience and scorn.

"Wayne Moore's dad. I want the charges against him dropped, and I'm trying to think of some demand I could make that would mean you never bother him again, but to be honest, knowing the way you operate, I'm struggling."

"I can get his charges dropped with just one phone call to the forensics lab," announces Peterson. "My bloke there will provide a lab report confirming that the substance found in his car was not cocaine or any other controlled drug."

"Well, I would like you to do that now, please."

McCoy gives Peterson the nod and he leaves the office, hopefully to attend to obtaining the report.

"I've got a bone to pick with you, Gary," says McCoy. "I've got a new client called Mr. Holdsworth. Do you know him?"

"No, I don't think so. Should I?"

"What if I told you his neighbor is Albanian and that, according to Holdsworth, this neighbor likes to fanny about in Holdsworth's attic of an evening?"

"No, that still doesn't ring a bell."

"Come off it, Gary. You sent him here as what I would call an act of petty revenge, just to fuck about with my office. Do you realize that he is here every day when we arrive and that he's already lodged complaints against us with the local fucking MP. Worse than that, he's had the local coppers on to us claiming that Tommy assaulted him when he was being forcibly removed from the premises. Now, thankfully, DI Peterson should be able to look after that for us, but if it seems that I am not giving you the fairest of treatment here, Gary, then you can put that partially down to you gifting us the menace that is Mr. Henry fucking Holdsworth."

I'm pleased that I have caused McCoy some inconvenience, but that's tempered by the knowledge that McCoy and Peterson are fully in control of my destiny. I look at the glass-fronted display cabinet behind McCoy's head and notice a strange collection of seemingly unrelated items on display. There are beer glasses, ashtrays, two or three opened packs of cigarettes, a walking stick handle, three paper coffee cups and two china teacups, a door handle, various items of cutlery, a glue gun, a parking ticket, and lots of other similar tat.

"What's with the stuff in the cabinet? Do you collect tat or something?" I inquire.

"That is not tat, son. That is memorabilia from some of the

more interesting cases we've worked on—little golden nuggets my people have gathered for lifting fingerprint and DNA samples. We do a lot of evidence-gathering for our friend DI Peterson, and it's a lot easier for us to obtain it illegally than it is for the police to go through all the official channels. Mainly, though, it's just for identification."

"Does Peterson use it to frame people and bribe witnesses, that sort of thing?"

"No comment."

I remember my first meeting with Emily at the Grove Tavern, when I was the person under surveillance. She had made quite a fuss of returning my plate and cutlery to the bar. I also recall a detail from Brendan's document stating that Tommy had taken a wineglass from the bloke involved in the honeypot sting. The penny drops, and some verve returns to my outlook.

"I want my knife back."

"What knife might that be, Gary?"

"The one that Rowlett showed me at the police station, the one that Emily stole from me at the Grove Tavern. It's a steak knife. Oh fuck, are you trying to link me up with Brendan's murder? If you don't give me that knife, then fuck you, I'm taking the dongle to the press, Scotland Yard—I don't know, I'll take it everywhere."

"Calm down, Gary, just sit tight. I'll go and see how DI Peterson is getting on."

McCoy gets up and leaves the room, then locks the door behind him. I get up off my chair and pace the room, then check the cabinet for the knife. I even examine the window to see if it would be safe to jump out. I hear the door unlock, and in come McCoy and Peterson. I pick the gun up from the desk and point it at them.

"Give me the knife!" I demand.

"You going to shoot us, Gary?" says McCoy.

"No, I am fucking not, but I'm shitting myself and I'm out of my depth and give me the fucking knife!"

"Put the gun down, Gary," says DI Peterson, sounding like a genuine and concerned copper. "I'm sure we can come to some arrangement regarding the knife."

It's a chink of light, and so I lower the gun.

"What arrangement? Tell me what I have to do. Come on! I'm just a shitty little bloke. Why are you doing this to me?"

"You're not so little, Gary," says McCoy. "I'm average height and you're only a couple of inches shorter than me."

Peterson places a piece of eight-and-a-half-by-eleven paper on the table for me to read. I pick it up without letting go of the gun. It's a copy of a report from the Metropolitan Police forensics lab stating that in the case of *R v Moore* the sample submitted for analysis had tested negative for controlled substances. I've seen many of these reports before, and it seems legitimate. I grab hold of it and crush it into my jacket pocket.

"Thank you," I say, "but right now I'm more concerned with making an arrangement about the knife. I promise you that if I don't get it, then you will never get the dongle. Have you entered the knife into evidence yet?"

"No we haven't," says Peterson. "The photograph we showed you was just of the type and model of knife that we believe was used to slit Brendan's throat. We are pretty sure about that—it has a very unusual shape to the blade."

"And you just happen to have that exact knife with my fingerprints on it?" I raise the gun back up and point it directly at McCoy. "Give it to me."

"Or what?" McCoy grins.

"I don't know, but I'm losing it here, so who does fucking know? Not me for sure and I'm holding a gun."

McCoy walks behind his desk and sits down. "We'll give you the knife, son, as soon as we have the dongle. Let's just call it a fair exchange and we can do it at a location and a time of your choosing. How does that sound?"

"It sounds great, but I don't trust you. Let's do it this afternoon, at the play area in front of my block of flats where we spoke before. I'll give you a ring when I'm ready."

"Perfect," says McCoy.

"And is that the end of it? Does it all end there? Will you leave me alone?" I plead.

"Absolutely," they both reply in unison.

"As long as everything goes smoothly," adds McCoy. "Now give me the gun, Gary, and let's put it somewhere safe."

"No chance. I'm taking it with me," I reply. "You can have it back when I feel safe again."

"You wouldn't want a copper stopping you in your car and finding a firearm in there, would you, Gary? Because it can easily be arranged," Peterson says sarcastically, but maybe with a hint of irony—it is difficult to read him.

"No, I wouldn't, but I'll take a chance on that. I'll phone you up with a time and place for the handover as soon as I've fetched the dongle."

I usher Peterson away from the door and back out of the room before placing the gun in my jacket pocket and striding out of the offices. I can hear Peterson and McCoy laughing loudly at something that I assume is not funny. Some people do that a lot, and they are usually wankers.

When I open the door to the street, I'm met by Mr. Clown Shoes. Henry fucking Holdsworth. He is stood by the intercom, gurning into the camera lens. I hold the door open for him and gesture for him to enter.

"I think they are expecting you," I say as he strides up the stairs, his clown shoes squeaking at every step.

26

I DRIVE BACK INTO my estate and notice my squirrel mate and his girlfriend chasing each other round and round the trunk of one of the large beech trees. He doesn't notice me.

I call in on Grace, who is now fully awake and seems refreshed. We sit outside together on the walkway and have yet another cup of tea.

"Did you find her, then?" Grace asks.

"No, I think she's another girl who has up and left me for a better life."

"Ah well, never mind, plenty more chairs in the library. She was a lovely girl, though."

"Thanks, Grace, that really helps, but she wasn't as nice as you might think. She had a way of drawing you in, but it was for her own ends—nothing to do with affection or love or anything."

"Bit like you then, Gary."

"I suppose. Fair point. But I do want to confirm that I am sad about my loss and expect you to treat me like a prince in the coming weeks."

"I always do."

"Are you all ready for your operation tomorrow?"

"I've canceled it."

"Oh fucking hell, Grace, what did you do that for?"

"I'm not ready for it just yet. I got scared, scared that I wouldn't wake up, scared that it wouldn't work and I would be in pain for the rest of my life. I mean, I do all right as I am and we've got a pretty good thing going looking after each other, don't you think?"

"Well, yeah, I do most of the heavy lifting, but I reckon you're right."

"Can I ask you, Gary, when you first met me, did you want me to like you?"

"Definitely not. I thought you were a grumpy old bag."

"There you go, then. Maybe that's a lesson to be learned for you."

Back in my flat, I lie on my bed and try to think through my plan for handing over the dongle and returning the gun.

The only downside to handing over the dongle is the obvious one that McCoy and Peterson and their cohorts will remain free to operate. For better or worse, I have already decided that is not my primary concern. Truth is, even if I handed it over to the authorities, that would still be a million miles from actually nailing them, and what would the consequences be for me? There has to be a chance that I would suffer the same fate as Brendan. I am going to give them the dongle. It hurts me slightly that Emily will never suffer any consequences, but it's time to let that lady lie.

Whatever happens, I have to get that knife back. I'm unsure how they could ever use it to tie me in with Brendan's murder, but if I destroy it then the possibility disappears. Giving them the dongle is my only chance. So long as they have that knife, my life will remain an ocean of shit. As long as I have the gun to protect me, I feel safe that they won't simply overpower me and take the dongle when we meet.

It's time to make the phone call. I arrange to meet them in thirty minutes by the plinth where the seesaw used to be.

I put on my baby-blue hoodie sweatshirt, hoping it might give me a defiant, even intimidating air at the meeting. Unfortunately, when I check in the mirror, I look like a cupcake with a face. I decide to stick with my shitty suit but wear my training shoes in the hope that they might speed up my exit if I have to do a runner. I wash my face twice, then go into the kitchen to make a cup of tea. I'm out of milk so just throw the brew down the sink. I go back to the bathroom and trim the hair from my ears with my electric razor. The mirror is tainted with old water splashes and mystery blobs, so I breathe heavily on it and clean it as best I can with some toilet roll. My trainers feel a bit tight around the tops of my feet, so I retie them using a double for added security. I run through to the kitchen to assess their comfort and open the fridge door to examine the contents.

There's a Babybel cheese, a half-eaten tin of peaches that I had got in for Grace, a large half tomato, a sachet of chili sauce, a tub of margarine, a jar of peanut butter, and one of the almond croissants I bought for Emily. The croissant makes me sad, so I throw it in the bin and start to make a cheese, peanut butter, and chilli sauce sandwich. I have only the crust left from a sliced loaf, so I lay it on the surface and carefully cut off the crust side. I get my angles wrong and end up with a wedge of bread that is paper-thin at one end. When I open the Babybel, it has two blue spots of mold on it, so I abandon the sandwich and retrieve the croissant from the bin. One bite of it reveals that my mouth is too dry to achieve a successful chew, and so I spit it out into the bin and go back into the bathroom. I need a movement. Sadly I have used the last of the toilet roll to clean the mirror and so have to clean myself up in the sink.

Calm down, I tell myself as I walk back into the lounge and slump on the sofa. Within seconds I'm rubbing furiously at my thighs and my back has become clammy with sweat. I stand up and take off my jacket, then sit down again and take my training shoes off. I stretch out my legs and notice that one of my socks has a hole in the toe. I have a fresh pair drying outside on the wall of the walkway so step outside and fetch them. I take the opportunity to assess the situation in the play area. There's no one around, and the only activity I notice is Boiler Suit Man talking into his phone by the side of his van. He spots me looking his way and gives me a thumbs-up sign as he points to his lower back. He's clearly well pleased with the nettle treatment. I knew I was onto something with that theory and promise myself I will also tell him about the pain-reducing abilities of willow bark if I ever get the chance.

Back in the flat, I put on the fresh socks and step back into my trainers. They feel just right; a fresh sock can have that effect. I go back through to the bathroom and wash my face again, then into the bedroom, where I straighten out my duvet and plump up my pillows. I take note of a tea or beer stain on the floorboards next to the mattress that is exactly the shape of Italy. I need a drink so go back through to the kitchen and down a pint of water in one. I shake the last dregs into the sink and place the glass upside down on the draining board. I check the time on my phone; there are still twenty minutes to go. I scroll onto my music app and select "Keep on Movin'." I jiggle around like a dad at a barbecue as it plays.

> *So get on up when you're down*
> *Baby, take a good look around*
> *I know it's not much but it's okay*
> *We'll keep on movin' on anyway*

It doesn't have the same effect as when I played it in the car with Emily. In fact, it brings me no joy at all. I turn it off and leave the flat.

The play area is still empty as I sit down on the plinth and survey my surroundings. I can feel the weight of the gun in my pocket tugging on the shoulder of my suit. The sun is shining and I can hear the sound of the traffic on Peckham High Street and kids shouting and screaming in the nearby park. From one of the flats beyond the play area I can hear the strains of Bob Marley's "No Woman, No Cry." I sit on my hands while rocking back and forth and pray that the dongle exchange will release me from this torture.

They arrive in two cars, Tommy's red BMW and a small silver Japanese hatchback. Both cars park up on the grass verge of the play area. Tommy revs his car engine hard after it comes to a standstill to alert me to their presence. Peterson and McCoy emerge from the silver hatchback, and the three of them walk slowly towards me. I notice as they approach that both Tommy and McCoy are significantly bowlegged, and it gives the moment a bit of a country-and-western vibe. I stand up to greet them and place my hand in my jacket pocket to indicate that I am armed and a potential safety risk. Tommy does the same with the pocket of his brown suede bomber jacket. McCoy is the first to speak:

"How appropriate to be meeting a little prick like you in a children's playground, Gary. Have you had a go on the swings, or do you need one of your parents present before you'll risk it?"

"Is that a remark?" I inquire.

"Just hand over the dongle," says Peterson.

"I'll hand it over as soon as I have the knife."

Tommy reaches into his pocket, so I immediately reach into mine and hold the gun pointed directly at him. Tommy withdraws his hand and barks at me:

"HEY, CALM DOWN, LAD, HA HA HA. THE KNIFE IS IN MY POCKET, DO YOU WANT IT OR NOT?"

"Bring it out dead slow. I mean really slowly, like it could bite you or something. I'm pretty jumpy here so hurry up but keep it slow," I reply.

Tommy laughs at me, then does as I have requested. Little by little the plastic tube emerges from his pocket. He holds the tube towards McCoy in his closed hand.

"SHALL I GIVE IT TO HIM, BOSS? WHAT DO YOU WANT ME TO DO? I COULD JUST RIP HIS HEAD OFF IF YOU'D PREFER?"

"Just give it to him," replies McCoy. "To be honest, I'm sick of the sight of him. The sooner this is done the better."

Tommy tosses the plastic tube, and it lands at my feet. I bend down and pick it up to examine its contents. It is definitely the knife from the Grove Tavern, complete with the little chunk of wood missing from the handle. Things seem to be going well. Then Lassoo appears at my feet and proceeds to sniff everyone's legs in turn.

"Hi, Gary."

It's Grace waddling her way over to us.

"Sorry, but Lassoo needed to go. Hope you don't mind me joining you?"

I guess that this is my situation to handle, so I reply: "No, not at all, Grace, just having a meeting with these clients. They are interested in developing some houses on the play area."

"But where is my Lassoo going to do his dirts? You know fine well this is his favorite spot."

"Hello, darling," says McCoy. "Lovely to see you again. You remember I helped you search your flat for the dongle that you misplaced?"

"Yes, I do, and I also remember Gary telling me you were a nasty bit of work and an arsehole to boot. You're not trying to buy this land; you're up to something dodgy. Do you want me to phone the police, Gary?"

Peterson removes his police badge from his inside pocket and displays it towards Grace.

"No need to do that, love, I'm a police officer and I would ask you to leave us now as we are on official business."

"Do you want me to leave, Gary?"

"Yes, I'm fine, Grace. Just one thing, though: could you take this knife and tube back to your flat and clean them with bleach, Brillo pads, nail varnish remover—anything you can get your hands on."

Grace looks at me suspiciously, then turns towards Peterson:

"Show me that badge again."

He obliges.

"And are you okay with me cleaning up that knife?" she asks of Peterson.

"Absolutely fine. It's nothing to do with any ongoing inquiries, so if you could toddle off now that would be great."

"I'll get that done, then, Gary. I've got some window cleaner with ammonia in it—that should do the trick. And remember the best advice is to keep your trap shut when dealing with the police."

I give Grace the tube, and she slowly makes her way back across the grass to her flat. I half expect Tommy to chase her and retrieve the knife, but he doesn't. Lassoo stays with us and sits down at my feet. He looks up at me with an expression that suggests, *Don't worry, kid, I'll look after you.*

"Come on, Gary, let's be having the dongle," says McCoy.

I hesitate. There are a few things I want to clear up before handing it over.

"Have you dropped all charges against Wayne and Derek Moore?"

"It's all in hand, Gary," says Peterson. "We were never going to see it through anyway. It was all just a gentle reminder to his family to behave themselves."

"You've ruined his life, you know."

"And he wanted to ruin ours, Gary, so that's not nice, is it?" replies Peterson. "Hand it over, or shall I ask Tommy to come over and take it off you?"

"I haven't got it on me so I wouldn't bother. It's nearby, though, so don't get a panic on. Listen, before I tell you where it is, I want to know how you lot found out that I had the dongle and that I had chosen to hide it."

McCoy takes a step forward.

"How do *you* think we found out, Gary?"

"I think you planted Emily into my life to keep an eye on me and she told you."

"That's not quite right, Gary," McCoy begins. "She definitely helped us, but she didn't know that she had. Do you remember when we left Tommy in your flat to search for the dongle? Well, while he was in there, he took the opportunity to put simple listening devices in the plug sockets in your lounge and bedroom. We could hear everything you said to Emily, and like the wanker that you are you let your mouth run off. Dongle blah blah blah . . . password blah blah blah. It's our job, Gary, to listen to people when they don't want us to. Don't be upset; you're far from the first to suffer. You in love with her or something?"

I look at Tommy; he has an inane, unsettling grin on his face.

"Where is she now, Tommy?" I ask.

"Somewhere safe. Somewhere she can't cause any trouble. I doubt very much you will ever be seeing her again. You need to REMOVE HER FROM YOUR FUCKING THOUGHTS," he replies.

"Are you and her still together?"

"No, and I can't see her being with anyone ever again, especially not you," replies Tommy.

"Are you going to beat me up?"

"Yes, very badly, but I'll wait till the dust has settled and you will never know where and you will never know when, just like your mate's dad, Derek Moore."

"Is she safe?" I ask.

"That depends on this transaction," says McCoy. "Let's

just say that she is our security should you try to serve us up a wobble. Hand it over, Gary, and don't forget the password."

I put the gun back in my pocket and text the novelty sock shop number to McCoy. I point to the edge of the plinth where the seesaw used to be and indicate exactly where the dongle is buried. Tommy steps forward and gets down on his knees to pick out the dongle from its hidey-hole.

As he pokes his fingers around to locate it, I notice that the soles of his work boots are covered with what looks like confetti. The stupid thought that he has forced Emily to marry him crosses my mind. McCoy and Peterson as bridesmaids and Emily in tears as the ring is forced onto her finger. Stupid thought.

Tommy raises himself up off the grass with the dongle in his hand. "Take it back to the office," instructs McCoy. "Check that it's legit."

Tommy gives me another grin.

"SEE YOU SOON, LAD. I'M LOOKING FORWARD TO IT. HA HA HA." I watch as Tommy goes back to his car and drives away from the estate.

"Thank you," says McCoy. "I hope for Emily's sake that it's the genuine article. Listen, you've done the right thing and, provided we never hear from you again, and you don't ever mention these events to anyone, you will be left in peace. You might get a kicking from Tommy, but you'll survive, I'll make sure of that."

"Do you not want your gun?"

"Oh, yeah. You feel safe now, do you?"

"Well, Grace is on the walkway up there watching us, so I don't think you'll do anything daft."

I look up to the walkway to see Grace waving at me and giving the *"zip your mouth"* motion across her lips with her fingers before stepping back into her flat and shutting the door.

"She'd be better for you," says Peterson. "You need a mum not a girlfriend."

I hand the gun to McCoy, and he immediately raises it and points it straight at my face. Shit.

27

EMILY

IT'S DARK, IT'S DAMP, and my feet are freezing. I'm sure that before long my toes will fall off. I'm sat on a concrete floor in a room that measures about twelve feet by ten. The walls are brick, and the only door is a thick metal panel without any handle. There is a bucket by the door that I assume I am meant to use as a toilet. My arse is proving troublesome; it seems to absorb the cold from the concrete floor like a sponge. The chill revolves around my buttocks and then intermittently shoots up either side of my spine. I wish I wasn't wearing the green cotton trouser suit that Grace gave me. The only warmth it gives is on the shoulders, where it is heavily padded. There is a tap mounted on one wall, and in one corner is a plastic crate filled with sweet and savory snack bars. A draft occasionally wafts into the room through a vent high up on the wall opposite me. A few shards of light shine through the vent, but not enough to dissolve the darkness. If I had to guess, I would say I am in the basement of an empty detached Victorian house. I never sense any movement above, below, or to either side of me. During the day I hear the constant rumble of traffic and the occasional police siren. Every now and then I shout at the top of my voice for someone to help me. They never come. This is no way to treat a lady.

Tommy brought me here about four hours ago. He grabbed me at Gary's flat. I thought it was Grace knocking on the door or Gary returning early from the police station, but no, it was Tommy, and he was quietly furious. He instructed me to collect up my stuff and leave the flat with him. At first I refused, but there was that familiar dead look to his eyes that meant there would be dire consequences if I failed to comply.

"This is the second time you have done this to me. I made the mistake of forgiving you the first time," he said in a calm and measured tone. "But I guarantee it won't ever happen again."

"What are you going to do? Kidnap me and lock me away until I beg for you to take me back?" I asked.

"Yeah, something like that, but I won't ever be taking you back. Just get your stuff together and let's go."

Tommy leered over me from the bedroom entrance as I packed up my rucksack.

"Where did you get that awful suit?" he asked.

"The nice lady next door gave it to me," I replied.

"What, so you're a beggar now, are you? It makes you look fake and unremarkable. You are unremarkable. I fucking hate you."

I put my copy of *The Clementine Complex* in my messenger bag, thinking that a book might provide some comfort as events unfolded.

He drove me to this place without saying another word. I wasn't particularly scared or anxious. I'd seen him in these dark moods many times before; they usually only lasted a couple of days or occasionally a couple of weeks. I had made my choice and was going to stick with it. I supposed this was Tommy's way of processing the breakup. I owed him the right to see that through. The journey lasted around twenty minutes, and throughout it Tommy made me lie across the back seats with a jacket over my face.

If I had to guess, I would say I'm somewhere near Blackheath, or Lewisham, or maybe Sydenham. I didn't get the sense that we had crossed to north of the river. When we arrived, he put a bobble hat on my head and pulled it right down to below my mouth. Through the holes in the weave of the hat I could tell that we walked around to the back of the house and went through two doors before descending some concrete steps down into the basement.

"Take the hat off," instructed Tommy. I could hardly see him in the darkness. "This is your new home. I hope you like it. Hope you find the time to think about what you've done and what the consequences might be for you."

"Listen, Tommy, I'm sorry, really sorry, but—"

"Oh shut the fuck up, princess, and let me tell you, whatever happens to you will be nothing to what happens to that wanker you've shacked up with. That, my darling, is a promise." With that, he turned away and slammed the metal-faced door behind him.

It's strange where your mind takes you in a situation like this. The first thing it compelled me to do was pace out the room and measure its size. Then I walked around the entire room, rubbing my hands against the brickwork to see if I could find any feature or detail that might allow me a better mental picture of the basement. The walls were damp to the touch and occasionally, as I felt my way, little lumps of mortar or plaster would drop onto the floor. I picked up the bucket and had a good smell of its plastic surfaces. I turned the bucket upside down and climbed on top of it to see if I could inspect the air vent, but it was just beyond my reach. I crawled up the concrete steps to the door to the rest of the house. It was locked solid and definitely impossible for me to open. I couldn't locate a handle or a keyhole. I turned on the tap and lowered my mouth to take a gulp of water; it was cold at first but then ran slightly lukewarm. It tasted metallic, and the taste seemed to cling to the walls of my mouth and my tongue. I opened a snack bar and took a bite. I think it involved oats and blueberries, but the overall sensation was of eating a square of damp and abandoned plasterboard.

Then I couldn't think of anything else to do, so I put the bobble hat back on and sat down on the concrete floor. My arse bones started to panic almost immediately. My problem was that I had left the flat wearing a pair of stiletto-heeled shoes that Grace had given me to go with the trouser suit. My DMs were in my rucksack, which was still in Tommy's car. How I wished I had them now. My feet were freezing and aching due to the stilettos, but if I sat on the concrete, within minutes my arse would cry out for relief. My compromise was to alternate between sitting and standing, with my feet forced deeply inside the bobble hat at all times.

I've tried to second-guess Tommy's intentions. Maybe this is just a simple punishment, and I will have to suffer it here for some hours or maybe at worst a night or two. Maybe it is just a move in this business with the dongle. They hold me here in the hope it will persuade Gary to hand it over. This scenario doesn't worry me unduly, as I'm certain Gary will hand it over to McCoy, and I will be of no further use to them. Worst-case scenario is that Tommy wants me to rot to death here in this basement as his final revenge. I dismiss this pretty quickly. Tommy is still in love with me, and his end goal is to have me back by his side and at his beck and call. I will just have to wait and see. At least I'm still moving forward. Not necessarily happy, but living my own life. Then I hear a loud banging on the back door of the house.

28

"WHAT ARE YOU DOING?" I plead as I find myself staring down
the barrel of McCoy's gun. I instinctively place my hands out
in front of my face hoping they might absorb the bullet and
just leave me with shit hands.

"I'm going to shoot you, Gary, as a thank-you for giving
me the dongle and sending Henry fucking Holdsworth into
my life. You ready?"

I try to answer him, but not a single word will come out
of my mouth. For a brief moment the image of Emily's face
staring up at me before our kiss on the promenade bench
comes into my mind. My legs then turn to jelly, and I fall to
the floor. McCoy adjusts the angle of his arm so that the gun
is still pointing directly at my forehead. I feel sick with nausea
and still can't find the switch in my brain that would allow
me to speak.

"Cheerio, Gary," Peterson says. "Don't worry about your
lady friend. We've got plans for her."

McCoy pulls the trigger.

I shut my eyes tight and utter, "I love you, Mum," despite
the fact she has been dead for many years.

In the darkness I hear the tune to "Happy Birthday" and the

sound of Lassoo barking just a few feet in front of me. I open my eyes. McCoy is still pointing the gun at me, but I haven't heard a shot fired and I'm not aware of any injury. McCoy and Peterson are laughing at me, and from his demeanor I think Lassoo is in on the joke. Then I realize that the tune is coming from the revolver in McCoy's hand. It's some sort of replica item intended for practical jokes or as a laughter generator at an office party. I find the ability to speak again.

"Fucking hell, McCoy. I mean, what the fuck? Was that meant to be funny? Jesus, what's the matter with you?"

And then it all goes hot banana apeshit.

From just beyond the play area, I hear two or three men bellow: "PUT THE GUN DOWN! PUT IT DOWN AND GET ON THE FLOOR!"

I turn my head to see Boiler Suit Man and two armed police officers running towards us.

"PUT THE GUN DOWN AND GET ON THE GROUND!" they repeat.

McCoy tosses the gun away and slowly gets down on his knees. Peterson stands stock-still and simply places his hands up in the air. I turn over flat onto my stomach and force myself as far into the ground as I can. Lassoo runs over to the gun, which is still churning out the "Happy Birthday" tune and barks at it as if it is the key to his wildest dreams.

Boiler Suit Man kicks me on my side and tells me to get up. I pull myself off the ground as Peterson and McCoy are being handcuffed by the two armed officers. Peterson calmly declares: "I'm DI Peterson from the Lewisham Serious Crimes Squad. This is an ongoing inquiry that you are placing in jeopardy."

"You're not a police officer," announces Boiler Suit Man. "You're a fucking disgrace, that's what you are."

One of the armed officers reads them both their rights. Peterson looks deflated, but McCoy remains defiant as he addresses Boiler Suit Man. "You've screwed up here, son. This is going to cost you your job."

I turn to Boiler Suit Man. "Ask him if that's a remark," I suggest.

He seems amused by the idea. "Is that a remark, McCoy?"

"No, it's a promise," he replies.

A couple of marked police cars arrive in the side road and the armed officers lead Peterson and McCoy away from the play area towards them. I hold my hands out in front of me in the expectation of being handcuffed.

"No need for that, Gary," says Boiler Suit Man. "I know we've met before, but I've never properly introduced myself. I'm DS Marks from the anti-corruption unit at Scotland Yard. We've been investigating Peterson's squad and McCoy for months. The death of your mate Brendan has brought the whole thing to a head. To be honest, Gary, you have been very helpful to the inquiry. We are not going to arrest you, but we trust we can rely on your total cooperation with the investigation."

"Yes, of course," I reply.

"Good lad, then tell me: Where is the fucking dongle?"

"Jesus, you lot as well. How do you know about it?"

"We've been listening in on McCoy's office for the last six months. That's what we do: we listen in on people. We very nearly came in heavy-handed during your last meeting at his office, but you managed to get yourself out of there in one piece so we decided to wait and see how it played out. I'm glad we did. So, the dongle, Gary, where is it?"

"I thought you would have seen. They gave it to Tommy to take back to the office."

DS Marks takes a police radio out of his jacket pocket and passes on this information to his colleagues.

"Listen, Gary, why don't you go back to your flat and rest up? We will need to talk to you at length, but that can wait until tomorrow. Go on, fuck off, and take that dog with you."

"So I'm free to go?"

"For the time being."

"How's your back holding up?"

"It's not too bad thanks to you. I use the nettles whenever it plays up and it seems to do the trick."

I think about recommending that he chew on some willow bark to help with the pain from the nettle rash but decide against it. All of a sudden I really want Boiler Suit Man to like me. I walk back to the flat, still shocked by the events but slightly elated that it might all be panning out in my favor. When Marks and his crew get hold of the dongle, that will be the end for McCoy, Tommy, and Peterson. I will have nothing to fear.

Grace greets me on the walkway outside her flat. She has been watching the events unfold.

"That all looked very exciting. I couldn't really tell what was going on. Are you okay? Did you keep your trap shut?"

"I don't think that will be necessary now. They were the proper coppers and I reckon they're on my side. They seem to know that I am just a circumstantial prick."

"They're right about that. Oh, sorry, Gary, I haven't cleaned the knife up yet. Shall I do it now?"

"There's no need. The police know it's something that McCoy's lot were using as a potential plant. I expect the police will want it, and I'm going to do everything by the book from now on. Do you mind if I go and have a lie-down? I need to think this all through and untangle my mind."

"Maybe you should have a bath and a mug of hot Bovril. Liquid beef is a powerful pick-me-up."

"No, I think I'll save up a bath and a Bovril for when my spirits have lifted and are no longer bent towards the desperate."

Back in my flat, I immediately take the cover off the plug socket in my living room to check for a listening device. I don't know exactly what I'm meant to be looking for, but as soon as I remove the cover it's apparent that this is not a standard household socket. There is an incongruous little electronic unit with a SIM card slot and a very advanced-looking attitude inside. McCoy had been telling the truth; Emily was not knowingly working for them.

I need to see her and ask forgiveness for my grubby suspicions. I want to make sure she's safe. I have to find her. My first thought is that she will either be at McCoy's office or Tommy's flat in Walworth. I pick up my car keys and run out of the flat, down the stairwell, and over to the parking bays. DS Marks is nowhere to be seen, but his mobile mechanic's van is still parked up. I drive myself straight over to Emily's flat on the Grange estate. There is no sign of Tommy's BMW, so I chance it and climb the stairwell to the front door of her flat. I bang on the door and shout her name through the letterbox, but there is no response. I go back down to my car and rest my back against its hood, hoping to come up with a better idea of where she might be. A squirrel appears under the cherry tree next to the car and sits up on its hind legs to have a chat.

"Whoa, look at you, mate, all confused and agitated. You got a dilemma that needs attention?" I ask on his behalf.

"Yeah, a big one as it happens. I think Tommy's taken my girlfriend and is holding her somewhere against her will."

" 'Girlfriend,' is it? Is that official or just a fantasy?"

"You're right to ask. It's nothing official, at least for the time being."

"Against her will, you say? Have you thought around whether she is quite happy enough to be where she is?"

"Well, from what's been said to me it sounds like she's somewhere she doesn't want to be. That's my dilemma; I won't know either way until I find her."

"Why don't you leave it to the police? Let them do the legwork. Have you thought around how much more suited to the job they are than you?"

"Yes, and they might even have her already, but that doesn't mean I shouldn't try. I can't really rest until I know."

"I think you need to get more motivated about resting up, mate, let things take their natural course. Have you thought around the fact that most of the moves you make tend to work out towards the shit?"

"Yeah, I know, but there must be something I can do?"

"What makes you come to that conclusion? *We* all know you're a hopeless shortarse, so why can't *you* see that?"

"That's a bit harsh. Can I ask you something?"

"I can't stop you asking, if you think around our relationship here. You're the one pulling the levers."

"Okay, so tell me: Why do people feel so free to have a go at me and treat me like a soft touch?"

"Simple. It's because you are so desperate for people to like you, it's written all over your face and permeates your whole outlook. They know there will be no comeback on them; you will soak it up like a sponge. You should think around not getting all tarty about it. It's your choice; you're the one to blame, and if it's not working out for you, have a think about growing up."

At that moment the squirrel drops his front paws onto the ground then raises them up again to resume his cute hind-legs stance. I notice a couple of pieces of cherry blossom have stuck to his front paws as he rubs them off against his cheeks. They look like pieces of confetti, and with that thought, I instantly guess where they are hiding Emily.

"I think I know where she is," I exclaim.

"Well, tell the police, you big-nosed clown."

"Do you want a kick in the nuts?" I ask.

"That's more like it. Good luck finding her."

I wave him goodbye, jump into my car, and head off in the direction of Sydenham. On my way through Camberwell, I notice a number of police vehicles and a little clump of interested onlookers outside the offices of Cityside Investigations. Maybe they already have Tommy and perhaps Emily, but my instinct spurs me on to continue with my incredible rescue mission.

I arrive at Brendan's house within ten minutes and enter

through the front gate. It clunks shut behind me with a metallic bang and probably puts paid to any chance of my arrival going unnoticed. There is police tape sealing the front door. I begin to wonder if Tommy would really have the bottle to take Emily here when it was so recently searched by the police and definitely part of an ongoing investigation. Then again, Brendan wasn't killed here, and the place has obviously been searched and processed. Maybe it's actually the perfect place to hide her. The path round to the back of the house is still carpeted with cherry blossoms, a good inch thick in places. The back door had also been sealed with police tape, but it has been removed and dumped on the path. I knock on it a few times with no response, and then from below me and to my left I hear a muffled female voice shouting.

"Hello! Hello! Is somebody out there?"

My stomach takes a twirl as I recognize the voice belongs to Emily.

"Hello? Emily? Is that you? Can you hear me? It's me, Gary. Are you okay?"

Her reply comes back a lot more clearly. "You've got to get me out of here, hurry up!"

I can sense that her voice is coming from the other side of a vent just above the level of the small concrete patio. I bend down onto my knees and tell her to come to the back door.

"I can't," she replies. "I'm in the fucking basement. You need to get inside and see if you can open the basement door."

"I don't have a key, Emily."

"Well, smash a window, then, or break down the fucking door."

"Are you okay? You didn't say when I asked you."

"Yes, I'm fine. I've got a bobble hat for my feet. Please, just get me out of here!"

I pick up a large terra-cotta plant pot and throw it at the back door to break the circular glass panel. The pot shatters into many pieces as it falls back onto the path, but it has made a significant crack in the glass on impact. I try to finish the job with my elbow but don't have the confidence required to use enough force to smash through. I look around the small garden for something I can use to finish the job, and my eyes set upon a tall bird feeder in front of the rear hedge. It's a tall, thin metal pole with little branches towards the top from which to hang bird food. I work it around in the ground, and the six or seven inches that are beneath the lawn soon work free. I have myself an avian-friendly spear-cum-lance, and use its pointy end to smash out the rest of the glass panel from the door. I reach my hand through and release the latch on the lock. It leads into a hallway with the kitchen to my left. I know that Emily is directly below the kitchen, but a quick check reveals there is no doorway inside that room. I carry on through the hall and see a doorway under the first flight of stairs. It's secured by a large metal bar placed between two upright metal brackets. Emily starts shouting from the other side of the door.

"I'm in here! I'm in here!"

I kick upwards on the metal bar, and it pops out of its fixings without too much resistance. I open the door and there she is, still wearing Grace's green trouser suit and still looking as magnificent as ever. She throws her arms around me and gives me an adult hug.

"Thank you, Gary, thank you *so much*. Jesus Christ, my feet are freezing."

"Who put you down there? Was it Tommy?"

"Yeah, I don't know what his plans are for me, but I think we should get out of here in case he returns."

"But you are okay, yeah?"

"Yes, of course, apart from my fucking feet."

I hug her as tightly as I think is acceptable, but not as tightly as I want to.

"I know it wasn't you," I say.

"What are you on about?"

"It wasn't you who told McCoy I had the dongle and had hidden it away."

"Why would you think that?"

"I don't know, but I did, and I was wrong and I love you."

"No, you don't."

"Yeah, well, maybe not, but you know what I mean."

"Yes, of course I do. Now come on, let's get out of here."

She leads the way down the short hallway to the back door. As we step out into the garden, we are met with the sight of Tommy walking towards us from the path to the side of the house. We are trapped; the only way out is blocked by his lumbering bulk.

"Fuck," I half whisper.

"Oh do fuck off, Tommy," shouts Emily.

"OH MY WORD, BOTH OF YOU. IT MUST BE MY LUCKY DAY, HA HA HA," he replies.

We stand staring at each other for a few moments. I sense Emily step back into the house behind me.

"Was that a remark, Tommy?" I inquire.

"Oh, a bit of talkback is it, lad? You found your bottle, have you? Fancy your chances, do you, shortarse? Ha ha ha!"

says Tommy, his face breaking into one of his lifeless smiles. I pick up the bird feeder spear from the floor.

"Tell me, Tommy, did you kill Brendan?" I ask.

"Yeah, of course I did. It's my job. What of it?" he replies as if he is talking about a pizza order.

"Why?" I ask.

"Because I was told to. Now shut the fuck up and, like I say, do you fancy your chances, short bloke?"

Emily steps back out of the back door holding the metal bar from the basement door in her hand. She answers on our behalf:

"Yes, Tommy, we do fancy our chances."

"Whenever you're ready," I add. I don't have a sweat on. My fear is way above that level. Maybe my internal organs are sweating, though, because all my insides feel like jelly.

Tommy walks slowly towards us. I direct the pointy end of my bird feeder spear towards him, and Emily raises the metal bar above her shoulder.

"McCoy and Peterson have already been arrested. The police have been watching you for months," I blurt out to Tommy. "I've told them Emily was here," I lie, "so they'll be arriving any minute, I reckon. You should just fuck off, Tommy. That's your best bet, mate."

"I disagree," he replies.

My courage is fading with every step he takes towards me. He is now only a few feet from the end of the spear. It's now or never, and sadly I can't do it. Tommy wraps one hand around the shaft of the spear and pulls it out of my hands with one great big Yorkshire tug. He then points the tip at Emily's face.

"Go and wait for me in my car out front," he instructs Emily.

"No chance," she replies as she raises the metal bar higher above her head to make her defiance even more crisp.

"Just do it, Emily," he says. "You don't want to witness what I'm going to do to this pathetic prick."

"No. Fucking. Chance," says Emily.

"Just do as you're told," says Tommy. "You know it doesn't end well when you force my hand."

"Tommy, it's over, we're finished. Just leave and find someone else's life to ruin," replies Emily, seeming perfectly calm and together.

"Well, that's just it," says Tommy. "There aren't many girls like you around anymore, these are strange times we are living through. Don't you agree, Gary?"

I can't think of an answer. He lowers the spear so its tip is resting on the lawn.

"So, my lovely Emily, is this you choosing him over me? Because I think that would be a grave mistake."

"I'll tell you what would be a grave mistake," says Emily. "If I was ever to give you so much as an inkling that I would ever take you back. I hate you, I hate your face, I hate your pockmarked bald head, I hate the way you speak, and I hate the way you treat me. You know what? I felt more fucking free sat in that basement than I ever did living with you. You sicken me, and it took meeting Gary to realize what a real fucking companion should be. I never want to see you again—EVER!"

I can see by the slight quiver in Tommy's cheek that this tirade has hurt him. I feel a sea change in the air.

"If that's what you want then that is what you shall have, my sweetheart," and with that, he raises the tip of the spear off the ground and thrusts it straight through the top of Emily's bare foot. She screams in agony and falls to the ground, the spear somehow managing to stay lodged in her foot as she lies on the lawn in agony and confusion. I immediately bend down to comfort her, but as I do so Tommy dives at me and takes me down onto my back. He then straddles my chest and pins my arms to the ground with his knees. I can hear Emily whimpering and breathing heavily over towards the back door. His large medieval face is looming above me, full of pure Yorkshire gristle and hate.

"Fucking hell, Tommy, what are you doing?" I plead.

By way of reply, he punches me full on the nose.

"Fuck off," he says, and then punches me again and again, each punch accompanied by an increasingly angry "Fuck off." I can feel blood running from my nose and down my cheeks. My lips are being mashed up, and I can taste the blood in my mouth. He stops hitting me and grips either side of my mouth with one hand so that my lips pucker up into a figure of eight. I notice that he is now holding a knife in his other hand, the tip of which is only inches from my cheek. I can't speak. Fear has once again shut me down.

"Come on, Gary. Let's have a little singsong before I finish you off," he says. I hear Emily yelp and let out an agonizing scream. "Come on, let's sing together. It's such a lovely way to say farewell," says Tommy as he begins to sing the national anthem:

"GOD SAVE OUR GRACIOUS QUEEN
"LONG LIVE OUR NOBLE QUEEN
"GOD SAVE THE QUEEN

"COME ON, GARY. SING ALONG. EVERYONE LOVES THIS BIT," commands Tommy as he releases the tight grip he has on my mouth and starts to force the tip of his knife into my neck. I stare defiantly into his eyes, silently begging him to just do whatever it is he intends. He raises the volume of his singing:

"*NA NA NA NA*
"*SEND HER VICTORIOUS!*
"*HAPPY AND GLORIOUS!*"

I see a flash of green behind him, from which Emily's face emerges, then a burst of energy from the green goddess as she brings the metal bar down on the back of his neck with all her might. He slumps forward onto me, and I feel the full weight of his bulk on my face and chest. I manage to roll him slightly and crawl out from underneath him. I stand above him on the lawn, catching my breath, not knowing whether I should try to finish him off or attend to Emily. His eyes are shut, and his chest seems to be gasping for air. Emily has fallen back to the ground, and I can see that the big gaping hole in the top of her foot is bleeding badly. I run into the kitchen, grab a tea towel, and start to tie it tightly around her foot in an attempt to stem the flow of blood. The tea towel is covered in images of brightly colored novelty socks.

"Shit, Emily. Are you okay? It looks really bad . . ."

She doesn't reply other than with a strangled whimper. I hear Tommy let out a short, sharp gasp of breath, then see him move one of his hands slowly onto his chest. I have to get her out of here before he comes round. I finish tying the knot in the tea towel and lift her up into my arms.

"Put her down," says Tommy.

I look over to where he is picking himself up off the grass. He is pointing a gun directly at me.

"Put her down," he repeats. "We don't want her getting shot by mistake, do we?"

I do as I am told and place her back on the lawn as gently as I can. The gun he is holding looks identical to the one in McCoy's office. "That's not a real gun, Tommy. Come on, let's pack this in and get an ambulance for Emily. She's hurt really badly."

"Would you rather I shot you or shot Emily? It's your choice. I couldn't give a fuck," he says in a tone that suggests he absolutely and resolutely really could not give an actual fuck. I look more closely at the gun and begin to doubt that it is the same type as the one belonging to McCoy. It seems to be bigger and has a different sheen to its surface. I could be in real danger here.

"Maybe just don't shoot anyone, Tommy?" I say.

"It's an option, but not one that I favor. Go on, if you had to choose, which of you would it be?"

"Shoot me, Tommy," I say. "Yeah, go on, shoot me and see how that turns out for you. And I tell you what, why don't you just shoot yourself straight afterwards and let Emily live her life like you've never let her?"

I hear the sounds of a police helicopter and numerous police car sirens in the near distance. I can see by Tommy's glance into the sky that this has registered with him as well.

"Thank you, Gary, that's made my mind up nicely," he says as he slowly adjusts the angle of the gun and points it directly at Emily. Emily's eyes are now wide open and trying to come to terms with the events unfolding around her.

I see Tommy's expression change and any indecision within him disappear. He tightens his grip on the trigger. I take a step and drop myself on top of Emily to shield her from any bullet. As I land on her, I hear the roar of the gun being fired twice and then silence as my brain tries to establish whether I have indeed been shot. I can't register any pain and raise myself off Emily to see if she has been hit. I glance towards Tommy to check if he is about to shoot again and see that he is lying flat on his back on the lawn. A big chunk of his face is missing from around his left eye, and his eyeball itself is hanging from its socket. He has shot himself.

I turn again to Emily as she lets out muffled yelps of pain. She is lying flat, holding her right hip. I gently move her hand to one side but can see no obvious sign of a wound. I take hold of her tan bag and pull it away from her hip. There is blood on the side that was next to her hip and a hole where the bullet has entered through the other side. There is a book inside the bag, and I can see that the bullet has passed through the book and into Emily's hip. There is very little blood, but there is no doubt that Emily has been shot.

"Lie flat on your face with your hands behind your back!"

It's an armed police officer with his gun pointing directly at me.

"Both of you! Lie flat on your face with your hands behind your back!"

I let go of Emily and do as I am told.

"She's been shot, shot in the hip. He shot her then he shot himself. You've got to help her," I shout as I feel the cold hard metal of handcuffs being placed around my wrists. I'm pulled up to my feet by my arms and find myself facing DS Marks, who has just entered the garden still wearing his boiler suit.

"What the fuck are you doing here?" he barks. "I told you to stay in your flat."

I start to cry, just from the sheer madness of the whole thing. I can hear Emily sobbing between her grumbles of pain.

"Thank you," I say to him. "Thank you so much."

I can hear the siren of an ambulance approaching.

Marks places a comforting hand on my shoulder. "Her foot looks really bad and your face is a mess," he says. "I'm sure you'll both be okay, though, just be thankful he didn't kill either of you."

A uniformed officer is kneeling down next to Tommy searching through his pockets. He holds up a small yellow dongle.

"Is this it?" he shouts over to DS Marks, who looks at me for confirmation.

"Yep, that's it," I mumble. "It's password protected, but I can give you the password—it's on my phone."

The paramedics arrive and tend to Emily. One of them confirms to DS Marks that Tommy is deceased. My cuffs are taken off, and I'm led to the ambulance, where a paramedic checks me over and starts cleaning up my face. Shortly afterwards Emily is rolled into the ambulance from a gurney, and we make our way together to the hospital. I hold her hand all the way there, and after about ten minutes her face breaks out into a half smile.

"Has anyone ever told you that you are a total shithouse?" she asks.

"Funnily enough, yes. In fact, nearly everyone I've met this past week," I reply.

Emily raises her head slightly to check that the paramedic is out of earshot and half whispers, "You know that dongle? I was just thinking, maybe my name is mentioned in it. I did help Tommy with a few jobs here and there. I could be in the shit."

"Don't worry, you're not mentioned."

"How do you know?"

"I just do. Don't you worry about it."

It is hard to know if the conversation is registering with her as she is pumped full of painkillers, but she continues: "I've been shot in the hip, haven't I? How bad is it?"

"Not half as bad as it would have been if you didn't have that book in your bag."

"What book?"

"*The Clementine Complex*. It saved your life."

She smiles again and asks: "Would you really have preferred that he shot you rather than me?"

"To be honest, I didn't think it was a real gun, so I just said that to impress you."

"I don't believe you," she replies.

She offers me up her lips for a kiss but falls asleep before I can accept.

POSTSCRIPT

SIX MONTHS OR SO after the back garden shooting, I left my final meeting with DS Marks and his team from the anti-corruption squad. I wasn't to face any charges arising from their investigations but would be called to give evidence should it be required. A total of eleven officers from various south London police stations and three members of staff from Cityside Investigations were currently on remand in prison awaiting trial for charges ranging from perverting the course of justice to conspiracy to murder. DS Marks was hopeful that McCoy and Peterson would get a minimum of twenty years each. Brendan's document had proved to be the final nail in their coffin. Emily was not among those charged. I had accompanied her to both her police interviews and ensured that she offered "no comment" to all questions. It was clear from the questions they asked that they had no knowledge of the couple of jobs she carried out on behalf of McCoy and Tommy.

To celebrate what felt like the end of this dongle nightmare, Emily suggested that myself, Grace, Lassoo, and her all take a drive to Brighton for a day by the seaside. Inevitably we ended up sat on Emily's favorite bench, looking out over the gray-blue dishwater of the English Channel. We each had an ice-cream cornet made with the draft variety of ice cream that falls out of the machine on the pull of a lever. The sun was shining, the seagulls were arguing about immigration, and the promenade smelt of hot pepper and seashell vapors. I was happy. I think we all were. Emily hadn't mentioned Tommy or the shooting in the garden for a couple of months.

"I've been speaking to my mum," she announced. "My father left the hotel to her in his will and he expressed the wish that I take over the running of it and Mum says she would be cool with that. It's either his final attempt at a reconciliation or his final punishment from beyond the grave."

"Does that appeal to you?" asked Grace. "It is very lovely down here. A lot nicer than bloody Peckham."

"Well, I do think I could make a go of the place—bring it up to date, attract some younger people, freshen the whole thing up. I've got a lot of ideas and it could be an amazing opportunity. I hardly get any pain from the operation now, and I reckon I'm ready for a challenge."

"You should do it," said Grace. "No doubt about it. Don't even dwell on it; just say yes and start a new adventure. It's like I'm always telling him, you only start living once you leave your comfort zone."

"Would you come and help me run the place?" Emily asked me. I wanted to say yes immediately, but felt it best to fake some caution:

"What about my job?" I asked.

"You hate your job," said Emily.

"You hate your job," said Grace.

"Maybe so, but it pays okay and keeps us ticking over."

"The pay is crap and it's not as if you couldn't get a job in the law down here," said Emily.

"She's right. There's a lot of law down here," said Grace. "You can feel the legal opportunities in your bones."

"Maybe, maybe not," I replied. "Even so, I don't think I could bear to leave Grace alone on that estate. We rely on each other; it just wouldn't be fair."

"Grace could move down too. She could look after the IT and update the systems," said Emily.

"Systems have to be updated, Gary, that's just a fact of life," added Grace.

"And would you want to move down here, Grace?" I asked her.

"In the blink of an eye," she replied. "Did you know that my daughter lives just a few miles away, in Lewes. Maybe you could help me to get contact with my granddaughter—oh, and I could get my hip operation done here. What a lovely place to recuperate . . ."

I was feeling slightly ambushed.

"I thought you were loving it in Peckham," I said to Emily. "Sharing the flat together, working in the coffee shop with Wayne, having a drink in the Grove, going to the markets on the weekend . . ."

"I do love it, but it's your life, Gary. I sometimes feel like I've just tagged myself onto it and am just enjoying the ride until we run out of steam," replied Emily, with a surprisingly earnest look about her face.

"That's what always happens with his girlfriends. He's admitted that to me many times," added Grace with a surprisingly self-satisfied look on her face.

"This would be for *us*, Gary, a great big daft adventure with all sorts of possibilities."

"Yeah, we could go bankrupt and end up on the streets scavenging like these seagulls."

"So what? They seem very happy," said Emily.

"Have you two been talking about this behind my back?"

"No," they both said in unison.

The conversation took a rest as we all tucked into our ice creams. There was a lot to think about for sure. Eventually, Emily broke the silence.

"Grace, are you still annoyed with me for ruining your trouser suit?"

"Don't be daft," replied Grace. "I was never upset with you." She pointed her cone at me and continued, "It was *his* fault. He should have finished that bloke off when he had the chance. He is such a shithouse."

"Isn't he, though?" added Emily.

They both laughed, and Lassoo wagged his tail so hard it seemed he was trying to propel himself into the future.

ACKNOWLEDGMENTS

Thank you to my editor, Holly Harris, for her support, invaluable feedback, and encouragement.

Thank you to my son, Harry, for designing the cover of the book. He was the first to read the initial draft and pointed out many important failings and ways to improve the story. He also willingly watched hours of football on the TV with me when I needed a break from thinking about Emily, Grace, and Gary.

Thank you to my old friend Charlie Higson, who gave me a comprehensive list of the book's failings to address. I took most of them on board. He is an effing stalwart if ever there was such a thing. Love him.

Thank you to Lisa Clark and my brother Simon, both of whom took the time to read early drafts and gave sufficient praise for me to continue with the project.

Thank you to my wife, Lisa, for her excellent systems.

Above all, thank you and farewell to my friend and confidante, Mavis, who left my lap forever just as I was finishing the book. I miss you every day.

THE CLEMENTINE COMPLEX

BOB MORTIMER

This reading group guide for The Clementine Complex includes an introduction, discussion questions, and ideas for enhancing your book club. The suggested questions are intended to help your reading group find new and interesting angles and topics for your discussion. We hope that these ideas will enrich your conversation and increase your enjoyment of the book.

INTRODUCTION

Bob Mortimer, beloved comedian and #1 *Sunday Times* (London) bestselling author of the memoir *And Away . . .*, returns with a delightfully quirky mystery in the vein of Richard Osman and Nita Prose.

Unremarkable legal assistant Gary Thorn goes for a pint with his coworker Brendan, unaware his life is about to change. There, Gary meets a beautiful woman, but she leaves before he catches her name. All he has to remember her by is the title of the book she was reading: *The Clementine Complex*. And when Brendan goes missing, too, Gary needs to track down the girl he now calls Clementine to get some answers.

And so begins Gary's quest, through the estates and pie shops of South London, to find some answers and hopefully some love and excitement in this page-turning, witty, and oddly sweet story with a cast of unforgettable characters.

TOPICS AND QUESTIONS FOR DISCUSSION

1. We get to know Gary quite well in the first several chapters, as he opens up about his appearance, career, vivid imagination, and social life (or lack thereof) in London. How would you describe Gary's personality and attitude toward life?

2. Consider Gary's earliest interactions with his neighbor, Grace. Besides their fondness for pie, what initially draws Gary and "Dog Woman" together as friends?

3. When Gary first encounters Clementine, he observes her burgundy Doc Martens with blue laces tied in double bows and "clinically straight fringe lying across the middle of her forehead" (pg. 16). During their second interaction, Gary notes that Clementine's "fringe was no longer perfectly set and her hair was distressed and ruffled. She was wearing a gray dressing gown, and her Doc Martens were untied" (pg. 61).Compare and contrast Gary's first encounter with Clementine in the pub to his surprise arrival at her stairwell. What does Clementine's

change in appearance represent? Why do you think she lets Gary keep her book?

4. DC Bailey tells Gary in chapter 10 that "nobody in the major investigation team had heard of Brendan Jones and there certainly was no ongoing investigation into his death" (pg. 101). He also confirms that there are no officers connected to the police station by the name of Wilmott or Cowley. What do you make of this revelation? Do you agree with Gary's assessment that Brendan is still alive?

5. Gary forms a habit of communicating with his "squirrel friends" about Clementine and the events unfolding in his life. What sort of conversations do they have? How does Gary's active imagination aid his character as well as plot progression?

6. Part two begins with a new narrator. We are introduced to Emily, whom we gradually discover is the woman Gary knows as Clementine. Just like Gary's opening chapters, we learn a lot about Emily in a short amount of time. How would you describe Emily's character? Does she seem like a reliable narrator?

7. When Gary meets Wayne for a statement about his arrest, Wayne tells Gary that he looks like a "carpet salesman or a card-shop owner" and that "it's not fitting with [his] status" (pg. 139). This is something Gary is told repeatedly throughout the book. What role do clothing and physical

descriptions play in the shaping of Gary and the supporting characters? What physical descriptions stand out and why? Think back to other observations of appearance, such as the description of Emily in question 3.

8. In chapter 15, Emily shares that Tommy is a workmate of Brendan's at Cityside Investigations. We learn that Emily was in the pub on the night she met Gary to "identify the person [Brendan] was meeting and more specifically watch to see if Brendan handed any documents, or in fact anything at all, over to that person" (pg. 168). Readers are privy to this information before Gary.

   What purpose does dramatic irony serve in the unfolding of this mystery? How does Emily's version of the night she met Gary enhance or contradict what we already know about "Clementine" from Gary's perspective?

9. Gary is met with another shocking piece of news when he learns from DC Bailey that Brendan has now been found dead behind a warehouse in Peckham. With the information we know at this point in the story, who do you think killed Brendan? What evidence leads you to this belief?

10. On a related note, what part do you think Emily continues to play in Brendan's murder and Gary's mix-up in the investigation? Before she spends the night at Gary's flat, do you believe her story about breaking up with Tommy?

11. Gary's relationship with Emily is the centerpiece of the story. However, Gary's friendship with Grace is equally important to the plot and character arc. After an emotional moment over losing the corncob dongle, Grace admits her loneliness to Gary. Gary confesses that this "was a topic I had never raised, and hearing her mention it made me panic. It wasn't something I wanted to address, probably because I was lonely, too" (pgs. 177–78). Grace later shares with Gary how she became estranged from her daughter and granddaughter (pgs. 242-45). What do these two moments of vulnerability reveal about Gary's relationship with Grace? How has their friendship progressed throughout the novel?

12. Even in climactic moments, Bob Mortimer embraces the humor of both his characters and their absurd situations. Consider the "gun" McCoy points at Gary, which turns out to be nothing more than a prop for practical joking. Think about the moment Gary wraps Emily's injured foot in one of Brendan's tea towels that's "covered in images of brightly colored novelty socks" (pg. 288). Analyze specific moments where the author relies on comedic choices. How does humor affect the overall tone of the story?

13. The book ends with Gary, Emily, and Grace celebrating the arrest of McCoy and Peterson and an end to the "dongle nightmare" (pg. 293). They take a drive to Brighton for the day and discuss the possibility of Emily taking over her father's hotel. How have our three main characters

evolved from the beginning of the book to the end? Did any predictions you made throughout this mystery come true?

14. Back in chapter 6, Gary reads the blurb on the back cover of Emily's book: "*The Clementine Complex* is a novel about loneliness, lack of identity and cultural and moral corruption. Its characters are confused but compelling. A haunting meditation on love and loss and everything in between" (pg. 55). How accurately do you feel this blurb reflects the "real" copy of *The Clementine Complex*—that is, the book you are presumably holding in your hands?

ENHANCE YOUR BOOK CLUB

1. Gary regularly visits South London's pie shops. Do you have any pie shops where you live? If not, recreate some London cuisine in your own home! Gary mentions mince and potato and steak and onion as two of his favorite types of pie. See if you can find these recipes online, and give them a try.

2. *The Clementine Complex* is filled with many twists and turns—the perfect material for an interactive mystery. As you read, have members of your book club write down predictions about Gary's relationship and ties to Brendan's investigation. Throw all these guesses into a bowl to be shared with the rest of the group when the book is finished. Those with the most accurate predictions win prizes! Perhaps, a free pint of beer?

3. Emily has a favorite wooden bench in Brighton that overlooks the English Channel. She shares this bench with Gary during a vulnerable conversation, and it is also

where our three main characters end their story. Do you have a space that brings you immense peace, joy, laughter, or happy memories? If possible, spend some personal reflective time in this space. Alternatively, share this space with a friend or two. Explain to them what makes it so special.